To Caylin —
Caylin —
Enjoy this pla[y]
x Caylin
C. Sullivan ♡

LESLIE O'SULLIVAN

WILD AZURE WAVES

ROCKIN' FAIRY TALES
BOOK THREE

WILD AZURE WAVES

LESLIE O'SULLIVAN

CITY OWL
PRESS

WILD AZURE WAVES
Rockin' Fairy Tales, Book 3

MYSTIC OWL
A City Owl Press Imprint
www.cityowlpress.com

Cover Design by MiblArt. All stock photos licensed appropriately.

Edited by Lisa Green.

For information on subsidiary rights, please contact the publisher at info@cityowlpress.com.

Print Edition ISBN: 978-1-64898-325-2

Digital Edition ISBN: 978-1-64898-324-5

Printed in the United States of America

PRAISE FOR LESLIE O'SULLIVAN

"Submerging readers into a fantastical world, *Wild Azure Waves* is a love story swimming with music, mysticism, and magic… Villains deliver with evil schemes and diabolical characteristics that readers will hear their sinister chuckle every time they are on the page. Leslie O'Sullivan's whimsical fantasy tale is an interesting take on sorrow, second chances, and soulmates." — *InD'tale*

"*Gilded Butterfly* is a unique and magical mashup of fairy tales, Shakespeare, and lore, unlike anything I've read before. At its heart, is a beautiful story about family, the destructive power of chasing fame and money, and the healing power of love. The twists, turns, and magic sprinkled throughout create an engaging story that brings a new kind of fairy tale to modern Hollywood." — *Megan Van Dyke, author of Second Star to the Left*

"*Pink Guitars and Falling Stars* is a fast paced and very engaging read, with a constantly evolving main character and a colorful cast. The adventure wraps up nicely, and ends with a hint of what is next in the Rockin' Fairy Tales series. This is a great read if you are looking for an action-packed modern fairy tale with aspiring rock stars who fall from the sky." — *Paranormal Romance Guild*

"Leslie O'Sullivan's narrative style in *Gilded Butterfly* celebrates truth, love, and heritage, and reads as pure poetry from the opening line until the end." — *InD'tale*

"As full of heart and soul as the music it describes, *Crimson Melodies* drew me in with a fresh take on a classic tale, masterfully combining celebrity and monster romance vibes to give me everything I wanted and more!" — S.C. Grayson, author of *Beauty and the Blade*

"Submerging readers into a fantastical world, *Wild Azure Waves* is a love story swimming with music, mysticism, and magic." — *InD'tale*

"*Pink Guitars and Falling Stars* is an interesting take on the story of Rapunzel...O'Sullivan has definitely nailed the initial animosity between Justin and Zeli. As they become closer, the relationship jumps off the page and morphs beautifully. There are awesome love scenes with a lot of description which pull the reader right in and keep a tight grip... A fascinating remix of a popular fairy tale with some very sexy differences. One to add to the e-reader and to be read list!" — *InD'tale*

"With wickedly clever wordplay, fresh and lovable characters, and an utterly unique take on a classic fairytale, *Pink Guitars and Falling Stars* is one of the swooniest romances I've ever read. You'll be cheering for B.A.S.E. jumper Justin to help Zeli escape her tower in the heart of Hollywood's twisted music industry and fall equally hard for their chosen family on the Boulevard. A romantic, heart-in-your-throat read!" — *Sarah Skilton, author of Fame Adjacent*

"*Pink Guitars and Falling Stars* reads like glitter and stardust, like a song of the heart set free and realizing every dream." —*Fairrryprose*

Hot Set is a 2023 Holt Medallion Winner for Mid-Length Contemporary

Pink Guitars and Falling Stars is a winner of a 2023 Gold Author Shout Reader Ready Awards "Top Pick."

To my beloved daughter, Melissa,
who taught me the wonder of believing in mermaids.

ROCKIN' FAIRY TALES
BY LESLIE O'SULLIVAN

Pink Guitars and Falling Stars

Gilded Butterfly

Wild Azure Waves

Crimson Melodies

Emerald Spire (Winter 2024)

"O, wonder!
How many goodly creatures are there here!
How beauteous mankind is!"

The Tempest
Miranda Act 5 Scene 1

1

SEA SONG

EACH STROKE OF MY OAR CUTTING THROUGH THE WATER SINGS.

Shuuush.

I'm alone in the channel between Lalale Island and the Santa Barbara, California mainland, writing a song with the sea as my co-composer. As I gift the ashes of my loved ones stolen by fire to the waves, I'll raise my voice in fresh notes of farewell.

A tap of the metal band around my wrist against the oar lock sounds a clear *ring.*

Shuuush, ring.

For percussion, I s*lap* the flat of the oar against the side of the canoe.

Shuuush, ring. Shuuush, slap.

The ocean adds notes of *hissssss* to soften our composition as my bow cleaves whitecaps. The water and I agree on momentary silence. Every song needs beats of silence to allow time for the music's energy to fill a soul.

Ring, ring, slap. Hissssss.

Silence.

The wind chimes in.

Oooooo-whip.

That's it, our song's missing bridge.

Shuuush, ring. Oooooo-whip. Shuuush, slap. Oooooo-whip.

I join my voice to the progression of notes.

"Time to fly. Farewell. You will soar. Farewell."

Silence.

"Beat, beat wings. Sailing. Seek Cloud's Path."

Silence.

"Farewell. Farewell."

As I near the mid-point of the channel, I'm still weighed down by the thick sorrow that hung in the air earlier when I crossed the sands of the island to the canoe. Members of the artist commune I'd lived with my entire twenty-five years watched me carry the four urns in my arms until I nestled the ashes of lost ones in the bow of my friend, Juan Luna Azul's, tomol. He's proud of this canoe he built with his grandfather, Juan Estrella Azul. The family learned the art of building tomols, the traditional plank canoes used for generations by the Chumash, from a boat builder who joined our artist commune on Lalale Island when my parents were kids. Neither Juan Luna nor I are Chumash, but he thought it fitting I use the traditional vessel for this burial at sea.

My parents, brother Piyo, and his fiancé, Tani, would hate any type of melancholy sendoff, so there'd never been an official memorial, but sadness is still etched on the faces of their friends nearly a year after the fire.

Whenever we lost friend or family, my parents said, "*Death is cool, Rai, a beginning for the next adventure.*" I smile. To them, everything was *bitchin'*, *boss*, or *cool* with the occasional *groovy* tossed in. The Lalale Island artist commune that birthed our family company, Cloudpath Music, will forever languish in a sixties time warp.

Only Emerson, Tani's father, walked all the way with me to where the sea lapped at the shadowed sands of the lagoon. Now, I look down on his thinning, gray hair. For many years, he was the one looking down on the once scrawny son of Lucas and Corinne Cloud.

"It'd be cool if you rowed out with me, Em," I'd offered.

The moon rose over his shoulder as he shook his head. "I've said good-bye to my Tanya. This fabricated ritual is something you cooked up for your own closure."

Perseverating on Emerson's dig ruins the rhythm of my stroke, and I stop singing. Tani hated being called Tanya. Damn Emerson for bumming my night. For years before he adopted his Mr.-Serious-Business-Dude persona, he bought into the laid-back vibe of what he now labels a *hippy dippy* island commune. The rest of the commune understands the respect I'm trying to show with my ritual. Emerson avoided disparaging my intentions in front of our friends, especially Tutu, Juan Luna's grandma. She'd string him up to the closest palm and throw rotten fruit at him.

I dismiss the negativity of his sendoff. My heart knows my family would welcome a joyful song of farewell as I steer the tomol toward the deepest part of the channel.

The urns rattle in the bow, and my heart clutches the way it does every time the gravity of my loss rises to the surface. I press a fist to my chest and speak to the ashes. "Your peace will come soon, I promise."

Peace is key here. I can't send these spirits off with bitterness in my gut. It's wrong of me to be angry with Emerson. He's dealing with death in his own way. He lost a child, a potential son-in-law, and dear friends. Pushing people away is his coping mechanism. I, on the other hand, am lost, a man floating through each day while I wait for reality to define its edges instead of keeping me adrift in the shapeless blur my life has become since the fire.

My gaze follows the silver-white path painted by a near full moon on the sea. The night is a melody, punctuated with flashes of moonlight catching the tops of swells. I welcome the lunar energy flowing through me, a river of the peace I desperately need. The moon is the spiritual touchstone I feel most connected to. I crave its presence tonight. Away in the distance, I see the Santa Barbara shore. Behind me rises the familiar shape of Lalale Island. It's time to begin.

First, I cradle the matching, deep red ceramic urns of my parents in my arms. Their wedding rings hang on thin silver chains around the tops. "Thank you, Mom, for making Lucas my father and Piyo my brother. Thank you, Mom and Dad, for giving me a cool life surrounded by love and belonging. I will always cherish the connections you taught me to find with island, sea, sky, and the creativity within me."

One at a time, I raise each urn to the moon and snap a mental picture of its silhouette against the bright disk before I dip my parents' urns into the water. "I gift you to earth and sea under a watching moon. Walk the Cloud Path to your next adventure."

I'd be lying if I didn't admit to hoping for an otherworldly surge or some other sign of connection to the spirits of my parents as I sink the urns. Nothing ethereal or supernatural goes down as they disappear. Disappointing.

Next, I tell my brother how much I love him and send him on his adventure. The moment Piyo's urn is out of sight, tears blur my vision. I've said so many good-byes to my family before I fall asleep and again when I meet each new dawn alone. Giving them to the sea is the deepest cut.

I wipe my eyes to find a darker sky. Lines of flat-bottomed, gray clouds cut across the moon. Beneath me, the canoe pitches left and right as swells smack its sides. I check to make sure the oars are secure in the locks.

I'd settle for a much calmer sign of my family's spirits finding their Cloud Path than an agitated ocean.

Tani's urn rattles. I lunge forward to grab it before it spills.

The moon, wearing a red ring, reappears from behind storm clouds. In the commune, Old Granny Blossom, our resident green witch, read signs of nature and conversed with the unseen. She gave me a moonstone charm to represent my spiritual energy, which I planned to give to Tani but never did. Before Piyo and I started school, Granny Blossom watched us while my parents poured crazy hours into creating Cloudpath Music. One night, she dragged us out to see a moon with a red ring. The wise witch called it a killing moon and warned us to take shelter whenever we see one.

I'm looking at the same creepy moon now.

Did I summon a freaky red ring and clouds that look like they want to squash me with my self-created ritual? Totally not my intention. This is the good-bye I crafted to please my family. I meant no offense. Tutu would tell me to get out of my head and finish.

The plank canoe stills its choppy dance. Rowing out to the middle of the channel at night doesn't feel as poetic as it did when I planned the ceremony. I'll say my good-bye to Tani and get my ass back to the island.

I look at the green sea glass urn adorned with a delicate gold leaf pattern and pause, unable to speak. As soul scarring as it was to commit my parents and brother to the deep, it's worse letting Tani go. She was my first love. My only real love to date. We told secrets. We laughed until we couldn't breathe. We dreamed together. We shared first kisses and fumbling explorations of each other's bodies. We moved together from childhood to adulthood on the island.

And then she chose Piyo.

They loved in a language beyond what I understood. She was better off with the steady Cloud brother instead of the one who listens for the songs of trees. Tani and Piyo moved past me in the ebb and flow of life, and I accepted it.

At least, I thought I had. I clutch the urn to my heart. "I love you, Tani." There are no other words that matter. I raise her urn to the moon as forks of lightning slice through clouds to bury the tips of their sabers in a circle around the canoe with an unnerving *sizzle*.

The storm breaks above and around me like a beast on the hunt. I am powerless prey. I wedge Tani's urn between my knees and try to take up the oars. The boat shimmies, twisting my insides. The bow rises only to thwack down with teeth-shattering violence as it rides the swells. I attempt to pull the oars in, but the sea bests me.

I hunch over the urn, my mind searching for the best strategy not to get killed. I wedge my body as low in the canoe as possible. The next wave nearly topples the tomol. The possibility of riding out the storm looks grim. Tani and I may be fated to find our Cloud Path together after all.

I listen for a song in the storm to calm myself. I hear only fury. Spray drenches my hair, the bare skin of my chest, and my trunks. The stern of the canoe lifts. Under a cascade of lightning, the Santa Barbara cliffs rise in sharp relief. Suddenly, to the south, a blinding burst of gold splatters across the sky like a gilded lace curtain. The shine is beautiful, and I wonder if it's the gate to my next adventure, opening to receive Tani and me.

Instead of the canoe slapping down, it's catapulted upwards by an unforgiving wave. I'm airborne along with Tani's urn. I reach for it, but green glass meets bow. The urn shatters, its fragments mixing with spray.

"Tani," I scream in the instant before my head collides with the curved stern of Juan Luna's tomol.

2

TANI'S AWAKENING

FAINT TINKLING BELLS SOUND AS SPARKLING GREEN CHIPS RAIN around me. Beyond my glassy curtain, a flock of golden birds splash across the sky. I lay a hand over my heart, awed by this beauty.

A phrase echoes through my mind. *"I love you, Tani."*

Tani. My name.

Beneath my palm, a heart shivers as if awakened by the words, then settles into stillness. I yearn to respond to the voice but don't know the way.

I love you.

Who's calling? Who loves me? Who do I love?

A bright flash erupts around me, sprinkling the water with a full spectrum of hues like a rainfall of candy drops that flare and then melt back into the blue palette of the sea. With the blast comes a flood of memories relearned, fighting to take shape in my confused thoughts.

I float. Instead of rising, I fall. The roll and sway of...

Water...this is water, surrounding me, cradling and rocking like the arms of a lover. I look up to discover the muted...

Moon, the big, round, white ball nestled on its bed of wobbly stars in a dark...

Sky...yes sky.

I know sky. I remember my moon and stars but not these that waver and fragment.

This altered state is familiar. Swirling thoughts fall into order with a rush. A memory of friends and nights where reality played games with my mind. An island. Juan Luna. Is he the one who calls to me?

No, he is not a love. I connect strange perceptions to Juan Luna, a man, a friend. Did I eat one of Juan Luna's special brownies? I remember those. Am I tripping in a weirdscape of half memories?

When I taste salt on my tongue, awareness leaks into my consciousness, a stain across cloth. I'm in the ocean. It's a curtain of tide between the sky and me making moon and stars quaver.

What the fuck am I doing underwater?

White tendrils the color of a full moon twist, snakes in this untrustworthy current knocking me around. I try to escape. The white lines follow. I reach out to push them away and see my arm, my hand. One strand of bright white wraps around my finger. I try to capture a fistful of moon-colored strands, but they float through my grasp. It's my hair. How can this be? My hair is the color of maple syrup. Tani's hair. My hair. I am Tani. What turned my hair white?

Slowly, like dawn glow over the horizon, my vision brightens, and reality whiplashes back to me. I don't belong underwater. I'm frantic, kicking for the surface. My body shudders, but not from cold. When I should be freezing in the sea at night, I feel nothing.

Halfway to the bobbing line that separates water and air, I pause. Moonshine lightens the space around me. Instead of the familiar, murky, gray-green water I've swum in my whole life, sapphire currents gently swirl around me. The moon above the surface says night. Here it's as bright and lively as day. Fish dart by as if I'm nothing to see. One bold, yellow-and-red pest swims through my hand. I watch his jaunt to the ocean floor where every detail is in crisp clarity. Sea plants rising from the sand twist and bend in a colossal game of tag with hundreds of fish.

"*I love you, Tani.*"

The voice is louder. It searches for me. I squeeze my eyes shut and grab my head as the edges of this watery dream sharpen and cut.

My lips move soundlessly. "Tell me who you are."

There is no answer. Instead, the sea around me transforms, dropping me straight into hell. An orange and red conflagration bursts around me, sizzling my core with flesh-melting agony. I strain to open my eyes to make sense of the new torment. I try to touch my face. It's gone with the rest of me. In my watery reality, I had a body. In this fiery place, I'm a molten blob. What the actual fuck is going on? Realization flares like a flaming spear in my brain. This nasty-ass vision is the retelling of my death. Fire took me. I died alongside my fiancé Piyo, Corinne, and Lucas Cloud. Fate is a merciless teacher.

I am Tani, and I am dead.

As quickly as it came, the horror flash disappears. My arms circle next to me while those strange, whitish strands of my hair draw paths through the water. I kick my legs, swivel my body. What is this bizarro version of me? It's not life. If it's a dream, it's the crappiest one ever. Confusion molts into frustration. How am I underwater but not drowning? I'm undefined. Screw it. I need answers.

I swim up, up until I break the surface and gulp air. It's an empty gesture with no result or feeling. What brand of freak exists above and below the water without the need for breath?

The sensation of panic sizzles in my chest. I scream for Piyo. Surely, he's the one trying to find me in this head trip. There is no sound. I dive again and scream. There's not the smallest movement of water around my lips.

I surface again and raise my arms, half expecting to see corpse white limbs to match my hair. Moonlight brightens a transparent version of my caramel-colored skin. Thunder teases the clouds above. Electricity cracks the air, warning me away. I dive.

I grab for my head and feel nothing but water. I unleash a silent scream to a sea that ignores me.

Curling into a ball, I allow the current to choose my movement. If I'm dead, why do sobs crush my chest? Is this freak zone really my end game?

Well, shit.

"*I love you, Tani.*"

The amplified voice warbles through the water closer than before. I whip around, trying to see where it's coming from. Is Piyo thrashing in a crap world of fire dreams and underwater daylight with me?

Not far off, a shadow plunges into the water shrouded in a white cocoon of bubbles that quickly fades. The black lump doesn't move at first, then it unfolds to sink into the depths. Holy moon—it's a person, a man. Not someone like me, hanging in the sea without breathing. The person is for real drowning.

The tide twists the body. A lingering bolt of lightning from the storm blasts through the water to reveal a broad chest covered with a familiar pattern of tattoos.

I must still have a soul because it quakes. The voice that ripped me away from death is clear now. Rai. The Rai I once believed would be my forever.

"*I love you, Tani.*"

It is Rai, Rai Cloud, saying he loves me, and he's drowning.

Am I real enough to save him? Are the fates torturing my soul with Rai's death because I caved to my father's expectations and chose Piyo over him?

Don't think, Tani. Swim.

In my split second of hesitation, a dark shape like a bird of prey on the hunt flashes past. The power of its surge through the water sends me tumbling backward end over end away from Rai. The beast hurtles violently through the water toward its target. I can't let it destroy him. With surprising power, I blast in pursuit of the threat. All I make out are the powerful thrusts of the thing's greenish glowing tail. In moments, I've closed the distance and reached the predator. I grab for the tail, but it whips through my grasp as if my hands are not there at all.

Of course, they're not. I'm not the Tani that was. I'm nothing. I'm a freaking shadow or spirit or soul plunked into the sea. What an idiot to think I could save anyone when I have no clue what I am.

My gaze locks onto Rai, and my mouth falls open. The sapphire undersea light partners with the moon to illuminate my scene, and I see the truth. What I believed to be a ravenous sea monster is a creature from a picture book. The body of a woman is encased in a luminous green tinted sheen. Long strands of dark blue hair course through the water around her, dozens of streams searching to find the river they mean to rejoin. From waist down, the iridescent shine of her shape sculpts into the magnificent tail of a mermaid.

I watch an honest to goodness mermaid cut through unnaturally blue water. What other familiar faces or unreal creatures populate this liquid hell?

Beat, beat, beat.

Her tail strokes the water, bringing Rai toward the surface. She carries him across her back. The mermaid covers his hands with hers to clutch her hips. Rai's fingers disappear into the top rim of her tail.

I follow. I pray the mermaid swims quickly enough to a place with lifegiving air. Rai deserves to breathe and sing again. He can't be banished to whatever freaking mess I've landed in.

They break the surface, and I hear her murmur.

"Breathe."

I stay hidden where the waves break since I don't know if they see me. I stare at the cliffs. This is not the Santa Barbara mainland I know. Where did she bring him?

Under the moon, the mermaid's skin shimmers more blue-green than the rainbow hue of an abalone shell. Tiny droplets shine along her body and tail like tears of the moon. She is stunning. If I had breath, the grace and beauty of the mermaid would steal it as she skims rapidly to the shore.

Gently, she lays Rai on the sand and tucks in next to him. The water laps at her tail fin. Sliding fingers to something dangling near her hip, she plucks out a pair of flat, shiny ovals and places them in Rai's palm. The mermaid squeezes her hand around his to prevent her iridescent gifts from leaking onto the sand.

"Breathe."

She rests a cheek over his heart. Hair, a brighter blue out of the water, splays across his bare chest. Abruptly, she raises her head. A smile bright enough to compete with the near-full moon lights her face. Did she hear his heartbeat? His breath? Oh, please let that be the case.

The mermaid traces Rai's lips with the tip of her finger.

His eyes open, and he speaks. "Are you a dream?"

Her answer is a kiss. She presses her lips to his and lingers way past peck. An unexpected rush of jealousy burns my hollow insides. *Shake him awake. Turn him on his side and pump the sea out of his lungs. Anything but a kiss.* How dare she?

The mermaid begins to sing. I want to storm out of the surf and tell her to shut the hell up and get away from my Rai. I follow the next wave in closer, rise out of the water, and walk to the sand. When I reach the edge of sea foam, a sound freezes me in place. Rai joins the song with one pure note, a perfect harmony to the mermaid's melody.

He's alive.

Rai finishes his part of their song and closes his eyes. The corner of his lip curves into the trace of a smile, one I know well. One I wish belonged to me as it once did.

Shouts sound from the top of a nearby bluff. A cluster of people wave their arms and call to us. The mermaid hears them too. In a flash, she scrapes away the objects she placed in Rai's grasp. With a twist and flip of her tail, she folds into the tide.

I run to Rai and reach for him. My hand passes through him. I draw back until my ghostly palm hovers above his tattoo. I see rather than feel the rise and fall of his chest. "Rai," I say, imploring him to open his eyes to me the way he did for her. I try to raise my voice in the call and response song we used to sing as we hid from one another behind palm trees on the island.

Seas roll slow
Sand will blow
Find me soon
With our tune

Rai does not give me a single note.

The group from the cliffs race across the sand. I recognize the pop stars Zeli and Justin Time, Chorda Lear from the reality show "Kickin' It With Midas," and another man I don't know. Their attention is fixed on Rai.

"Is he breathing?" asks Zeli.

Chorda drops down next to Rai, flattening her palm against the tattoo of the moon on his chest. "Yes, thank Bríg," she says. "He's freezing. Adair, give me your jacket."

The man, Adair, yanks off his hoodie and lays it over Rai. He pulls a phone from his pocket and starts hollering into it.

Zeli brushes hair from Rai's face. "Oh, my God, this is Rai Cloud." She gently pats his cheek. "Rai, can you hear me? It's Zeli." She looks wide-eyed around the group. "We need to warm him up." She rubs one of his arms while Chorda kneels in the sand to attend to the other.

Justin slides in next to Zeli and raises his volume to be heard above the waves. "Rai, dude, wake up." He grips Rai's bicep and firmly shakes.

Not a single person acknowledges me. I continue to be nothing.

Slowly, I back into the surf until the water is deep enough for me to submerge. Only my head is above the spray.

A voice floats between waves. "You're Rai Cloud."

I twist to my right. The mermaid is a few feet from me, gaze fixed on the beach. I can't make out details of a face through the thin aquamarine shroud covering her features.

"Rai Cloud." The mermaid sings his name.

I slap the surface with a crack. "Hey you, mermaid." I need to chat about *operation underwater rescue* and the lovesick expression on her face.

Her attention remains riveted on Rai.

"You, over there. Answer me. Can you hear me?" I don't hear me. I'm aware the words push out of my mouth, but they don't make a sound.

Cheers erupt from the beach. Rai sits, coughing like he's trying to eject a boulder from his windpipe. Justin Time thumps him on the back while the women hold his hands. He slumps forward, and Adair attempts to fit him into the hoodie. Rai's bulky arms mercilessly stretch the sleeves. It doesn't come close to covering his chest. He was better off using it as a blanket.

Rai shakes his head, flicking water all over his rescuers. "Where's the woman?"

Justin Time is on his feet, scanning the beach. "No clue, Dude."

Rai grips Chorda's arm. "You saw her, right?"

The mermaid they can see. I hate her for that.

"She was here for a sec," says Chorda, moving sand-matted hair off Rai's face.

"Then poof," says Adair.

"Poof?" Rai says and starts a new bout of coughing.

"She sang to you," says Zeli.

Rai grasps his throat and nods. "Yes. So, beautiful." He searches the shoreline. "Did you see where she went? I have to find her."

Commotion near the base of the cliffs catches their attention. A pair of EMTs drag a backboard down the path. Justin jogs over to intercept them.

The mermaid sighs. "I will find you, Rai Cloud."

On shore, the rescue team covers Rai in a silver blanket and goes to work on him. I long to be the one next to him, singing a song to return him to life. Instead, I'm a voyeur lingering in the waves.

A splash between breakers draws my gaze. The fluke of mermaid tail slips under the surface. I glance to shore. Rai is safe. He's alive, thanks to a creature straight out of legend. I may not be able to figure out what my story is yet, but I can get some answers about the woman encased in a wet, silky skin. A woman who happened to be near Rai Cloud when he fell into the sea and pulled him ashore miles down the mainland across from Lalale Island.

Did she mean to revive him then claim him far from his home so no one who knew him would interfere? The only way to learn the siren's plan and possibly keep Rai away from her is to catch her.

She's three mermaid lengths ahead of me. I pump my legs and push my arms against the current. I'm awkward, achieving pathetic forward movement. How did I move before when I tried to get to Rai? I will my body to cut through the sea. To my shock, it does. I slip forward, and the water offers no resistance. I soar through gleaming layers of gemstone ocean.

I stop to marvel at the sensation. Where else can I fly?

Movement ahead yanks me back into the pursuit. I'm losing the mermaid. Aiming myself in her direction, I take off after her like a rocket, careful not to get too close and scare her. She didn't take notice of me near shore, but this is the ocean, the realm of mermaids. I want answers from the fish babe. I have no clue how reality works here or how I work. The woman seemed gentle, but there are too many stories about sirens and selkies with sharp teeth. It'd be idiocy to confront her before I understand more. Once

I see where she's headed, maybe I'll give her a breather before I knock on the door of whatever coral castle she hangs out in.

A shadow falls across the water, turning sapphire into midnight. I glance up. The surface is out of sight. We've been diving. Here's the sea I know. Dim and near impossible to see through. In my beat of inattention, I lose the mermaid. *Damn.*

Part of me is reluctant to move deeper into the shadow. I must follow the mermaid. As my father always says, "*Tanya, stay the course to gain the prize.*"

I hate being called Tanya.

Following Rai's savior is a short-term goal I refuse to give up. If I do, I'll be forced to examine whatever brand of freak I've become.

I squint into the shadows to find the steady movement of a shape through water. I sprint after the mermaid until a series of yellow circles of light cuts through the darkness. As I close in, they take on bulbous shapes embedded in a metallic structure nestled against an undersea wall of rock. I know this place. It's the Miaqua Research Station repurposed to be the Miaqua Music complex. One summer, Rai and I went to music camp down here. He, of course, was the star of the session. I ended up singing backup chorus with the other mediocre voices.

Piyo and I were here last month to hear The Mermaids, Miaqua's resident artists, in concert. Was it last month? How do I judge time? Rai looked the way he did the last time I saw him at my engagement bonfire. The one that...

I shudder.

...killed me.

The silhouette of the mermaid glides in front of the lights. Is this creature drawn to the music of her namesakes? They do make beautiful, almost haunting music. Perhaps her human side feels a connection to the six musical sisters.

As the mermaid swims past the farthest window, I snap out of my thoughts and hasten after her. Once I pass the end of Miaqua, all I face is barren landscape. The rock façade of the sea wall looms off to the side. There is no coral castle or flick of a shiny mermaid tail. It's desolate, dark, and lonely past the complex. I sense I'm trespassing in a place where something might spring out and swallow me.

I slip backward into a splash of quavering yellow light from Miaqua's windows. What now? I wish for blackness, for the nothingness that must have existed before my current state of non-being. Shit, this is mind-blowing. I hate it. I don't want to feel. I don't want to know what I am now or remember who I was and ache for the people I loved. I don't want to be aware I am nothing.

Does this mermaid know of magic in her world to fix me the way she saved Rai?

I draw in a not-breath because I do not breathe and open my eyes. Above me, a tall figure, a woman with broad shoulders, stands in the light of a grand window. I lift my gaze to her face, and the world around me blasts with the same rainfall of colors that first sharpened my consciousness in the sea.

The statuesque lady fills the space of the window, staring directly at where I flounder in the water. She lifts a hand in greeting.

I am seen.

3

DON'T CALL ME KITTY

EMERSON WAITS FOR ME TO SPEAK AS HE STEERS THE SHIP ACROSS THE channel to Lalale Island. He's pissed. Nothing new there. He's always pissed at me these days. He brushes off my explanations about the dulling white noise that plays constantly through my head since the near drowning in June. It's as if I'll never overcome constant fatigue or get my full reason back. Only one thing quiets the racket and gives me impetus to move forward, the memory of her voice, the woman on the beach.

She lingers in my mind when I walk along the shore of the island. I hear notes of her song in the waves. When I sleep under the stars near the lagoon, I swear she watches. I even imagined her presence drifting through the love song Zeli sang at Chorda and Adair's wedding last week.

Juan Luna is my sole confidant because he speaks the language of *out there*. My friend indulges my spaciness and longing, even though he chalks it up to lack of oxygen to the brain during my extended underwater plunge.

No one witnessed the act of my near-dead body being pulled from the water, but Zeli, Justin, Adair, and Chorda saw my rescuer on the beach with me. The memory of her is so real I feel the touch of her lips on mine and hear her song that called me out of the gray, murky end the sea ordained. I know in my heart if not for the storm-shadowed woman, I'd be with my parents, Piyo, and Tani on the Cloud Path. My memory of her, the sense of connection to this stranger, refuses to fade. The months since are no more than moments in my soul.

I told Granny Blossom I believe the mystery woman was sent by a force beyond our day-to-day consciousness to wrestle me from the sea. My mother never wavered in her surety of the spiritual power of the moon. All my life, she read Piyo, Tani, and me stories of moon goddesses such as Selene, Artemis, and Chang'e, along with other lunar deities and spirits, to illustrate the viability of the moon's influence. Mom swore my creative energy was absolutely tied to the moon because I was born at the full moon. It's true, I feel my most inspired alone outdoors bathed in moon glow. The moon tattoo on my chest, which, according to Juan Estrella, was ordained by his connection with spiritual intention, further cements my affinity with the enigmatic orb watching over the Earth.

When I spoke of my savior from the storm, the green witch gazed deep into my eyes, smiled, and repeated the words my mother whispered to me as a child each night before I fell asleep.

"See the unseen. Sense the unknown. Suspend the common belief."

Granny's message confirmed what my heart already knew. I am meant to find the woman who saved me.

Emerson clears his throat as he slathers sunscreen across the back of his neck. He burns while the August sun turns my skin a deeper shade of summer brown. "I take it you weren't impressed with Midas Lear's offer, Rainn."

Emerson, the C.F.O. of my company, and Midas Lear, C.E.O. of Golden Pipes Records, hammered out the financial particulars of a potential sale inside the Lear's Waterfall Palace in the Hollywood Hills. I escaped to one of its terraced gardens with the newly minted Mr. and Mrs. Adair Holliday. They both reiterated their story. One moment, they saw a girl on the beach hovering over me, and the next, I was alone, one tick shy of being a sodden corpse.

"Did you call out for her or look for footprints?" I'd asked.

"Absolutely," said Adair. "We all agreed the best move was to leave you alone, barely breathing, to go all Hardy Boys and Nancy Drew in search of a mystery woman who clearly wanted nothing to do with us."

Chorda's scowl sliced through Adair's sarcasm, her words kinder. "You probably scared the woman to death, washing up at her feet out of nowhere while she dodged lightning bolts. The storm was intense, Rai. What was she supposed to do, drag you across the sand? You're not exactly petite. She opted for what any sane person would: self-survival."

I'd frowned at Chorda's explanation. "And not come back when the storm passed to see if I was still alive?"

"Dude," Adair said. "We were with you by then. If she was watching, she knew you had help."

I still can't wrap my head around why she seemed bent on saving me and then disappeared.

"Well, Rainn?" says Emerson, interrupting my thoughtscape.

He uses my full name to get a rise. No one calls me Rainn. I'm Rai. I've always been Rai. It fits. I'm an island kid raised on an artist commune. It's a control thing with him, like the way he called Tani, Tanya. My gut clenches with guilt. I haven't told Emerson the way I botched Tani's burial. I can't. The failure haunts me.

Fate made no mistake. Tani was better off with Piyo than she ever would have been with me.

I used to dream of Tani even after she and my brother got together. Once we believed we were fated, blessed by the moon to live as one. Our convictions were no more than dawning adolescent philosophies fed by the *nature speaks* beliefs of the commune. Tani and I heard what we wanted nature to say, until it told her something else. She hasn't visited my dreams since the night of the storm, part of my cosmic punishment for fucking up her eternal farewell.

"Do I need to make an appointment for your attention, Rainn?"

Space man Rai on duty. I refocus on Emerson. "I need time to process."

Emerson presses his lips together and glances down before speaking. "The way you're still processing offers from Rampion Records, Tempest Tunes, and Caliwood Inc.? These companies are desperate to acquire Cloudpath Music. We need to act while we've got guilt over helping poor Rai Cloud sell his parents' company working to our advantage."

I squeeze my eyes shut to keep from blasting him for leveraging my parents' death and remind myself he's trying to give me a financial future. A pair of deep breaths later, I reengage. "I'm not positive I want to sell at all."

He smacks the steering wheel. "We've been over this a thousand times, Rainn. Selling, and selling soon, is the only way to salvage any hope of a profit."

"Em, I'm ready to hunker down and work on the new direction I'd like to take Cloudpath Music. You said we have the resources."

Emerson cuts the engine. We bob on the water while he stares at me.

I lift my chin. "What?"

"I said that three years ago when you first asked me. Three years ago, when Corinne and Lucas started the handoff process to you and Piyo. Resources dry up. Even if you could get your act together enough to cut a new album or even a fucking single, and it does decently—"

I shake my leg to vent my frustration. "My act is together." My act is so not together, yet. But there's the hope of it coming together.

He raises hands in surrender. "Let's say you do. First, you've only got the one stale hit from your win on *You've Got a Gift.*"

Emerson can take his *stale hit* ding and shove it up his ass. "'Fire Capped Waves' still gets decent play and downloads on Tuneful. It's evergreen, man." My chest tightens the way it always does when Emerson tries to push me in his direction instead of mine.

"You haven't cashed in on your fame in five years. Even back then you only did what? Three live appearances, a handful of podcasts and TV spots?" He drums his fingers on the dash of the speed boat. "I get it. Five years ago, you were finishing college. Rai, your audience is in their mid-twenties now, different people with different tastes, different goals. You barely even post on social. Rai Cloud is stuck, wandering in circles, waiting for inspiration to drop from the sky. You are fading from view." He runs a hand through his hair and tugs. "Your brother saw the hopelessness of trying to hold on to Cloudpath."

I bite my tongue to keep from lashing out at him for the cheap shot. We're both screwed up from loss. I try to see myself the way he does. He's right. I am not Piyo. My brother had the business brain, and I am the right-brained artist. That's why my parents left the company to both of us, balance.

I'm all there is now, the Cloud son who lays in a hammock listening to sounds the island makes in the hope of reinventing them as music. Not the new age soundscapes Cloudpath is known for, a new sound where nature meets an irresistible rhythm. I've been gathering material for years and dabbling in a musical genre I believe can redefine Cloudpath Music. My vision was always missing something until one night on a beach after a storm when I heard the voice that tied everything together.

I find the voice. I find her, and I complete my vision.

I force myself to chill instead of butting heads with Emerson. Bottom line, I'm his boss. "Let's agree my fluid sense of timing spilled over the rim of the glass, but I'm almost ready to go into studio to make island rock reality."

Emerson shouts. "Almost ready. You've been almost ready for years, Rainn. Almost isn't action. Almost is too late to matter."

He's asking me to sell my parents' dream. Losing Cloudpath Music is another death, and I can't handle the ones I'm already dealing with. I believe I can turn the company around with my new brand of music when I find the storm woman.

I rub my lips together. So far, my search is a bust. When the story of my rescue went public, I blasted a plea on social media asking my rescuer to post a video of the song she sang to me on the beach. The avalanche of responses freaked me out. Juan Luna helped me sift through DMs and messages but found nothing solid hidden in the sheer amount of bullshit and false claims. No sign of the wondrous voice.

"Em, what about our soundscape contracts with submarines and anywhere with an elevator?"

Emerson barks out a laugh. "The Cloudpath Music brand of pleasing noise ran its course. There are a dozen apps with more variety. Those make us obsolete."

I know he's right. My parents and brother hoped my new sound could usher in the next generation of relevance for Cloudpath. I never produced for them.

My lofty search for a missing piece is just one more excuse.

Emerson thumps me on the upper arm. "Look, Rai. This is not entirely on you. We raised you kids with the same go-with-the-flow philosophy our parents celebrated at the commune."

I'm surprised he even references his own flower child upbringing. Em went full corporate tight ass as soon as Dad brought him in as C.F.O. of Cloudpath. Tani and I used to joke that tight assery was her pops's latent superpower.

He studies the island in the distance. "The sentiment has its merits, but that way of thinking isn't the best fit for business."

A gust of wind rocks the boat, and I grab the side rail. "I realize things are crap and crumbling fast. You've been trying to protect me, Em, and I appreciate it. Bottom line, how bad is it?"

While his face shifts from bright red to dark pink, he fires up the engine but idles instead of surging toward the island. I've pushed almost all his buttons.

"Taxes are a nightmare. Piyo and Lucas were working on a few contracts to dig us out of debt, but then..."

Emerson doesn't need to finish. It seems the bonfire that killed my family used Cloudpath Music as kindling as well.

"How long do I have to at least attempt a save?"

Emerson eyes me with a calculating look. "We need to sell by the end of the quarter before October first or we go under."

My face heats. "That's barely over a month."

He looks guilty. "I own not being clearer with you about the timetable. Given your lack of interest in the company at all, I assumed you'd be happy to lose the burden of Cloudpath Music and go solo with another label."

"Happy to lose the artistic vision my parents built?"

"Built and then let atrophy."

I clench and unclench my fists to clear my head.

"Be real, Rai. Since the fire, you haven't exactly been present for me to lay out a game plan. Grief is a bitch, but life doesn't push pause." His gaze bores into me and his volume skyrockets. "I don't even know where you are for days when you turn off your phone and traipse around the island. Then you almost get yourself killed with that canoe-hugging burial ritual you and Juan Luna cooked up."

I look away to avoid unleashing words I can't take back. He guns the engine to cover the silence.

We pull into a slip at the marina near a pink stucco building that looks like a smaller cousin of the Royal Hawaiian Hotel in Waikiki. My parents took Piyo and me to Oahu on a splurge vacation when were toddlers and fell in love with the hotel. They were making enough bank to raze the old headquarters and rebuild Cloudpath Music's studios and offices to echo the vibe of their cool pink Hawaiian dream palace.

Responsibility battles with my natural tendencies of avoidance. There is no clear winner. Emerson has valid points. I haven't acted like the decision maker of a floundering record company should. He shoulders that yoke.

A sharp bark wakes me from my Rai daze. Skittering down the dock to greet us is Kitae, the island fox injured in the fire who adopted me. I hop out of the boat onto the gangway to tie the stern line around the cleat and scoop up Kitae. He licks the underside of my chin and then wriggles to be set down. With his signature yip, he tears along the dock to the sand. Once there, he runs in little circles barking at me to join him.

I grab the bow line from Emerson. "I'll take the meeting with Sulaa Kylock tomorrow at Miaqua Music and then you and I will consider all offers on the table."

Emerson hunches slightly as if the air keeping him inflated leaked out.

"But—" I jerk my head to flick a stray hair out of my eyes. "I will hustle to put my new music out there before the end of the month. If it catches, I expect you to work with me to reassess."

Emerson shakes his head slowly, watching me secure the boat. When I reach out to help him onto the dock, he pulls me into an embrace. "I don't want you to lose your inheritance, Rai. With Lucas and Corinne gone, I'm the only one left to advise you. I feel responsible, and I do care about you."

I thump him on the back, and we break apart. "I know you do, Em. It's a shit time for both of us, but I'm a big-ass man who needs to make some big-ass decisions."

He tries to pet Kitae, who snaps at him. Emerson pulls away in time to avoid a mouth of needle-sharp teeth. "You're a real peach, Kitty."

"My man, Kitae, takes offense at your use of Kitty. He keeps score."

"Stow your beast away from tourists on craft fair days, Rainn." He emphasizes my full name. "If we get hit with a lawsuit over a fox bite, then selling the company will be a moot point."

I leave the marina with a backward glance at what's left of Cloudpath Music's headquarters after my parents downsized these past two years. They leased half the pink palace to a Lalale Island tour company. I see the big pic with more clarity following my stress chat with Em. My folks sensed the company that flourished in their heyday wasn't thriving anymore. Piyo knew it as well. No one looped me in much since they figured head-in-the-clouds Rai didn't give a crapping damn about business except as a vehicle for his own music.

They were right.

I viewed Cloudpath as a delivery system waiting on standby until I was ready to create new music. My attitude must have driven my family crazy, but they never pushed me. Moon, I'm an entitled ass.

Once it's just palms, Kitae, and me on the path to the lagoon, I inhale deeply to allow the scents of sand, sea, and island flowers to seep into my soul. Reality check. It's ridiculous to use the missing notes of my mystery woman's song as an excuse to stagnate any longer. My first big-ass man move must be to get island rock out into the world without her.

I kick a rotting hunk of wood. Fickle fate gifted me with the voice to perfect my new sound and then left me zero clues to find her? What did I do to piss fate off so badly? First, it robs me of giving Tani the farewell she deserves, and then conspires to rip Cloudpath Music from me just as I may have a shot at reviving it.

The better question is: What does a dude need to do to get fate to mellow the hell out and cut him some slack?

I follow Kitae along the shoreline toward the lagoon and my hammock. I'll rock under a blue sky and listen to the advice of wind and trees to conjure a successful path through this mess. In the words of my parents, *find the flow, baby.*

4

MIAQUA

THE SOUND QUALITY IN MIAQUA'S CONCERT HALL IS MIND-BLOWING. The hall was off-limits the summer Tani and I came to music camp here as kids. The Mermaids aren't singers, they're alchemists, blending resonances alongside intersections of acoustic shadows in an otherworldly, bone-piercing experience. I've downloaded every note the sister group ever recorded, but a one-step-removed interaction didn't prepare me for the richness of their live concert.

Juan Luna leans in so close his breath tickles my ear. "I'm tripping on the gestalt here, Bro. Dig that floor. Is it driftwood?"

I check out the stage which tilts in a slight rake to the audience. He's right. The floor is a tapestry of twists and gnarls through grayed wooden strands shot through with a dozen veins of various blues for a marbling effect. It's an art piece. The slightest bleed of white through the thick layer of varnish suggests clouds drifting across the sea-inspired stage floor. Slowly moving patterns from overhead banks of spotlights saturate the air both onstage and in the audience with crisscrossing beams and dots of blues from aqua to cobalt. Everyone, performer and spectator alike, exist together in this transformative experience filled with illusions of currents and gentle whirlpools.

Juan Luna drops his head back, eyes closed. "I'm massively into the moment." His shoulders rock, joining the flow of the song. I half expect him to kick his legs and attempt to swim up through an imaginary tide.

Emerson shoots him a *shush* glare. I brought Juan Luna as a buffer for the pressure valve Em cranks higher by the hour. My laid-back friend also serves the purpose of flustering Emerson, pulling focus off me.

I melt alongside Juan Luna's tripping and let my eyelids drift shut. The Mermaids sing the texture of rip currents through their musical bridges and echo the ocean roar from inside a conch shell during refrains. One song blends into the next as they tame the essence of shrill whale song into seductive harmonies. With my eyes closed and one finger tapping out the progression of verse to pre-chorus to chorus, I don't merely listen, I bond with their music.

Emerson nudges me. "If only your parents had made an offer to scoop up Miaqua Music in its infancy, they might have given Cloudpath a second wind."

My eyes snap open along with a burst of defensiveness. How dare he diss my folks when he's on the brink of dismantling their dream. I watch him watch the sisters, and realize it wasn't snark. The Mermaids move even the ole number cruncher. His eyes brighten at the next tune when silken slings in multiple shades of blue drop from above.

The song is new to me. It conjures the hiss of a bow through the water. Half the sisters perform an arial ballet, twirling and gliding through fabric high above the stage floor while the others mimic undulating movements of mermaids below. Instead of giving off a circus vibe, the choreography is poetic, a dead-on perfect counterpoint to their song.

I mutter under my breath. "The Mermaids would totally get what I'm trying to do with island rock."

Emerson's frown proves my comment rankled. "Sell to Sulaa,

and maybe she'll sign you as an artist if Miaqua Music and Cloudpath merge."

Em sees rows and columns where I see spirals of color woven between notes.

The Mermaids lure my attention back to the stage. The level of impact and immersion their performance provides is exactly what I ache to create with my island rock. I need to make music that connects the essence of a person to wind, moon, and the spirit of Lalale Island. I'll weave an ethereal tether between audience and music with the acoustic reflections and rhythmic punctuations of my island world. My artform will not be the new age, spacey soundscapes of my parents' generation. I will make music to incite dancing, singing, and joy. The undertone of something deeper will hold the listener captive until I choose to release them.

The song ends to the inadequate applause Emerson, Juan Luna, and I can produce. The Mermaids bow, maintaining their unique fluidity, then fade behind a beaded, deep blue curtain. A handful of beats later, the curtain parts in the center, and Sulaa Kylock appears. She opens her arms wide.

"My daughters appreciate the honor of performing for you, my friends." She glides to the edge of the slanted stage. Glide isn't the right word. Meanders with purpose? Slinks? I flip through mental files to connect movement with intention and shudder when I land on the match. Sulaa hunts, not with the focus of a bloodthirsty predator but with possession as her goal.

Emerson gives a slight bow. "The Mermaids are a wonder, Sulaa."

I prepare for a now-familiar round of negotiation hidden under the veneer of mutual kiss-assery. It's been the same story with all the labels interested in buying Cloudpath Music.

Strange unease skitters in my gut. My parents were superstitious about Miaqua. They never allowed Piyo and me to hit the rehabbed research center for concerts or the annual undersea festival hosted by Sulaa and Miaqua Music. Tani went every year and slipped us cool souvenirs like singing shells or coral flutes. I'd only scored a stint at Miaqua Music Camp the summer my parents left to scout new soundscapes in the rainforest. They left Piyo and me with Emerson, who didn't waste brain space stressing that Miaqua might be a denizen of dark ocean spirits. Piyo bought into my parents freak-out and passed on camp. He was always the more tentative of us Cloud brothers.

The folks flipped when they found out about my time at Miaqua. They made me wear a bracelet of black tourmaline beads for a year to cleanse my chakras and flush any dark forces I may have picked up. It was the first time I'd heard them refer to Sulaa as a sea witch.

Sulaa's gaze locks on mine, then Emerson's, and finally, it flicks cursively to Juan Luna, who actually purrs. I nudge him to shut up.

It's near impossible not to be captivated by the woman. Her height appears to increase as she draws closer until my six-foot-two frame feels like a child in the shadow of a grand figure. Sulaa is an undeniably large presence, not in a bulky way, but a commanding one. Her white, off-the-shoulder, satiny gown captures every subtle difference of blue from the spotlights in its folds. A golden trident on a thread thin chain in the hollow of her throat shines in brilliant contrast to skin that reminds me of the perfect shadings and luster of a polished teak statue. Lines of opalescent gems the size of an infant's palm dot her shoulders and give off their own light.

"You must be Lucas and Corinne's son, Rai," says Sulaa in a voice, pouring over me, the first wave of heat from a newly lit fire.

My attempt at a polite response is cut off as Sulaa seats herself with the pulsating grace of an immortal sea jelly. She curls long legs beneath her and leans on one arm, composed and in control. She could be a goddess lounging on a velvet couch at Olympus.

I reel within the cocoon of her company, unable to utter a single word. Of all the fascinating pieces in the composition that is Sulaa Kylock, her hair renders me mute. Every strand, instead of being the width of a dime, is as thick as my finger and a distinct shade of teal, peacock, lapis, cyan, bluebell, or azure. I suck in a breath, registering the origin of each hue. They are distinct color matches to the names of Sulaa's daughters, The Mermaids. Her locks chase around her head in an alluring pattern of twists and braids culminating in the shape of a crown.

Sulaa Kylock's entire being is performance art.

The three of us gravitate toward her like tides to the moon. Juan Luna is there first. He reaches out, and Sulaa places her free hand in his. The idiot kisses Sulaa's knuckles. "Ms. Kylock, your daughters unravel my soul."

Sulaa laughs, tilting her chin to study him. Juan Luna's head lolls in concert with her movement, his eyes wide and dreamy. My friend is smitten. There's uncomfortable attraction rising in my chest as my gaze travels the length of Sulaa's body. I quickly turn away. This woman is a business venture and my mother's age. Checking her out is big time bad. I squash Juan Luna's foot with my own to snap us both out of our Sulaa daze.

Sulaa's glance flicks downward, catching my stomp. A lazy smile spreads across her wide lips. "Please meet my ladies?" She fans her arm with the grace of a ballerina to the upstage curtain. "The Mermaids love to connect with fans."

A bead of sweat rolls down the side of my face. The woman blows my mind.

Juan Luna boosts himself on stage with the determination of a high jumper. "We'd love to." He holds out a hand to me.

I wave him off. "Go ahead. I'll meet you in a few. The three of us are going to chat."

Emerson raises an eyebrow as Juan Luna scrambles up the slanted stage to meet The Mermaids. "The three of us, Rai?"

Sulaa's fingers rest on my shoulder. "I admire a man who protects his interests."

Her hand locks onto my body. It's unnerving. Trying for subtle, I create distance until her touch has no choice but to slip off me. This is one freakish sitch. First, I start to be hot and bothered over the woman, then she frightens me. All those sea witch comments borne of my parents' paranoia mess with my head. For a sec, I wish I'd worn my bracelet of black tourmaline beads for peace of mind.

Em gives me the out. "Sulaa and I have a few negotiation points to iron out. Go reel in Juan Luna before he makes a fool of himself. I'll text when we're ready for you to join."

"Cool," I say with a nod. A savvy businessman I'm not. Instead of following Juan Luna's athletic lead to storm the sisters, I head up a ramp next to the stage and step behind the shimmering curtain.

My friend is the center of a sister tangle as they laugh and fawn over him. He's busting out the knuckle-kissing routine he used on Sulaa. Juan Luna possesses a deadly fun sense of humor. His new face is probably a novelty to this group of women who rarely appear outside Miaqua. If memory serves, all the sisters choose to make their home here underwater. Hey, home is home. I can't imagine living anywhere besides Lalale Island. They must feel the same about Miaqua.

Why leave? There's a full-blown recording studio in addition to their performance spaces and a wing still functioning as a research center. Lots of peeps who work the Miaqua shows and annual sea faire live down here as well. I remember when several families from the commune relocated at Miaqua for a new experience despite my parents' misgivings. I dig the appeal of an undersea zip code. It's exotic, just not my brand of bitchin'.

A melodious laugh catches my attention. It's familiar. I stare into the group, afraid to believe my ears. Did I hear the voice from the woman on the beach?

Juan Luna calls to me. "Dude, join the party."

I make my way to the women, my hearing finely tuned to the sounds of their laughter. A few still lounge in the silk slings from their finale. Other sisters relax in the wheeled contraptions they glided across stage in.

"This is my man, Rai Cloud," says Juan Luna. "Okay, I'm going in." He rubs his hands together and gestures at the tallest singer. "Rai, meet Teal."

"One right," answers the sister who must be Teal in a sing-song voice. The name matches the color of ringlets cascading over her shoulders. Not the voice of my dream.

"You should quit while you're ahead," says another sister. Her voice is dainty and sweet, but unfamiliar.

Juan Luna's bounces his lips together. "Good plan, ah..."

"Bluebell," she says.

"I was totally going to say Bluebell," says Juan Luna, and they all share a laugh.

My gaze drifts over their heads as I sharpen my hearing. It must have been a bout of wishful thinking, taking me back to the mystery woman. As if one of these women grew fins and a tail to pluck me out of a stormy sea.

"Listen to this," says Juan Luna, tugging at my arm. He holds up one, then two, then three fingers. The sisters sing his name in a multi-part harmony. Juan Luna points to me. "Now do his." They oblige.

The sound of my name resonates in my chest. "Wow. Amazing." Amazing with a side dish of disappointment as my hope of a miracle fizzles.

She is not here.

I'm at a loss where to continue my search. I've walked the stretch of Malibu beach where she saved me and lingered under moonlight until dawn with the hope she'd walk out of the shadows to find me.

"Your performance was equally beautiful. Thank you."

"Maybe these lovely ladies will allow you to sing with them when Sulaa buys Cloudpath Music," says Juan Luna.

"Sounds like a party," says the sister with hair the color of a lapis lazuli gemstone.

An empty silk sling off to the side catches Juan Luna's attention.

"Mind if I give this a whirl?" he asks. The sisters close in to give him pointers as he awkwardly wraps himself in stretchy fabric.

With The Mermaids entertained, I decide to do a bit of poking around offstage. There are bent wooden acoustic reflectors and artfully placed speaker arrays with gauzy covers. I mentally catalogue these factors that create The Mermaid's on-brand undersea sound.

Through an open double door past the wings, a flicker catches my eye. I follow the light to find a corridor lined with a series of round windows. Through their glass, I see a second wall separated from the first by a few yards. The sight beyond stops my breath. Past the far bank of bulbous-shaped windows is the sea.

Shafts of sunlight knife through greenish water. A school of silver-blue fish weave back and forth, causing the flicker I saw before. Layers of kelp dance in the currents below the windows. I sway to their watery rhythm.

"*Mmmm, wah. Mmmm, wah*," I hum, trying to orchestrate the music of the kelp.

A shadow flits past a window to my right and breaks my concentration. When I turn to look, there's nothing. I walk to where the shadow disappeared. Is someone in the second hallway watching me, listening?

I glance farther into the narrow space but see no one. No doubt, another trick of fish through sunlight. Facing the bright streaks from above, I close my eyes to imagine the warmth they carry through the cool ocean. Blowing air from my lips, I make an *ooooooo* sound. It doesn't work. What sound would light through water make?

Beyond my closed eyelids, something blocks the light. As I snap my eyes open, a fleeting wisp of blue slides away outside the window nearest me. This time, I press close to the glass, trying to follow the dash of color. A face pops up in front of me.

"Holy shit." I stumble backward. First, I catch the reflection of my open-mouthed shock, but then I see a riot of bright blue hair surrounding a heart-shaped face that tapers to the curvy point of a chin. The woman's laughter is muffled behind glass. She taps a finger to the window and drops out of sight.

"Hey," I call out. "What was the jump scare for?"

Off to my right, there's a tap on the glass. I dash over to find the woman waiting for me. She's stunning with eyes a shade lighter than her hair. The slight upward curve at the outer corners of her eyes set them in a perpetual smile. Her words warble through the window. "What are you doing out here?"

Her expression is playful, so I join in the game. "Looking for you."

With a slap to the glass, she winks, long lashes brushing cheekbones, and disappears. I don't catch movement to the right or left. Where did she go? Her reflection in the windows to the sea give me the answer. I find her crouched low near a window to the left, looking upward. Tricky. I see her strategy. She'll follow my shadow to catch me unawares again. My competitive side kicks in. *No, you don't.*

I hunch down and move a trio of windows away from her and then lean nonchalantly against the glass, waiting for her arrival. She darts up, and I yawn. We both break out in laughter at our flirty game of hide and seek and then take in the look of one another.

I lay a finger against the window. "Who are you?"

She flicks her blue hair and shoots me the *"Are you really that stupid?"* look.

Of course, I know she's one of The Mermaids. I mimic her hair flick and sing a few bars of one of their hits. She licks her finger, draws a tick mark in the air, and points at me.

I rephrase my question. "Which sister?" Who bailed on the meeting of the Juan Luna fan club to follow me out here?

She lifts a handful of bright blue hair and lets it fall in layers to her shoulder. Okay, we're playing *Name That Blue*. I stare at her. I'm guessing she's about my age, twenty-five. Ah, she's the youngest sister. They're named in reverse alphabetical order which makes her...

She raises her hand, five fingers outstretched. One by one, she lowers them, counting down. If I win, I'll ask for an invitation to her side of the glass as my prize. When her last finger is left, I smile. "Azure." Ah, this woman is the daughter of Sulaa Kylock and the president of Tempest Tunes, Prospero Tempesta. I guess Sulaa won Azure's recording contract in their divorce. It would be a crime to break up The Mermaids' incredible synergy by removing any one of the sisters.

Azure taps a finger to the tip of her straight nose and smiles.

"I'm Rai Cloud." I'm rewarded with a *Do you really think I'm that stupid?* expression. "Loved your show. Big fan."

Azure pats her chest, points to me, and hums a short phrase I recognize from my one hit, *Fire Capped Waves*. Glass muffles the quality of her voice, but I catch the familiar progression of notes. Her smile is shy, and color deepens the shadowed apricot of her skin.

"At least, I've got one fan left."

She shakes a finger at me, chiding my sarcasm. Her gaze flows down my face from brow to lips.

"Thanks," I say and press my palm against the glass.

Azure spreads her fingers against her side of the window. I take the opportunity to stare at her gentle smile. Our gazes meet with matching interest.

"How do I get to where you are?" I ask, jutting a finger to her double-windowed breezeway.

When Azure raises a hand to show me the way, I draw back in alarm. For a hot second, I swear I catch a face peering at us from outside a seaside window behind her. Azure whips her head around to see what freaked me out.

"There you are," chimes a voice behind me. Sulaa and Emerson emerge from the stage door.

I spin to face them. My body blocks the window. "I was checking out the space, and I ran into..."

When I turn to the window, Azure is gone.

"Ran into?" asks Emerson.

Something inside tells me to keep my flirt with Azure on lockdown. "This cool bank of viewports."

"Yes, I'm sure you enjoyed a lovely view," says Sulaa with a half-smile. There's an unnerving *caught you* gaze in her plum-colored eyes.

5

SULAA'S GARDEN

I PICTURE MY CHEST RISING AND FALLING WITH AIRLESS BREATHS. RAI
looked stunned when his gaze met mine—if he truly saw me. My
face was plastered to the window where I watched the game
between the singer I recognize as Azure from The Mermaids
and him.

If he did see me, it couldn't have been more than a glimpse
before I ducked. It was probably a shark or an ugly-ass barracuda
with an underbite swimming behind me that spooked him.

My father took me diving into the unnaturally warm currents
that swirl around Miaqua creating an anomaly of an ecosystem
with tropical critters, including barracuda. Several artists from the
commune came to work at the research station to photograph and
render the bizarre mix of species drawn to the out-of-place coral
reef surrounding Miaqua. For a hot second, I considered becoming
an aquatic illustrator, but diving was never my happy place. I snort.
Isn't this irony 101?

I move along the windows, hoping to see Rai when someone
dives into the water near a corner of Miaqua. My first instinct to
hide is quickly shattered when I lock onto the figure barely ten feet
from me. It's Azure. She glides through the water completely naked

without any air tanks. Is this a *who can last the longest in the sea* challenge The Mermaids play as a dare to one another? Instead of circling back to whatever door she jumped out of, Azure cuts through the water with a twirl as a neon, lime-colored covering flows down her body. In seconds, the woman's legs fuse into a tail. Holy, moon. Azure is not just one of The Mermaids, she's a legit mermaid.

One I've seen before.

She darts off after the bright yellow shuttle, leaving Miaqua for Lalale Island and follows at a distance. Azure is following Rai. A phantom sensation of unease and distaste flows through me. Azure is the mermaid who saved Rai when his canoe flipped. I witnessed her powerful fish tail propel them with inhuman speed through the stormy sea.

A more powerful urge overtakes me. I've got to protect Rai. What game is the mermaid playing? Is she a myth, a siren with an agenda to lure him into some dark mermaidy fate? Did Azure save him from death to toy with him now, possess him for sport in phase two of her fluke-flipping plan? I can't allow the sparkle of interest in his eyes as he flirty peek-a-booed with the blue-haired liar to burn any brighter.

I cut through the water until I'm abreast of the shuttle window. "Rai Cloud," I shout, testing my voice with no result. The mermaid takes no notice of me. I surge around to the other side of the vehicle. I'm about to pound on its metal hull when I see my father. A rush of sadness overtakes me, and I let the teardrop shuttle speed away with Azure in its wake.

My dad was right there, close enough to touch. I want so badly to feel him clutch me to his chest and promise me the strange new reality I'm stuck in will go away. I'm overwhelmed with loss. There must be a way to tell my father or Rai I'm still here.

I want a bridge back to life, to the world I was ripped out of by the fire. Did I blow my chance when I swam away from the woman at Miaqua who waved to me the night of the storm? I was so messed up and confused that fear and mistrust overwhelmed me. I fled for home, Lalale Island, and comfort when I should have connected with her. Leaving sea for land was shockingly effortless. It was a rush to rise off the ground and nest in the treetops. I swim, I walk, I fly, but I'm invisible to the living, except the woman in the window. Will she give me a rewind?

The shuttle is out of sight. I'm left behind. Again.

I have a single thread connecting me to the life beyond my reach, and I pray she's still at Miaqua. I must find her. Determined to not chicken out, I swim back to the exact place outside Miaqua I lingered on the night I woke in the sea to the sound of Rai's voice saying he loves me.

The windows are empty.

Broken bits of kelp float through my body. I'm nothing but another hunk of sea trash.

I judge time from the shifting light above the surface. Time doesn't matter. I've nowhere else to be.

The moon brings her. The figure is as imposing as I remember. She doesn't wave. Is the freakishly tall babe real or a manifestation of my intense longing to connect?

I lift a hand in greeting.

Our gazes lock. She raises one finger. A rich, commanding voice slithers through my head.

Wait.

She does see me. I hear her in my freakin' brain. How...

The explanation is as simple as it is terrifying. Is this the sea witch Granny Blossom warned us about?

Does *wait* mean she wants to chat? Or... Damn. I'm unnatural. I'm wrong. Is her plan to lure me in to wipe me out of existence because I'm a blight on the balance of reality?

I dart toward the sandy bottom. My urge to survive as whatever I am blows away the need to connect with a sea witch. A bed of buttercup-shaped, crimson flowers flutters below me. They're not tall enough to hide in. I skirt the bottom of Miaqua station and press against steel, blending into shadow. Moonlight doesn't reach my hiding place. When I try to sneak farther away, a voice crackles through the water.

"Hey, you down there."

I flatten my body behind one of the metal spines.

"Sulaa sent me with an invite for you to join her in the garden."

Sulaa. Sulaa Kylock, the Sea Witch. Is she truly the woman who saw me, who waved? I'd never seen her. She had nothing to do with music camp and keeps an invisible visual profile in the media. I only caught a quick peek at her once in the conference room on the island years ago when Cloudpath and Miaqua Music were fighting over a band. She'd been seated behind a laptop in shadow. The only piece of her the light caught was a blue rainbow of snaky-looking hair. Rai and I were busted, trying to check out the woman rumored to be a sea witch. We earned beach cleaning duty for a month.

I peer around the girder and quickly duck back into hiding. The thing I see can't possibly be speaking. It's got the head of a lionfish, with crusty brown stripes, a frowning pout mouth, and finny spikes surrounding two small bulging blue eyes. The body and limbs below the monstrous head are gangly with what appear to be ragged cloth hanging off a human frame. Its tattered, rust-colored shirt bobbles in the current. The thing's feet are hidden beneath bright yellow swim fins.

It flows closer. "Cut the hiding crap. I don't have time for it. Monsters can see monsters."

I push off the station and raise my fist to the beastie. "Screw you. I'm not a monster."

Its spikey fins ripple, and a watery chortle bubbles through the water between us. "If I had a nickel for every...never mind. Follow me."

I hold my ground. "Who the hell are you?"

"Who the hell are you?"

This dude is an irritation I don't need. "If you don't know who I am, maybe you've got the wrong person."

"Monster," he corrects like a teacher counting the days until retirement.

"My name is Tani, not monster."

"Tani/Monster, sea star/star fish, tomato, tomahhhto."

"Shut it," I snap and swivel to swim off. Truth smacks me across the face. "You hear me?"

"Monsters hear monsters."

"I'm not..." I trail off. I can hear me, and not just in my head. Water swirls near my lips. I'm making sound. My gaze snaps up to the lionfish dude. This is totally a *does a tree make a sound when it falls in the forest if there's no one to hear it* moment. "Who are you?"

"My friends call me Calliwag. Well, they would if I had any." His swollen eyes circle in a freaky, blinking loop. I can't look at them.

"You work for Sulaa Kylock?"

He makes a watery sniff. "Do not torment me. I work *with* Sulaa Kylock." He straightens as much as a lionfish monster man can.

I move out from underneath Miaqua to stare at the windows, looking for Sulaa.

"Bottom line, Tani monster, Sulaa wants a word. Don't say no. The lady boasts a short fuse." He rests hands over the gills on his head.

Fear sizzles through me. If Sulaa created this Calliwag freak, she's not a person to piss off. Demented curiosity replaces fear. Sulaa wants to meet with me. If anyone has answers I'll never find on my own, it's a sea witch.

"Okay, Calliwag. Let's see the garden."

He bounce-walks through the water instead of swimming. It reminds me of old videos of astronauts on the moon. His flipper feet knock wavering kelp stalks out of the way and smack a few neon-striped fish. Graceful, he's not. I swim to follow, opting for the more elegant way to move.

Calliwag mumbles about turning me into a barnacle if I don't speed up as I trail behind him alongside Miaqua through the turfmoor of an underwater swamp. If he didn't border on ridiculous, I might be afraid. Calliwag is clearly a messenger, not a witch's enforcer, or he'd be dragging me to Sulaa wrapped in seaweed. We break free of the tangles to leave the station behind and curve around a protruding seawall of black rock. Cut near the bottom of its obsidian face is an archway with a door made of chalky, petrified driftwood. He pulls a long, old-fashioned key that looks like it belongs on a dungeon keeper's ring from his ragged pocket and unlocks the door.

"Welcome to Sulaa's Garden." Calliwag gestures me inside. "Some of my best work."

I float outside the entrance. "After you."

He snuffles and his head spikes flatten. "Right. The bigger monster inside will eat me first. Such an uncaring, selfish plan to sacrifice poor Calliwag."

This guy's personality is pricklier than his head. "You're a party in a box, and in case you're not reading me clearly, I mean you are on my last nerve."

"Not the first time I've heard that, Tani Monster." He leans against the side of the archway. "In or out, your choice."

As if any choice besides floating through my weird-ass existence is even possible. I raise my chin and swim through.

As I cross the threshold, a gust of what feels like air nearly knocks me over. The odor of fish overcooked in a microwave slams into me, and I wave a hand in front of my nose. It's the first time I've smelled anything since I popped into being. My non-breath hitches as it becomes real breath. I raise a hand to discover warmth against my palm as I blow onto it. My hair trails, not floats across my shoulders. Arms dangle at my sides instead of bobbing in water.

I dart a look to the walls of the garden. Just beyond them, the sea appears to lap against a transparent boundary. I'm in a bizarre air pocket beneath the surface.

The "garden" is eerily familiar. Beneath a dome of craggy black stone is an underwater version of the forbidden caliche forest on the northern tip of Lalale Island. Desolation filled with the calcified skeletons of once living trees and plants stretches in a circle nearly to the edge of vision. Thick white roots spill over rocks, petrified in place for who knows how many decades. Whorls and gnarls in trunks appear like the melting faces in a Salvador Dali painting. Nothing moves. My feet drift to the ocean floor and crunch over broken fragments of shells or bones covered in a layer of ash. It's a garden of death. These fossilized remains of ruined beauty stand rigid and mournful here beneath the surface like their twin on the island above, a place of massacre and despair.

I can't stay here. My throat constricts in panic.

Before I turn and flee, Calliwag shuts the door behind us. He flaps past. "Have fun," he snorts.

I try to cry out for him to open the door. Words stagnate and refuse to come. He's not gone far so I start after him. My legs feel as if they are attempting to move through wet clay. I wave my arms but fail to catch Calliwag's attention. The monster navigates to a far niche in the wall of rock covered in shadow. He knocks. A door carved of stone opens, and the fish man drops to a knee, head bowed. Nearly hidden in the dim, a man hovers above Sulaa's lacky. The mystery dude's shadow bleeds across the ground like spilled ink. Calliwag gestures at me, and the man's head whips in my direction. In a flash, he grabs the monster's arm to drag him inside.

It takes a few moments for sound to reach my ears. I swear I hear the faint cry of a young child before it's drowned by a growl and then the slam of a door. That wasn't Sulaa. I definitely saw a man, not a woman, and he didn't want me to see him.

"What do you think of my garden?"

I startle at the syrupy voice and swing behind one of the white, stony tree trunks.

"Don't be afraid, dear one. I'm a friend. Come out, let's chat."

It takes a few swallowing motions before I can speak. Through a split in chalky, dead tree branches, I find the woman who waved at me from the window of Miaqua, Sulaa Kylock, the Sea Witch. I keep the trunk between us. "Your garden is nasty."

She laughs. "Merely a deterrent for unwanted visitors. Close your eyes, count to three, and look again."

I make it to two before I open my eyes and gasp. The deathly vibe of the caliche forest is gone. There are no broken shells beneath my feet. I wiggle my toes in twinkling, silky, silver sand. The fragmented white tree trunks grow tall and fatten into pastel magentas. Each wears a halo of aquamarine leaves that remind me of broccoli flowers. Rising all around me in delicate tapered pedestals is coral in varying shades of greens from hunter to lime, interspersed with stripes of blood red. Bright yellow fingers of young coral polyps to rival sunflowers gently sway in batches around the garden. I've fallen into a design of the neon-colored tie-dyed T-shirts the commune sells at beach fairs.

The scent of fruity red wine suffuses the garden, driving out the stench of burnt fish. I ease out of hiding to face Sulaa Kylock. She presents like the statues of goddesses and heroes I've seen in museums on the mainland. The woman is taller than my father and far less wimpy. She'd give Rai or Piyo, the bulky Cloud brothers, a challenge in a wrestling match. A gold trident the size of a child's hand at the hollow of her throat gives off a slight glow. Whips of blue hair chase around her head, some meeting on top and others trailing over her shoulders. This version of Sulaa's prismatic paradise is also filled with air.

Sulaa lays a hand on my shoulder. The sensation of her fingers gripping my body freaks me out. "Beautiful, isn't it? When you truly look, you see the truth."

I pull out of her grasp. "You can feel me?"

"Of course, Tani."

At the sound of my name, my knees weaken, and I drop onto a seat of tangerine coral behind me. "How?"

Her laugh is deep and throaty, not unpleasant. "I won't insult your intelligence by pretending you don't know who I am."

"It's true then? You're a sea witch."

She purses her lips. "I prefer sorceress. It packs a bit more dignity, wouldn't you agree?"

"How did you know where to send Calliwag to find me?"

Sulaa reaches out and trains a strand of my newly silvered hair behind my ear. "Your pain, Tani. It runs through the sea like a dark river. The pain of a daughter is a blow to my heart, a song I know too well."

There's a familiar trickle falling down my cheek. I reach to find a pair of touchable tears.

Sulaa reaches a hand for me to take. "Come. I will show you."

When I lay my hand in hers, I feel warm skin. Her fingers wrap around mine, and I stare. "I don't understand how you can touch me as if I'm really here."

Eyes the strange color of bruises flare. "You are here. You are real. It takes the gift of true sight to find you." Her expression softens. "You're newly awakened, daughter of sea and island. I heard your cry through the storm. I watched you find your way to Miaqua, to me. I am the teacher, the mother you seek to guide you through this new reality."

I pull my hand away. "I don't want a new reality." I bury my face in my hands. "I want the old reality back." My hands clench into fists and pound the sides of my head. "I want the impossible."

For a flash, Sulaa's eyes narrow but then relax. "Wishes are not always bits of fluff that float away on a breeze or a current. Do not despair. Let's take things one step at a time."

I back away. "Ever since I was a kid, I've been warned about you."

She laughs and wiggles her fingers at me. "Beware the sea witch. Oh, dear one, people tell dark tales of things they don't understand." Her humor drifts into a gentle smile, and kind eyes fill me with a sense of belonging in this strange and beautiful place. "You've never feared the green witch, Granny Blossom, of your commune. I am no different."

The Granny Blossom who scared the shit out of us about Sulaa.

"Let me set your mind at ease." Sulaa raises an arm. Like gentle rain, a curtain of jellyfish descends beyond the boundary of the garden. Their transparent glory catches starlight from above the surface and splits it into ribbons of muted colors. We are inside a delicate rainbow. I spin to take in every angle and nuance of the breathtaking phenomena.

Sulaa threads an arm around my shoulders while I trip out on the jelly shower. It hits me like a kidney punch that the wispy mess I believed my body has become is natural and solid to the sea witch. "Come. Meet my daughters, and you will see the depth of devotion I hold for my dear ones."

With a wave of her hand, Sulaa transports us to a stage where a quintet of women rehearses a musical number. It's the Miaqua concert hall. I've been here for shows. I recognize The Mermaids at first glance. At second glance, I cover my mouth to stifle a cry of horror.

These are not The Mermaids I've seen in videos and live performances. These are distorted imitations of those women. Gills cover the sides of one singer's face from temple to chin. Another perches on the edge of something that looks like a dolphin stroller. Her body ends in a tapered stump just below her hips. In place of two legs, a third has a split tail covered in scrapes and scars. On others, there are fins where arms should be or mouths with rows of sharp teeth and slitted cat eyes.

I turn away, afraid I'll wretch in front of this shocking collection of malformity.

"Mama," cry the women in a single note of harmony. Sulaa pets and kisses her five daughters. As she touches each, the strand of her own hair matching that daughter's shade flares and then dims as she moves to the next. Strange magic connects mother to daughters. They are happy, a family. The group giggles and chatters, not a one noticing me.

I look at myself, afraid of what I might see in this theater of cold truth. I find skin, legs, and the clingy, sleeveless turquoise sheath dress I wore the night of my engagement bonfire. On my feet are peach-colored, beaded sandals Tutu made for my last birthday. I am the Tani I know.

A graceful voice sings, drawing my attention to the group. The Mermaid with deep cyan scales covering her in a second skin shares a new song lyric with her mother. Sulaa asks and answers a flurry of questions, daughters riveted by her words. There is great love here, no judgement or acknowledgement of the unnatural. Am I seeing true forms, or did the sorceress slap a weird filter over my brain for my first afterlife lesson?

I move to the far side of the stage, putting distance between me and the unsettling family confab. When Sulaa's back is turned, I crouch and then stretch, willing my body to fly the way I was able to do on the island. My feet stay rooted to the glossy driftwood stage floor. I strain against the gravity that's reclaimed me. Is this Sulaa's doing? The strange new powers of moving through air and water frightened me at first. Now I long for them. I'm suddenly aware I truly breathe because I start to hyperventilate. I lean against the wall to slow my breath and stare at the five damaged sisters. Five. There is a missing sister. Like a stab to the soul, I realize who it is. Azure. She's not among these tragic sisters with their collection of wrongness.

The dawn chirp of a joyful bird sounds from the audience. "Sisters." As if on cue, Azure runs up the center aisle of the theater and jumps on stage. "I've brought presents." The youngest of The Mermaids carries a small drawstring bag woven from seaweed. From it, she pulls out a paint brush, hair combs, necklaces, lipsticks, a small notepad, and pen among other treasures she distributes among her sisters. "And for you, Peacock, I saved the best for last." Azure pulls a long peacock feather from the bag and tickles her sister under the chin.

Peacock grasps the feather and waves it. Instead of words, her voice squeaks like a delighted dolphin as she clutches Azure in an embrace. The other women cluster around the pair in a sisterly group hug.

Sulaa stands apart from her daughters. Her lips purse as she studies Azure. "You've been to the surface."

Azure flips her hair. "I told you. Dinner with my father for his birthday."

After stalking Rai in the shuttle.

Sulaa's dark skin reddens to brick. The storm in her strange-ass purple eyes makes me retreat a few steps. My movement catches the sorceress's eye for a second before she refocuses on the women. Not going to air the dirty family laundry in front of the invisible visitor, eh? Interesting.

"I'm sure Prospero enjoyed the visit. You were careful?"

Prospero. Shit. That's right. Prospero Tempesta, head dude of Tempest Tunes, is Azure's father. The man they call Stormbringer. I always assumed the title was a tie-in to his record label name and his legendary public smackdowns with Midas Lear at Golden Pipes and Grant Gothel at Rampion Records. In this world of mermaids and sea witches, a fellow named Stormbringer may be more than he seems.

Azure pulls off a perfect imitation of her mother's lip purse. "I'm always careful, Mother, and I don't need your permission to surface. You've got me covered." She pats the seaweed pouch at her side.

Sulaa strokes her youngest daughter's hair. "No, darling, you don't. For safety's sake, I need to be in the loop on your trips out of Miaqua. What if the lure of the land overwhelms you and your scales dry? I must be ready to bring you home if you become too weak to do it yourself."

Azure leans into her mother's touch. "You worry too much. I'm an adult. I know the risks."

Scales dry? I don't see a single scale on Azure. She's as put together as I am or was. There are no signs of the oddities that plague her sisters except—

Azure was half-fish, half-human beneath the waves. Here, she stands, or rather runs, around on two legs. She was fully human, flirting with Rai. Azure can shift between mermaid and human, looking unnervingly hot in both forms while her sisters come off as hybrid mermaid experiments gone terribly wrong. Who spiked the punch at this party?

The azure strand of Sulaa's hair pulses. Azure lovingly runs a finger along the bright blue glow. "Calm yourself, Mama. You know even my fascination with my father's world..." She raises her eyes upward. "Would never tempt me enough to be careless, not when I've got my sisters to care for."

Sulaa takes Azure's face in her hands and kisses her daughter's forehead. "You are a fine young woman, my darling."

Blighted sisters, scales drying, above vs. below the surface talk... I have a thousand questions for Sulaa. Gathering my nerve, I straighten up, take a step toward the group, and open my mouth to make myself known. A sense of late afternoon fog rolling in wafts over me, and I tumble into gray mist.

6

WISH IS A FOUR-LETTERED WORD

I LAND IN A HEAP AT SULAA'S FEET. THE WITCH'S STARE BORES INTO me, a dark contrast to the vibrant garden around us. The energy of her power writhes through the air. It only takes a few seconds for disorientation to shift into wariness. I've never been at anyone's mercy, and this babe makes me feel caged. I should bust through the garden door and find a nice fat whale to hide behind. I gulp down the futility of my plan. Sulaa found me once, she'll find me again.

"Do you see, Tani, that I take care of those I love? My daughters know the sorrow of not being whole. I devote myself to give each what they need to experience a sense of worth and accomplishment." Her gaze softens. "I sense similar struggles in you, new daughter, set adrift in your fragile reality. Will you allow me to care for you as I do my own?"

New daughter? The title sends prickly sensations across my Sulaa-created skin. "I'm seriously confused here. I've seen The Mermaids perform live, in videos, on TV. They looked perfectly normal. None of the—" I move my fingers next to my cheeks to mimic fluttering gills. Sulaa gives me a patient look as if she's waiting for me to catch up. "How do you hide their..." I need to tread lightly here. Insulting Sulaa's daughters might be a trigger for her. "Differences?"

She smiles. "It's a sorceress thing, masking the truth of my sweet daughters' challenges from those who don't deserve their secrets."

I shake my head. "Can't your sorceress thing undo those challenges?"

Sulaa trails a finger along a golden-brown coral flower. "Sadly, that is beyond even my talents."

Her expression breaks my heart, and my nervous prickles smooth into renewed curiosity over Sulaa Kylock.

"Their imperfections must be a burden I carry."

"Azure looks put together," I say, not giving up the info. I've seen her all mermaided out. I only score a *hmm* in response at first.

Sulaa twirls a strand of azure hair around her finger. "She's my biggest challenge. The others are content in our beautiful home. Azure tests, pushes dangerously close to her limits. The world above the waves is not the friend she thinks it could be."

Before she elaborates, Calliwag's flippers bounce-slap along the path to our coral grotto. "Message from up top, Sulaa."

Her voice shifts from soothing mommy to business shark. "From Emerson? Did my offer get a bite from the Cloud kid?"

There's a quick pang in my chest, hearing my father's name. At the mention of Rai, the pang spreads into a pool of longing. As if sensing my feeling, Sulaa switches her attention from her servant to me.

He gurgles an answer. "For Azure."

Sulaa crosses her arms. "Well?"

His fins point up like a team of exclamation points. "We're into screening messages now?" Sulaa frowns, and Calliwag raises a human hand to the side of his grinning fishy mouth to mime, letting me in on a secret. "We are into that." Sulaa clears her throat, and the fish man snaps a salute. "An invite for Azure to meet Rai Cloud on Lalale Island."

This can't be good news for Mama Bear. She just complained

about reeling Azure in from her surface visits. It's not good news for me because the thought of Azure ramping up her flirty-flirty with Rai fills my gut with fish bones.

Rai Cloud loves me. Miss tail-swishing babe needs to back off.

A wave of lightheadedness swoops in. It doesn't matter if Rai loves me. I'm a non-thing. Still, pettiness pops a tattle out of me. "I saw Azure flirt with Rai at Miaqua, in the room with all the windows."

My tone is bitter. Each word brittle enough to snap in half.

Sulaa studies me with narrowed eyes, then turns to her monster. "I will pass along the message," says Sulaa.

He leans against a coral stack and checks his fingernails, rocking defiant nonchalance.

"The kelp beds need tending, Calliwag."

"Delightful," he groans with a slurpy sound. "If I get another otter bite, expect a strongly worded letter." The lionfish man flap-slaps down the silver sand path, grumbling.

Sulaa blows out a breath. "The seas will run dry if that hagseed ever yields a kind answer."

Azure and Rai can't get together. It's an impossible match. Her mer-reality will only crush him in the end. "Before you allow things go any further between Azure and Rai, please understand, he is a soul filled with light. He's a gentle, sensitive artist."

When she turns to me, sarcasm is replaced with dewy eyes. "Oh, my sweet daughter. Come." She opens her arms. "Your longing for this man crushes my heart."

"I don't... I can't. It's too late." I step away from her, but a pull draws me into her arms. I'd be lying if I didn't admit to a shade of envy when I watched her gush over her daughters. Being held, felt, and heard nudges aside some of the emptiness that has been living within me since I woke in the sea.

Sulaa croons in my ear. "The source of your pain is clear to me now. It's not about the life you no longer cling to. It's lost love."

My tears come with such force they stain her white satin dress. I dab my face and relish this single sweet reminder of what I used to be. The secret of my lingering love for Rai haunts my spirit. Finally, here is someone completely disconnected from my shame of trading Rai for Piyo with whom I can share truth without fear of judgment. "Yes," I murmur. "Rai Cloud. We should have been together. I ruined us."

Sulaa holds me at arm's length. "Ah, you scorned your fate."

I drop my head to avoid her eyes. I've never thought of my actions in such universal terms. Hearing them now, I know Sulaa is right. Rai is my heart's fate, and I turned my back on nature's plan.

Sulaa lifts my chin. "Tani, you've seen how I care for my daughters. Will you allow me to help you right your wrong?"

I pull away from her touch. "I'm dead. I know it. Rai is alive. We can't happen."

Sulaa shakes her head. "Oh, you dear thing. Death has not come for you yet. You are between. That is why I am able to embrace you as if you still bear flesh to cover your spirit."

I wipe my eyes and again marvel at my tears. I was nothing more than a wisp when consciousness sunk its vicious teeth into me. In Sulaa's presence, I've regained some sense of myself. "Between?"

"Accept there are choices still before you."

Choices? None of this existence feels like I have any choice, any power.

"To return to life or go forward to what waits beyond." Her plum eyes flare with super freaky, pinhead-sized sparks. "I am able to guide you along either path. It is the gift of mine I cherish most, granting peace to a spirit in turmoil."

"No offense. It's hard to buy into your explanation." I almost laugh. I've already bought into the fact Sulaa Kylock is a sorceress. I believe she cloaks The Mermaids so they appear normal to the world. The bottom line is the woman sees me, talks to me, touches me when I'm no more substantial than sea foam to the people who used to know me, to love me.

"Harder than buying into your reawakening? Why did consciousness return if not to allow you choice?"

Sulaa's claim is seductive. I want to go back. I want to be alive. Now that I know Rai Cloud loves me, I want a chance to fix the mess, the hurt I caused by leaving him for Piyo.

"If I choose to return, are we talking a memory wipe scenario for people who think I'm dead?"

Sulaa gracefully moves her arm to draw a figure eight. "More a reimagining of your Tani soul."

I don't speak this language of weird. "I don't get you."

She flicks a wrist. "Obviously, raising the dead is not a viable choice to reclaim any semblance of a human existence. I will change the vessel, but your true core will exist intact."

I want more details, but I'll save my thousand questions until it's time for me to blip back into the world. "You can make that happen?"

She nods. "All you need do is call me Mother and give me permission to be the guardian of your spirit on a new journey."

Not a tough call. Either float around as nothing for eternity or take a shot to reclaim my life. Even so, I sink teeth into my bottom lip until the sting convinces me this is happening.

I meet her gaze. "Okay."

She raises her eyebrows with a look parents get when you forget to say please. As a woman who was on the brink of marriage, I resent being treated like a child.

"Tani, dear, I need a bit more commitment than 'okay.'"

I riff on her previous words. "Sulaa, ah...Mother, please be the guardian of my spirit." The words are barely out of my mouth when Sulaa smacks her palm against my breastbone. Her fingers pinch and twist. She pulls shiny, gold and silver filaments from my body. It feels as if she's removing my ribs one at time. The breath I thought I'd regained is once again robbed from my lungs.

Sulaa raises her hand high, and a thick stream of filaments blast from my body to her palm, coalescing into a pulsing shadow. I collapse to the sand in agony as if she's splintered every muscle and bone.

A rumble in her throat explodes into a laugh. She shakes out the shadow like a wrinkled sheet and dangles it between us. Holy moon, the wavering shadow is me.

Sulaa wraps my shadow around her hand as if she's coiling an extension cord and stuffs it down her cleavage. The world around me transforms back onto the deadness of a ghostly caliche forest. My hand presses to my chest, searching for a heartbeat, the rise of breath, but I'm a void.

"Get up," says Sulaa.

Bent knees straighten and my feet hover inches above the ground of broken things. Despair as thick as oil runs within my spirit. "What have you done to me?"

"Lose the whine, it hurts my teeth." Sulaa shakes her head until the collection of blue strands trails over her shoulders. "I did nothing. You pledged your reality to me."

Anger shatters my woozy shell. "You promised to help me."

Sulaa fusses with her trident necklace. "And I will once you earn it."

"Earn it!" I flail an arm in her direction. "I didn't realize this was a deal. You acted like it was your divine purpose to help me with all your talk of choices. You fooled me."

Her grin is freakin' harsh. "Next time you make a deal with a sorceress, I recommend you ask more questions."

I squeeze hands into fists. She's right. I'm a total idiot. "How do I earn it? What exactly is my reality?"

Her lips curl into a sneer. "Your reality is my playground."

The urge to curse at her is quickly replaced by what's left of survival instinct, and I shut my mouth. There's only one choice for me now—figure out what I need to do to earn the help of a sorceress.

"We're going to see Azure. Pay attention to every detail between us so you'll be useful to me. She won't hear or see you. Don't get notions in your head about interfering."

Like being led with a rope around my neck, Sulaa drags me to the concert hall in Miaqua. We stand behind the last row of audience seats while onstage, Azure sits at a piano, picking out a song. Her voice brightens each note, traces of sunlight on a calm sea. The sound is pure, a perfectly cut diamond capable of reflecting any hue. She climbs higher and higher up the scale, singing notes completely new to me. There's no shading of a screech, rather the loveliest otherworldly tone. I want her to sing forever.

Rai would love her voice. The sounds she creates push the limits of convention, a goal he constantly strives for in his original music. I whisper. "Azure does have a voice to bring a man back from drowning." He's heard her voice before on a beach in the aftermath of a storm.

Sulaa's nails dig into my bare upper arm as she jerks me behind a pillar. "What do you mean?"

The sea witch isn't all-seeing. Good to know. Here's my shot to drive a stake between Rai and Azure so he'll be free when Sulaa finally helps me return to him.

"Azure busted out her mermaid skills and pulled Rai Cloud out of the sea the night of the freaky-deaky storm."

Behind the witch, a shadow rises twice her height. I swear it's outlined in a border of tiny flames. I cower.

"You've seen Azure's true form?" Each word pierces my skin like a knife tip.

"It was the same night I found myself in the sea. I was near his boat. She zipped past me and hauled him onto the beach." I nod at the stage. "Azure's singing brought him back to life."

Sulaa's shadow settles back into her skin. "Did he see her?"

"I don't know. He definitely heard her." Her eyelids tick lower in tiny increments and then flash open with the stare of a reptilian beastie. How does anyone think this woman isn't a witch? Should I mention Azure's dip out of Miaqua into the sea to follow Rai's shuttle or the kiss between them the night she saved him? I don't know if I'm more scared to withhold from Sulaa or nudge her anger farther than I already have. I tuck the tidbits away for now.

"You witnessed attraction between the two when Rai came to Miaqua?"

"That's a hard yes," I say, not bothering to hide the disdain in my voice. Surely, my news stacks the deck against Sulaa encouraging any meeting between the two.

She strokes her chin. "I sensed something behind his wanderings here." Her eyes switch from right to left, calculating. "So, Mr. Cloud's fool's agenda was to see if Miaqua might hold clues about his illusive rescuer. Not much of a stretch, is it? He was saved from the sea. We are sea dwellers." She heads down the center aisle toward the stage. "Follow."

Here we go. Sulaa will work her sorceress biz to keep Azure away from Rai, forcing the mermaid to keep her fishy secret to herself. He can't find out who saved him. I know Rai, he'd pledge his whole freakin' life to the woman.

"Your new song is transcendent, my dear," says Sulaa as she strolls upstage to the piano. I drop cross-legged at the edge of the stage.

"Not too unnaturally high?" asks Azure, tapping her bottom lip. "I want to expand the edges of my range but still sound—"

"Human?" says Sulaa, sliding onto the piano bench next to her daughter.

Azure closes her eyes for a long moment before meeting her mother's gaze and nods.

Sulaa pets Azure's jewel-toned hair. "You're every bit as human as you are my daughter."

Azure pops out a laugh. "Ever the diplomat, Mama." Leaning back, she braces herself on the piano bench. "Dad asked me to stay with him again. He's confident he'll find a way for me to live equally above and below the surface."

"Your father is a dreamer. That's where you get it. You know you can only stay on land until the scales in your pouch begin to dry."

Azure fingers the seaweed bag at her side. "He believes he's close to crafting a spell to—"

I dig nails into my palms. Prospero crafting a spell? Confirmation there's more than one sorcerer in the neighborhood. Score a point for Granny Blossom and her warnings of all the unfriendly magic within reach of Lalale Island.

Sulaa lays a finger across Azure's lips. "I won't risk your life for your father's pompous proclamations."

Azure lays her head on Sulaa's shoulder. "It isn't fair I can't come and go without limits between the sea and land as he does."

Come and go? Drying scales in a pouch? Pieces click into place. The scales hidden in her fashion accessory allow the mermaid to hang out on land. That's what I must have seen her place in Rai's grasp on the night she saved him. But why?

"Cheer up, sweet. I've got a surprise for you." Azure sits up, eyes wide. "An invitation from Rai Cloud to visit him on Lalale Island."

Azure blushes as I seethe. "I'd love to."

Her enthusiasm grinds my bones. Did I read Sulaa wrong? She wants Rai to figure out Azure plucked him out of the brine? That can't end well for anyone, especially me.

The Mermaid squints at the witch. "You're not going to give me a hard time about this?"

Sulaa stands and paces the stage before stopping to level a stare at Azure. "I know about the rescue."

Azure springs off the bench and grabs her mother's arm. "I swear he was barely conscious. There's absolutely no way he can figure out I was the one."

"You sang to him."

Azure lets go of Sulaa. "Only for a moment." Her entire body droops. "If you're going to insist I turn him down, why bring up the invite?"

What is Sulaa's game? She can't name me as a source. Azure

doesn't even ask how Sulaa knows about saving Rai. Does she know her mother's powers are strong enough to rat Azure out? Oh moon, I need a playbook on the extent of the sea witch's skills.

"I'm not your jailer, Azure."

"But?"

"But he cannot know what you are."

I feel guilty Azure's misery is a relief to me.

Sulaa pulls a strand of Azure's hair, smoothing a tangle. "How can I trust you'll never tell him?"

"If I say I won't, I won't. What have I ever done to earn your mistrust?"

This mermaid is a wily one. She already kept her role in Rai's rescue, her flirty-flirt through the windows with him, and her dash after the shuttle a secret until I told the witch. Azure is Sulaa's daughter. The kelp doesn't fall far from the stalk. I'll need to be wary of both.

"If you sing for him, he'll know."

Hope dawns in Azure's eyes. "I swear I won't sing. Mama, I need to see him again."

"Singing is like breathing to you. You'll slip."

Azure stares at the stage floor.

"Time to give it up, sister," I say, knowing she can't hear me. Sulaa can. She flicks a poison glance my way.

"Unless..."

Azure snaps her gaze back to Sulaa.

"Allow me to spell your voice."

The mermaid grabs her throat. "There's got to be another way."

"Relax. You'll sing freely under the water. On land, no more than a single note can be sung in the space of ten breaths. You won't be able to string a song together and give yourself away."

Azure runs a fingertip between chin and collarbone, thinking.

"It's a fair compromise." Sulaa softens her tone. "Darling, if song identifies you as his savior, that's all he'll ever see. Don't you want the man to know the Azure you truly are?"

Their gazes lock. For one kick-ass second, I think Azure will choose her voice over Rai, but to my disappointment, she nods.

Sulaa raises her hand. "One additional caveat... You must swear to show restraint with him. Anything beyond friendship makes you too vulnerable. Do you agree?"

Azure's shoulders rise and fall as she takes a deep breath. I grind my teeth. Curse Sulaa. This can't be happening. My gut-spilling to her was intended to keep Azure away from Rai, not serve the mermaid to him on a platter.

"I agree." Azure's right eye twitches. Sulaa doesn't seem to notice, but I do. Piyo had the same tick whenever he held something back. Is the mermaid lying to the sea witch?

I move next to Sulaa. "I didn't tell you everything. They kissed. It's already gone too far."

An invisible wave pushes me across the stage away from the two women. Sulaa's hands flow through the air as she chants words I can't make out. A pencil-thin golden thread crawls out of the witch's trident necklace to wrap around Azure's throat, soaking into her skin.

Sulaa conjures a pouch about the size of the purse I use for clubbing on the mainland. It's clamshell-shaped and dangles off a delicate chain. She hands it to the mermaid. "This will keep your scales moist longer than that flimsy thing your father gave you."

"Thank you, Mama." They hug. With a twirl and a skip, the mermaid dances off stage.

A moment later, Sulaa and I are back in her coral garden.

"You're making a big-ass mistake," I say, waving an arm toward Miaqua.

Sulaa roars with laughter. "I don't make mistakes. Azure is already smitten. She'll disobey every warning. And given no human can resist the lure of a mermaid, Rai Cloud will fall and fall hard for her."

Fury scrapes my insides raw, and I shout. "Are you doing this for kicks because I told you Rai Cloud was my heart's fate?"

She squeezes my cheeks with one hand. "Sweet fool, I'm taking steps to acquire Cloudpath Music." Sulaa releases me. "Azure's helping the family by being a delightful bargaining chip. Follow wherever they go and update me on everything. You'll assist me to insure Rai Cloud and my Azure tangle themselves in a luscious net of infatuation and unrequited lust."

"Unrequited?"

Tiny forks of lightning bleed from Sulaa's pupils into her irises. "Let their lust flow to the point of madness, but they must not consummate."

I'm totally on board with this rule. Sex is a promise to Rai. One he's only made to me. "How do I hit the brakes if things heat up?"

Sulaa flashes a smile that could scare the spots off a leopard shark. "You don't. I do."

A creeping tide of unease rises in my chest. "And then what?"

"We bring Mr. Cloud to the brink. He'll be so desperate for Azure he'll sign Cloudpath Music over to me for the chance to see her again. By then, I will illuminate for Azure the impossibility of their union. I didn't raise fools. She'll see reason."

"Encourage and then ruin them. That's cruel."

Sulaa's grin stretches. "Your perspective is all wrong. Rai and Azure sample the delights of an attraction, dripping with sexual tension. I expand my company, and you'll return to your lost love. Triple win."

This is wrong. I love Rai, and I'm no one's consolation prize. Sulaa grins, enjoying my turmoil.

"And if I refuse?"

With a snap of her fingers, the underwater caliche forest surrounds us. This time it's submerged in silty brown water that flows through my hollow body. I am exactly as I was when I first awakened, a shade in the sea.

Sulaa preens, unaffected by the change of scenery. She smooths black eyebrows with a finger and dabs at deep purple lips that match her eyes. "Oh, dear daughter, I failed to mention the third option you face with me as guardian of your spirit." She pulls my shadow from her pocket, twists it into a knot, and yanks it tight.

There's a single stab of pain, then the current twists me like a tissue dropped in water. Truth is a fist to my heart. I'm caught in Sulaa's net right next to Calliwag and who knows how many more. Mother my ass. She's my jailer.

"Tani, when you asked, and you did ask, I accepted you as my daughter. I have every intention to help you embrace the future you long for, but..." She rolls my shadow and tucks it away. "Don't begrudge me this teeny insurance policy you'll be an obedient daughter." She reaches out to squeeze my arm. I no longer feel her touch.

I pull away, finally understanding Sulaa's use of *daughter* has nothing to do with her adult offspring or me being her literal child and everything to do with being controlled. "Or I become Calliwag point two."

"Wise woman." Sulaa flies up to perch atop the wall of the caliche wasteland. Before she crosses out of sight, she points a long finger tipped with a glowing nail at my chest. "You will obey my pleasures, be they to fly, to swim, to dive into the fire, to ride on the curled clouds of sky or mad currents beneath the waves. The visibility of your spirit will adapt to fit my needs. When I want you seen, you will be seen. Otherwise, you are the shape of an afterthought, formless and insubstantial. Now, take your place as Azure's shadow."

Filled with helplessness, I collapse onto the watery ground of ash and shattered shells.

7

OUT OF THE SEA

AZURE DOESN'T SHOW. I WAIT OVER AN HOUR PAST THE TIME WE agreed to meet at the marina. My calls and texts to the number she left me all went unanswered. I scroll through messages to convince myself I hadn't imagined her acceptance of my invite. I finally pop off a text about rescheduling and decide to pound a couple of miles of sand with Kitae to run off frustration.

Once we hit the lagoon, my compadre nips my heel.

"Mellow out, Kitae."

He answers with a foxy version of stink eye and plods off to a shady spot under the palms. I toss my shoes and shirt onto the tufts of grass at the edge of the sand and wade knee deep into the surf to cool the burn of being stood up.

I splash water on my sweaty face and begin a pep talk to reinflate my ego. "Dude, something came up. Azure is *not* in Miaqua rolling her eyes over the dweeb who played peek-a-boo through the windows with her. She didn't bail on you."

Or did I make too much of my Miaqua flirt with Azure? For her part, our game might have been nothing more than a gesture of politeness to the doofy Lalale man on the other side of the glass.

I dunk my head into the lagoon and shake the water off the

three braids trailing down my back. "Reality check, fool." Azure's mother and manager, Sulaa Kylock, is salivating to buy my company like every other music mogul in Hollywood. No doubt, The Mermaids were charged with making my visit memorable. They did their job well, especially Azure.

I imagine Azure asking her blue-haired sisters for advice on how to ditch me once she got my invite. They'd answer "*Ghoooooost him,*" in perfect, five-part harmony.

I did feel a connection with Azure. Maybe not as strong as the pull toward the woman who yanked me out of the sea, but it was there.

Damn it, I've got to stop thinking about the night of the storm. Curse Juan Luna and his philosophies about my rescuer being a soulmate, a heart's fate. I bought hard into such possibilities before Tani dumped me for Piyo. Reembracing my belief in cosmic fated mates is not on the table. That's a sure-fire way to get my heart carved out of my chest and stomped on again.

My hand rests over the tattoo of a full moon on the right side of my chest. The nondescript silhouette of my mythical heart's fate, a dream girl, covers the left side, the heart side. A trail of stars rains down between the images. When a member of the commune turns eighteen, Juan Luna's grandpa, Juan Estrella Azul offers to gift them with a unique ink design. No one picks their tattoo. We trust the master to create his art, using us as his canvas. He taps into *mana*, spiritual energy from deep in his Hawaiian forefather's roots.

Mana chose my tattoo.

I got the ink years before Tani and I were together. Tani swore the tattoo was prophetic, and she was the woman etched into my skin. She chose the wrong chest.

Kitae barks and noisily chases something, killing my zone out. The clear cerulean water of the lagoon outdoes the bright afternoon sky. Blue, the color of peace. I drink it in like a potion and let the breeze be a salve to my soul.

The song, "*Moon Path*," I've been working on flows through my brain, and I sing.

Essence of the moon, my strength
Hear me in the light of day
Lead me past the waves that crash
Reveal my path to find love's way

I am lost to fortune's whim
Ever searching sky and sea
Sweetest voice of breath and life
Oh, dear soul who sang to me

I play with chords, keys, rests, but the song doesn't take shape nor do any more lyrics flow. I'm musically babbling about a woman I'll never see again. The whole song stinks. It's as if I'm not meant to sing about the soul who saved me. What should songs be about if they can't tell the story of life-altering experiences?

Sun beats on my shoulders and neck. I regret not grabbing a bottle of water before I took off down the beach to escape the humiliation of being stood up. I trek through the gentle waves of the lagoon toward shore and more realistic dreams of a super-sized glass of ice water.

"*Essss...*"

I stop, water lapping at my thighs, and look around. I swear I just heard someone sing a note. The only sound is the crash of breakers against the staggered half circle of rocks that form a natural breakwater for the lagoon.

"*...ence.*"

It comes again. Undeniably a voice. I scan the lagoon. On shore, Kitae gallops to the water's edge and barks like a fiend. He heard it too.

I close my eyes and recapture the note. "*Essss— Essence.*" My eyes pop open. It's the first word of my song and the notes are perfect, forming the illusive beginning I couldn't find in my dabbling.

I sing. "Essence of the—" I stall again. Do I stick to the key, or expand the musical vocabulary of the song?

"*Mooon*"

Yes, once again, the perfect note. Someone or something sings with me to fill gaps in my mess of a melody. Is one of my mother's famed moon goddesses taking pity on this broken song? It's daylight, but the moon never sleeps.

"*My*"

I whip around, searching for the creator of these singular notes. Surf splashing over sea rocks muffles the voice. I wade deeper into the lagoon until I'm swimming toward the craggy tops of boulders poking out of the sea.

"Who's out here?" I yell. "I hear you." Thank goodness Kitae is the only one watching a dude totally off his nut call to the sea for an elusive singer. I tread water. Off my nut is putting it mildly. Losing my shit is closer to the truth. I'm out here following notes in my head. There's no way a voice could rise over the racket of the sea. I've heard certain water birds can adjust their calls to cut through the sound of waves. People can't. It's the onset of heat stroke. I need water and an extensive dead-to-the-world nap.

I'm about to turn when first a head then the upper body of a woman rise over the edge of a large, slanted rock in the breakwater.

"It's me, Azure."

I swallow a gallon of salt water.

She executes a perfect dive off the rock into the lagoon as I sputter and cough. Within moments, she surfaces a few feet away. "Need a slap on the back?"

I shake my head. The braid with a moonstone disc woven into its end whacks me in the face. "Ouch, no." I rub my eye and stare at her. "Where did you come from?"

She waves an arm at the finger of island stretching into the ocean. "From the shuttle I took from Miaqua."

I search the distant sand spit beyond the lagoon. There's no teardrop-shaped shuttle that travels between the surface and Miaqua.

Azure follows my gaze and gives a nervous little laugh. It's the essence of sweet. "I parked around the far side."

I point toward her invisible ship. "You swam from there?"

Her arms trace a path through the water. "Yes. I love the water."

I move nearer. "It's rough past the breakers, bad rip currents. You lucked out."

She flips a strand of blue hair off the side of her face. "Skill, not luck. Don't worry your pretty little braids about it."

Without glass between us, Azure's beauty knocks me sideways. She's a groovy blend of delicate and confident. And that hair. Oh moon, it's not a dye job, the color matches the notes of a bright blue sky. The woman is a major key. I try to match her casual vibe as we float near the breakwater. A shiver blows my cool.

"You're cold," she says. "We should go in." Her eyes widen. She looks nervous.

"I'm fine." A chilly current from the open sea slithers in, and I shiver a second time.

"Don't feel the need to impress me with manly body temperature regulation." She shoots a wary glance in the direction of the shore.

"If you're more comfortable out here, I'm good to go." I spin in the water. "I'll take a few laps to heat my core."

Azure scrunches her face at the island. "It's fine. We can go in. I normally don't like to clock a lot of time out of Miaqua, but I'm up for a challenge."

Her right eye gives an adorable little twitch. Is she nervous about our meeting? Should I have arranged to meet her on her home turf?

"Don't get me wrong, I am glad to be here. It's new." She glances to check my reaction. "Newish to me, and maybe a little scary. I

don't quite understand how to interact with all this open space."
She fans an arm to take in the sky. "Does that make sense?"

Wow. To me, the sea is the mother of all open space. I never
considered how weird the shift from watching schools of fish
through a window to counting lines of palm trees under an infinite
sky might be for Azure.

We reach the shallows where we can stand, and the water is
warmer. I offer her my arm. "Rai Cloud, at your service to help
navigate the scary."

Azure slips her arm through mine. "Thanks." We take a few
awkward steps through the water, and she pulls away. "No offense,
I'd rather swim." Azure dives beneath the surface and speeds
toward shore.

I welcome the sun's heat on my skin as I join her on the sand.
She stands with arms wrapped around her middle. Her chest rises
and falls in the rhythm of calming breaths until she lowers her
arms. It takes a generous slice of willpower not to gawk at yet
another new perspective of Azure. The pairing of her hair with her
lagoon blue eyes is dazzling. Her body is covered in a shimmery,
iridescent emerald wetsuit that reminds me of a watermarked silk
scarf my mother brought back from a trip to Bali. The suit hugs her
lithe curves, hiding specific details. Around her waist, a thin gold
chain holds a clamshell-shaped pouch that appears to be made of
pearl. The breeze lifts the ends of her deep blue hair. It's hard to
believe this being who came from the sea is anything less than
enchanted.

Azure's gaze locks on my tattoo. "Beautiful. May I touch it?"

I nearly say touch anything you'd like but settle for, "Sure." I
want to touch her, too, slide my hands along the sides of her wetsuit
to learn its unfamiliar texture and the body giving it shape. My
fingers itch to pinch a strand of azure hair. Is it thin and soft or
thick and coarse? A bolder part of me twitches with baser inklings
completely out of bounds this early in our acquaintance.

Her fingers circle the moon on my chest and then draw smaller and smaller circles until she reaches its center. I hold my breath. It's been a long time since a woman touched me. Control is a language I need to brush up on. With the tip of her pinkie, Azure dots the stars across the dip between my pecs. She pauses at the feminine silhouette and pulls her hand away. "Blue instead of black ink?"

I swallow hard, searching for words, and pray her eyes don't stray down to the part of me that didn't get the message about control yet. I wasn't prepared to meet with Azure drenched in sea water while her fingers danced across my skin.

Kitae barrels over a small rise, coming to my rescue. The sand he sprays in his wake sticks to the damp hair on my legs, total foxy buzzkill to my cool first—or rather, second—impression. I scoop up the fox before he has a chance to draw blood from Azure's delicate ankle. "Careful, the little dude took Olympic gold in heel-nipping."

Her fingers reach out to scratch behind his pointy ears. He goes boneless in my arms and head butts her hand for more. I'm so astonished I nearly drop him.

"Your pet?"

"My associate by mutual agreement."

Azure moves closer and rubs her cheek against Kitae's head. "Aren't you a sweetie."

I set him on the sand, and he runs circles around us before licking Azure's leg. "I've never seen him use manners before. Careful, he may be tenderizing you for a good chomp."

She gives me a smile as sly as any island fox. "Beware the fox with no agenda?"

I may need to tread water on land to keep from going under in her presence. "Exactly."

Azure nods at the grass near the edge of the sand. "Any more beasties over there? I've heard nightmare stories about sand fleas."

I shake my head and the ornaments at the end of my braids clack together. Azure circles me to inspect my hair. "I've never seen a man with three braids or..." She drapes the braids over my shoulders and down my chest so they fall between us. "Toys in his hair."

My black braids are a stark contrast to her pale apricot skin. I cradle a small piece of abalone in my palm. "This was made from the first abalone my brother Piyo and I found when we learned how to dive. He wore a matching piece around his neck." I flick a braid. "Piyo didn't dig the long-hair look." I pinch a polished white disc with a hole through the center. "Moonstone stands for my spiritual inspiration, the moon." I cut off my last word. It's my first official convo with Azure, and I'm already laying commune speak on her. I try to read her expression. Talk of the psychic energies that are a constant in our lives at the commune don't always gel with outsiders.

Azure lifts my middle braid to discover a wooden whistle half the size of my pinkie. "And this one?"

Relief streams through me. I haven't weirded her out. "The first instrument my folks gave me. They claim I had perfect pitch from the time I was a toddler."

We meet each other's gaze over the whistle in her fingers. "I'm deeply sorry about your parents and brother, Rai." She settles my braids in place down my back.

Her sympathy is genuine, unaffected by cursory politeness. I want to fall into her arms and bury my face against her slender neck to sink into her kindness. The connection I felt with her at Miaqua surges forward, and I blurt out the thought that sent me plummeting to the depths of pity before she arrived. "I thought you stood me up."

A sunset blush colors Azure's pale cheeks, the contrast shifts her hair to a deeper blue. "I almost did.

My face heats.

Azure grips my shoulder. "Not because of you, Rai."

The sound of her voice wrapping around my name starts a flame in my gut.

"I knew coming here might be too overwhelming, but I had to

see you." Azure stares at her pale hand against my dark skin and
pulls away. "Am I being naïve, or at Miaqua did it feel..." She
shrugs. "Like there was something between us asking for more
time?"

I catch her hand and return it to my shoulder. I'm relieved our
silly window game wasn't a Sulaa-prompted nicety. I could snatch
Azure into my arms and twirl. "If you're naïve, I'm right there with
you. I asked you to come hang out with me to either explore what
this might be or to prove I imagined a connection."

A second hand finds my other shoulder. "Which is it?"

"I'm going with exploration."

Azure smiles. "I've never hung out with a guy above the
surface."

"What guys do you hang out with?"

She moves in ever so slightly. "Guys who live and work at
Miaqua."

I'm tempted to squash her against my chest and kiss away
memories of every Miaqua guy she's ever known. I'm determined to
respect her boundaries. Sexuality in the commune tends to be on
the less inhibited side. I need to be sensitive and pay close attention
to Azure's cues.

Testing the waters she initiated with proximity, I slide my hands
around to the small of her back. We're close enough that heat from
our bodies swirl together between us. "Boyfriends?"

"A few," she says, raising her chin.

"Recently?" My gaze drifts to her lips.

"Nope," she says, returning the favor.

Her hair tickles my chest. Is she wondering what it's like to kiss
an above-the-surface guy? I'm more than happy to answer such a
wondering. I dip my head to ease our lips closer to the same level.
She's shorter than me, but not neck-crimpingly so.

"And do you sing to them?"

As if I've suddenly turned into a hot stove, Azure pushes away from me. "I didn't sing to you." Hands fly to her lips, and her eye twitch goes full flutter.

I gesture to the rock. "The notes... You fixed the song I was writing. You're a super talented musician, Azure, and I'm thankful for the assist." I've blown it. I freaked her out. She did sing to me. Why is she flipping now?

Her head snaps to the pearly pouch at her side. She clutches it in both hands. "I've got to go." The woman hot-foots it into the lagoon.

"I'm sorry. What did I say?"

She looks over her shoulder and hollers. "Nothing. Everything's fine. I just have to get home." Azure plunges into the sea.

I dash to the water. Kitae nearly trips me as he runs too. "Azure, wait, please." Her head pops up midway to the rocks and she faces me. "I'll walk you to your shuttle."

"Thanks. I prefer to swim."

I splash in up to my stomach. "Can I see you again? I'll come to Miaqua."

She swivels in the tide. A soft smile brightens her damp face. "I'd rather meet you on the island."

Damn, this woman is tough to read. "Yeah, great."

"Tomorrow?"

The grin on my face hides nothing. "Sure."

"I'll be rehearsing all day. How about an hour before sunset here at the lagoon?"

I nod at Kitae. "My associate and I will be waiting."

Azure stills, staring at me in a way that makes my toes tingle. I match her look. As she moves to swim off, I call after her. "Don't swim to the lagoon so late in the day. It gets cold here once the sun goes down. Bring a sweater."

"Okay," she says, and disappears beneath the surface.

I stand, a goof in the water, half-believing I imagined this whole interchange. Did Azure really pop out of the sea, sing a few notes, chat me up, and then return to the wild waves? My gaze flicks to the rock where she appeared. Will she rise for one more look before she heads for her shuttle? I wait and stare and hope.

A growl of disapproval from the sand breaks my concentration. Damn, the fox has a point. I'm lingering here in the water instead of making sure Azure reaches her shuttle. She could get swallowed in a rip current or meet up with a shark. I'm a stupid fool for letting her swim alone. At the very least I should have gone with her.

I blast out of the water. It's too late to catch her by sea. I sprint around the palm trees lining the lagoon and head for the spit of sand where she said her ship is. When I reach the end of the island's finger, there's no sign of Azure or a Miaqua shuttle.

I drop onto the sand, gulping air. She made it, and I'll see her tomorrow to continue figuring out the *what if* between us.

It would be sweet if her boundaries allow me to kiss her tomorrow.

Or maybe she'll be inclined to kiss me.

Either way, it'll be cool.

My stroll back to the lagoon is filled with visions of Azure's lips, her hair, the sweetness in the way she's nervous about the island but promises to give Lalale another go. From the top of the small rise where I left my shoes, I gaze at the calm water of the lagoon. Shock smacks me in the chest.

Wavering on the surface of the water for the space of a heartbeat is the reflection of Tani's face.

8

TANI'S REWARD

MY MIND, HEART, AND GUTS TWIST IN RAGE.

Azure touches my Rai. Her fingers run over the moon tattoo on his smooth broad chest where I used to rest my cheek. The woman dares to lay a finger on each star where I've dropped a trail of kisses. My stars. My path to Rai's heart. When her mermaidy hand moves to the silhouette of Rai's heart's fate, I lose it.

My scream scatters clouds and dots the sea with whitecaps. Birds explode from trees. Kitae yips and scratches a paw against his ear to fight the unnatural frequency of my voice. Rai and Azure show no reaction at all.

Curse every impulse driving Azure toward Rai's lips. Dragging him onto the sand to keep him from drowning did not give her ownership. The woman is ten steps ahead of Rai, and he's clueless. The mermaid fell for him on the beach the night of the storm before she even knew him.

I swear a bruise covers my heart. Rai is worth falling for. He's wildly creative and kind. I'm the loser for leaving him. He's the perfect person for me. I will never see him as less. If only I could tell him, confess what a colossal fuckup I was casting him off for

Piyo. I can't let Rai move on now that I've heard his words of love for me. I'm ready to embrace him for eternity.

I am Rai's destiny. The soulmate tattoo Juan Estrella painted on Rai's flesh is me. I vow the half she-fish will not blind him to his true mate. Fortune and Sulaa Kylock hold the promise of a second chance. I will not screw up again.

I didn't leave Rai after Azure swam off even though Sulaa expects me to follow the Miaqua mermaid. His desperation to chase her tears me apart. I long to tell him there is no shuttle on the sand.

Mermaids don't need them.

Sulaa's magic ping pongs my existence between forms that suit her purpose. Is it the sea witch's plan that I exist in Rai's periphery? If so, do I dare hope he glimpsed my reflection in the lagoon and through the window at Miaqua? Does Sulaa intend me to be a reminder of love or a vision to plague his sanity?

Or could my connection to Rai be stronger than the sea witch's control?

I heard his voice in the sea. My only joy in this tangled reality is that I am still part of Rai's consciousness. I believe with my whole being he hasn't given up on me, and that if we weren't fated, any connection between us would be nonexistent. I wish Sulaa were approachable for explanations. Instinct warns, revealing Rai has seen me gives her one more thing to take away if this isn't her doing. She expects the game to be played her way.

I hate the game.

A sharp voice cuts through my thoughts. "*Tani.*"

Sulaa.

I drink in Rai's face with those burnt wood eyes, his beautifully crafted body from years of island workouts, black hair in its triple braids that reach to his waist, and those long, slender fingers, a musician's fingers.

He is my love. Mine is the name he called to the sea.

"*Tani, tend to your charge.*" Sulaa's voice is a command I can't disobey.

There's a tug through the middle of my chest as if a cord is fastened to my ribs. I'm dragged through the sea to Miaqua. Instead of being dumped in Sulaa's creepy caliche forest, I'm pulled through steel walls of the former research station into a bedroom. Azure and one of her sisters sit cross-legged, knee to knee on a bed.

"*Do not leave Azure's side again unless I direct you otherwise.*" Sulaa's voice blasts through my head like earbuds with the volume cranked full.

Azure grips her sister's upper arms. "Oh, Bluebell, he's sweet and funny." The mermaid pretends to fan her face. "And scorching hot."

Bluebell's hair is a few shades lighter than Azure's. I search her body for gills or a tail. She looks as unblemished as Azure. Two legit mermaid sisters? "Is he as good a kisser awake as he is practically drowned?"

Azure blushes. "You'd have kissed him, too, if he looked at you the way he looked at me."

"You saved his life. Don't confuse gratitude for love."

"I didn't say I love him."

Her eye does the twitchy thing. Shit, she's lying again. How dare she think of Rai and love in the same sentence?

"I know you, Azure. You're damn close to the big L with this guy. You've been gushing about him since the storm, and there's..." Bluebell reaches under a pillow to grab a small journal with a graphic of waves on the front. "Lotta love lyrics on these pages."

I feel the same pain as when Sulaa tied my shadow in a knot.

"*You can't love Rai. He's mine.*"

For a fleeting moment, I hope Azure can hear me the way Kitae did at the lagoon. The mermaid doesn't flinch. I fall into the familiar drift of being nothing.

Azure snatches the journal. "What are you, sixteen instead of twenty-six?"

"What are you, fifteen instead of twenty-five? You moon over him for songs and songs." Bluebell touches her forehead to Azure's. "You're headed for a heart smash, Sissy. It can't work with Rai no matter how much you bend rules to spend time with him. Your limitations don't change."

Azure pulls away. "It's not fair my father is able to live mainly above the surface, and I can't."

Bluebell huffs. "At least you know who your father is. All the rest of us know is that we're the product of a sexual flyby between mother's spelled womb and some random potential candidate for a mermaid daddy."

My stomach knots. Are Azure's sisters each a twisted mockery because of Sulaa's sick obsession to pop out a true mermaid?

Azure throws her arms around her sister. "Oh, Bluebell. Don't reduce yourself to that. Mama loves every one of us."

Bluebell squeezes her back. "Sorry. Terminal case of the bitters that flares every so often." She holds Azure at arm's length. "Would you trade being a mermaid to be full selkie like your father?"

Azure, part selkie? Selkie's aren't real. Neither are mermaids, sea witches, lionfish men, or whatever ghostly spirit thing I am, but here we are. A troupe of mystical creatures peeled out of stories and myths.

"Never." Azure slaps the pearl pouch resting on her hip. "But there's got to be a way for me to stay on land longer to be with Rai."

I thought I could do what Sulaa asks and endure watching Rai with Azure. I was wrong. It drains my last drops of tolerance to listen to Azure's longing to be with Rai. When they're together, all I want to do is scream.

Sulaa dangles a future with Rai in front of me. What guarantee do I have my eternal hell won't be as a voyeur to watch the man I love with another? I'd rather be lost in the ocean depths forever than witness their relationship shift from desire to fulfilled lust.

Behind closed eyes, I savor the coolness of Rai's moon tattoo against my cheek after lovemaking. The sensation of his fingers, his lips caressing the intimate places of my body until the rest of the world disappears is as real in memory as it was in life. I will dissolve into sea foam if Sulaa forces me to watch Rai give Azure pleasures that belong to me.

"Enjoy a light fling with the surface hottie, but be smart. Remember how close we came to Mama finding out when you slept with the marine biologist?"

Anger bubbles inside me. Little Miss Mermaid keeps quite the treasure chest of secrets. She's more dangerous to Rai's heart than I gave her credit for.

Azure grumbles. "Our love lives stopped being Mama's business a long time ago."

Bluebell grunts. "Oh, do tell her that, and let me watch. Seriously, Azure, you'd be smarter to stick to one of the guys here in Miaqua. At least with them, it's easier for you to sneak around and slip into the sea when you need to."

"Blue, what I feel for Rai is on a whole new level. As if he's always been part of my story, and I just hadn't turned to his page before the night of the storm."

I burn at Azure playing the fated mate card that belongs to me.

Bluebell squeezes Azure's shoulder. "Don't convince yourself you're in it for anything more than a dash of fun. Whoo hoo." She spins her finger in a circle. "Stay real." She kisses Azure on the cheek then shifts on the bed. "Scratch my betweens."

When Bluebell turns, I gasp. Along her spine is a row of stunted, thorny fins reminiscent of a sea monster in a children's book. Azure gently strokes each flat space between fins. Are we all monsters down here in Sulaa's realm?

With no warning, I'm twisted like a corkscrew. Colors of Sulaa's coral reef garden burst around me. I notice since it's just the two of us, she doesn't bother filling the space with air. The witch lounges on a throne of indigo coral polished to resemble blown glass. When she raises her arm, it continues to stretch beyond the nearly imperceptible upper boundary of her garden. The glowing nail of an outstretched index finger attracts a tiny sea butterfly which she skewers. In a flash, her arm retracts, and she pops the critter into her mouth. Sulaa's demonstration gives the term *far reaching* a sinister meaning. After a second fish succumbs to the fate of the first, she holds it out to me. The poor creature still wiggles, trying to escape.

"Care for a taste?" says Sulaa, waving the fish at me. "Oh, silly me. You don't eat." She swallows her snack. "Or breathe or touch."

Doubt pricks my soul like a swarm of needles. Each sting is a fresh bead of loathing for the sea witch.

"Unless I allow it," says Sulaa with a smack of purple lips.

The enormity of my stupidity flattens my heart. I rise from the shifting silver sand of her reef illusion to face her. "You promised me choices. How do I know you aren't using me for shits and giggles before you decide what my fate will be?"

Sulaa fans spidery fingers through the air. "What reason did I give you for doubting I will facilitate one of your desired futures?"

"Your game with Rai's and Azure's feelings for one. Let's toss in you giving me no choice but to watch the man I love fall hard for someone else."

"Choice. Now there's a loaded word." She leans forward, sparks returning to her plum irises. "We have an agreement, Tani. You keep your end of the bargain, I keep mine. Simple."

I take a few steps away from her fish-spearing nails. The rational part of me knows I should suck it up while the Rai/Azure debacle plays out until Sulaa brings me back to life. The emotional part is a slag heap. Can I bear to help Sulaa facilitate a brutal sucker punch to Rai's heart when Azure is ripped away from him? I've devastated Rai once. If I truly love him, how can I do that to him again?

"I'm not the best person for the job. Send Calliwag."

"Oh, but you are. You are invested, he isn't."

I need to spell this out more clearly. "There's got to be other things I can do for you. I really need to bow out of the Rai/Azure thing."

She drums fingers on the throne. With every tap, a sickly green swirl like the ripple of a pond surrounds her hand. "No."

"Isn't there something you can offer Calliwag, so he will invest?"

Sulaa offers me a pitying smile. "Dear, dear Tani. I understand your reticence, I do. Perhaps the teeniest smidge of encouragement will get your head back in the game."

With a wave of her hand, the coral reef transforms into a caliche forest. It's not the one camouflaging her underwater garden. I'm bound to a fossilized trunk in the real forbidden place at the tip of Lalale Island beneath cliffs blackened by ancient fires. Screams of terror and cries of children for help surround me. Metal clangs against metal so close I feel the whoosh of a blade past my ear. Faint gray shapes flee from obsidian shadows who cut them down with gleaming swords. The blows ignite clouds of red mist that swirl and coalesce before rising to form a crimson circle around the moon, a killing moon. Black cliffs, white petrified trees, and bloody mist close in on me. I'm trapped inside the centuries-old massacre between islanders and invaders that spawned tales of a curse to anyone who ventures too close to Lalale Island's caliche forest killing ground.

I attempt to shield my eyes, but the living horror and wails of death seep through my fingers.

"Stop, please stop," I cry.

With a hiss, the vision disappears, a sandcastle claimed by the tide. My chest heaves from phantom breath, then the horror begins again as if someone hit a replay button.

Sulaa's voice cuts through the vision. "This is the subtle version. I can dial up the resolution if you need more detail."

"No, please."

"Or perhaps a different scenario is more persuasive."

I sit between Piyo's legs, my back molded to his muscled chest. He kisses the skin behind my ear. I turn my head to catch his lips.

The oranges, golds, and reds of a bonfire reflect in his mourning-dove-colored eyes. All around us is singing and dancing. It's the night of my engagement party to Piyo, a beautiful night under a carpet of stars. Between the notes of a song, a distant whistle grows into a vicious howl as a rogue gust of wind collides with the bonfire. The world around us burns as licks of flame and ravenous sparks consume everything on the beach as tinder. The wind feeds us to the fire. Lucas reaches for Corinne. They do not escape. Piyo burns before me until he's a pile of ash. Smoke coats the stars. The fire chooses me next.

I burn. I scream. I die.

"Noooo," I shriek, elongating the word until the vision tears down the center, and I'm back among a lively palette of coral with a haze of doomed butterfly fish circling high above me. I fall to my knees in front of Sulaa. "I'll keep my bargain. I swear." The thought of either horrid illusion playing in a loop through my consciousness for eternity is more than I can bear. I'll do what the sorceress asks.

Sulaa strokes my hair. "See, incentive sets things right."

Her touch both soothes and repulses me. The push and pull are draining. One thing is clear, the only person with choices here is Sulaa. She's a monster. I'm a monster. Calliwag is a monster. Her daughters are their own brand of monster. Little did I suspect, the sea I once revered as the personification of our planet's changing moods is instead the skin of a beast—a sea witch that lurks in its depths.

"Someday, your obedience will allow you to cry real tears again, Tani." She twists my shoulders until we're face-to-face, allowing me to remember what touch feels like. I crave it. "Let me prove how dear you are to me with an act of good faith."

I wipe my eyes out of reflex.

"If you promise there is still trust between us I can count on, I have a gift for you."

Sulaa toys with me in a game where I can only be the loser.

Every choice in our relationship belongs to her. A stubborn knot forms behind where my breastbone should be. Unless I find a way to play her. If I'm a good little Tani and perform to her liking, opportunity may arise. Any power left for me to grab is in pretending to be all-in with Sulaa's sick manipulations.

I steel myself and reengage. "I suppose you would know the perfect gift for a gal between life and death."

Sulaa laughs at my snark. "There's the fire in you I appreciate."

I swallow my disgust and smile. "Great."

"I believe a visit to the island will make your task more palatable."

I clench my teeth. That's a shit gift, another session to grind my heart to dust as I watch Rai and Azure get cozy.

Sulaa wags her finger at me. "Before you judge my intent, hear me out. When you return, I will make you more...present."

Does she mean to give me substance so seawater, fish, and broken shells stop flowing through me like a sieve? I do want to walk on land again and float above the sand to find some semblance of who I was.

"To reconnect with your Rai."

My mouth hangs open, and a coral flake blows in. "I don't understand."

"He will see you again, dear one." She flicks her wrist. "As a spirit, of course. Touch will not be possible, but sight and sound are my gift to you."

"What's the catch?"

Sulaa leans back on her throne, teasing fingers through the spectrum of blue on her head. "No catch. This is a necessary step for you to gather quality insight for me on Rai Cloud's feelings for Azure. He trusts you. He talks. There's no rule against you benefitting as well." Her gaze hardens on me. "An itty-bitty warning or three." She twists long strands into a knot on the crown of her head and spears a twig of tangerine coral to hold it in place. After licking two fingers, she smooths her eyebrows. "Do not say anything to your once and future paramour to spoil my plans for acquiring Cloudpath Music. Limit your time with him to serve my purposes not yours. Make a connection, earn his trust, and then get back to Azure. Nothing more."

So, I'll be under a gag order.

"And you may not drop the tiniest hint to him about the possibility of you returning to the living."

Damn the sea witch. Did she pluck thoughts out of my mind like the poor butterfly fish who strayed too close to her claw? Those are exactly the things I'd tell Rai. First, the scheme of Sulaa's to get Cloudpath. Once he's repulsed by the manipulation, I'll urge him to hold on to the fated future we once believed we had. What's left to me? Haunt Rai and give him a coronary? I school my turmoil beneath a blank expression.

"Never forget, a vulnerable heart is ripe for the taking. If this man is your heart's fate, far be it from me to change the course of destiny. Allow him a small reminder of your value. I give you the gift of presence and a short visit to accomplish such a thing in addition to the benefits I'll reap from your renewed connection."

Hope. I can give Rai hope he will have a future after losing Azure. "When can I go home?"

Sulaa produces my shadow. Carefully, she undoes the knot through its stomach. When she shakes it out, I contort, bending at unnatural angles. In moments, it's over. I push off the bottom in a form with some substance returned. A skin of transparent energy covers my spirit form.

"I expect you back at Azure's side before she wakes at dawn. Give Mr. Cloud my best." With a dismissive wave, she begins to turn her back on me, then whips around with a sickening grin. A hand flutters to her mouth in a girlish gesture. "Oops, better not mention me. Ta ta." She sashays between coral pedestals as the garden shifts from underwater grotto to an air-filled dome. Sulaa throws open the door Calliwag used before in the sea wall.

I dart upwards as if I'm trying to outrun a sidewinder in one of the canyons on the island. Just before I cross the boundary of Sulaa's dominion, the sound of a slow clap and then a man's voice, much deeper and more menacing than Calliwag's warbles up to me from behind the door.

"Ah, Sulaa, I do love to watch you work."

The sea witch drops into an ill-fitting demure curtsey and disappears to join whoever waits behind the door.

I burst into the night through swells rolling atop the sea. The waning moon greets me with the pure white light of a hidden sun's reflection. My body imitates the act of breathing, and I imagine tasting a dose of clean, moist air. Floating here between stars and ocean is its own brand of Heaven. I linger in the bliss of rediscovered freedom until I remember this is merely a moment borrowed from a sea witch.

A trail of moon drops on the water leads me to Lalale Island. Thank goodness I'm on the channel side, not the far side that faces the open sea with the stunted peninsula where the actual cursed caliche forest lies. I shiver at the memory of the massacre Sulaa made me experience in real time.

As I near the island, a sound as dear to me as my own lost heartbeat floats up past the highest palm. Rai is singing. His ukulele paints the air with notes. The instrument looks like a toy against his broad chest and shoulders. I follow the song to the man I'd trade eternity to love again and pray the witch hasn't deceived me.

"Rai, I'm here."

9

HOMECOMING

Most of Juan Luna's wrecked tomol washed up on Lalale Island the morning following the storm. The chunk of bow I find half-buried in the sand of the lagoon is a melancholy surprise. I finish my song and attempt to work the water-logged wood free. A trail of embedded green glass chips pebble across its surface. These tiny flecks are all that's left of Tani's urn after I didn't stop it from shattering across the bow.

I run a finger over the reminder of my failure. Raising the plank fragment so the glass shines the way Tani's eyes used to in the moonlight, I force out words. "Forgive me for ruining your farewell, Tani. Spirits of the moon, I beg you to right my wrong. Take my dearest Tani over the Cloud Path to her forever." I drop a kiss onto the wood. "I love you, Tani."

"Rai, I'm here."

The bow piece *thunks* onto the sand as I stumble backward. My hand flies to my tattoo. Silhouetted against the moon is a figure of the woman on my chest. It's as if ink mingled with moonlight to conjure the image of my heart's fate Juan Estrella painted across my skin. She's here. My mystery woman has found me.

My heartbeat pushes against my hand as I take in the luminous shape lingering in the air above the lagoon. *In the air.* She is a vision, not my storm savior. This is a visitor from the realm of stars and faith. Could she be an incarnation of the moon's energy?

In the score of my imaginings, I never expected a spiritual message to appear to me in the guise of the woman upon my chest whom I'm destined to love. Years of one-sided convos with the moon have only given answers as sensations, intuitions, not face-to-face meet-ups.

"I love you, too, Rai." The apparition floats down to the beach and walks toward me.

"Love me too?" I wrack my brain. Did I ever tap into my mom's moon goddess beliefs to send me a lover? No. I sought wisdom, sure. The closest I've come to a love request is to seek a path to my earthly heart's fate. I've never drowned in mythological soup, asking for the love of my life to appear in the form of a realm-adjacent being.

The manifestation of my ink is close enough to touch. What the hell do I do? Take a knee? Hands to the sky? Bowed head? What did my mother's stories say to do? I stare, mouth bobbing open, and trip. A spirit decides to pay me a visit, and I ass-plant on a tangle of seaweed.

With the moon behind the figure, I can't make out details. I scramble to my feet and slowly approach, keeping a wide berth. I circle to put the moon at my back, hoping to see her face in greater detail. Palms pressed together, I bend at the waist, hoping it's an acceptable sign of respect.

She watches but doesn't speak, a familiar dynamic I can wrap my head around. I speak, she listens. "Are you sent by a moon goddess, come to answer my request to guide Tani over her Cloud Path?" I fall to my knees.

"Get up. You're coated like a piece of sandy tempura."

Finally, the moon illuminates the being. Instead of rioting to escape my chest, my heart stops. Standing less than a foot away is Tani, my Tani. It can't be. I'm losing my mind. Have grief and loss finally won, filling my thoughts with visions of rescuers that sing to you and dead friends coming to taunt you for ruining their burials?

"Please, messenger from the moon goddess, forgive me for assuming my pitiful ritual was capable of sending Tani's soul to its forever." My gaze sticks to the sand, waiting for absolution or at least respite from this crazy-ass mental breakdown.

"The way you said good-bye to me was beautiful, Rai. Please look at me."

With fear frothing on the crest of an adrenaline wave, I raise my head. It's not my Tani. The woman before me has hair the color of moonbeams like the color of the moon drawn on my chest.

"It's me, Tani." She kneels in front of me, her face inches from mine. "Hi."

The vision speaks with Tani's voice. Not an approximation of her tone and timbre, the real thing. I set disbelief off to the side, close enough to call if necessary. "Tani?"

She nods and smiles the smile that used to make me scoop her into my arms and kiss her senseless. "All me."

I stare at the piece of wood bearing chips from her urn and then to the person I once believed to be my heart's fate. "How? Why? Screw it. I don't care." I reach for her. She literally floats away. I run a finger over the moon on my chest. I'm tripping. "Did a moon goddess send you?"

Tani cocks her head to the side, studying me first then the moon. After a long moment, she answers. "I'm all Tani, here on my own juice."

Whatever juice sent her, a force born of myth or not, she is my Tani. I can't hold back another moment and rush to clasp her to my heart. My arms whoosh though air. Tani's body looks to be flush against mine. "I can't feel you." I'm tilting toward crazy. I rub the heel of my hands over my eyes. When I look again, she's put distance between us.

"Oh, Rai. It's not my choice to be apart from you. I ache for your touch." Slowly, she reapproaches. Ghostly fingers flutter on either side of my face. "I crave your deep, hungry kisses." Hands of wavering light trace the sides of my body. "Your body belongs against mine." Her eyes close. "The echo of making love with you fills my soul."

We're one hundred percent in the weird zone now. I scramble away from Tanivision. "Whoa. This is too out there." I sprint up the path away from the lagoon and head toward our tiny commune village. Is my brain finally erupting to fully mourn Tani? I've not allowed myself to go there. She was my brother's fiancé. I'm the castoff. I've kept my grief for her within boundaries, and now a visitation strips them away.

I'll seek guidance from Granny Blossom, the commune's conduit to the inexplicable. I pray she knows of herbs, crystals, or chants to counter my freak-out.

The Tani apparition blocks my way. "Stop, please. I'm sorry. Too much too soon. I'm new at this."

Dizziness rolls around in my head. Maybe if I pass out, I'll come to alone. I try to skirt around her. She counters every move. "What do you want from me?"

"I want you to go to the lagoon, sit your ass on the sand, and let me explain."

The ghost thing has Tani down cold.

"We've got shit to deal with, Rai." She crosses her arms, tucking chin to chest the same way Tani did when she was pissed at me.

My brain flips to the night of the storm and breaking Tani's urn. "Forgive me for ruining your burial. I never meant your urn to shatter. All I was trying to do was give you a sendoff with a beautiful moment under the moon."

Tani stares with over-bright eyes. It's unnerving.

"Shatter?"

I told no one, not even Juan Luna my ritual of sinking Tani's ashes didn't go as planned. Is this encounter penance for not coming clean about my dear friend's ragged ending? Or is it a chance to cleanse my soul? If I tell the truth, will the haunting end?

"A storm came out of nowhere. Tani's..." I take in the image of the woman before me and go all-in. "Your urn slipped out of my grasp and hit the bow. The wind drove your ashes and what was left of your urn into the sea. I'm so sorry." I rub my temples. "That's all I remember before waking on the beach." I omit the details about a woman who sang me awake. She doesn't belong in this reckoning.

"You're leaving something out, Rai."

Does she know about the woman? What's the cost of lying to a visitation?

Tani moves close. I should feel breath. "The part where you said you loved me."

An ice arrow plunges into my heart. She's right. My last words before I thought I was going to die in the storm were about loving Tani. Spirit woman might very well be here to force me to deal with buried truth.

I stare at her. Except for the hair, the Tani I know is in front of me. The expression on her face, the way she holds herself, the stubbornness is all T. Feelings I tucked in a box marked *never again* bust out. I loved Tani. I loved the way she didn't take shit from anyone, her acerbic sense of humor, the way she never ducked under a wave but met it face-on, and the tenderness she wrapped me in whenever we were alone under the moon.

I loved her even after she chose Piyo over me.

She chose Piyo over me.

My superheated body temperature melts the ice arrow. I turn away. "Leave me alone."

The spirit moves to face me. "I can't, Rai. Breaking my urn was nothing compared to what I did to you. I listened to the wrong people when I left you for Piyo."

My fists itch to punch. Does the ghost of Tani expect me to erase the fury of real Tani's betrayal? The fury I keep buried alongside the grief I can't release if I don't want to come off like a total jackass. I played nice. I wrote a fricking song for Piyo and

Tani's wedding, a song never to be sung. Outwardly, I was a good guy. Inside, fissures divided my heart into dead chunks.

Until a mystery woman on the beach gave me life with a song.

"I don't have to listen." I knock fists against my thighs. "I don't care if this is a dream or an omen, it's not my issue." I glare at my visitor. "I forgave Tani. I forgave Piyo. There's no point in reimagining the past. I'm done." I glue my gaze to the ground and stomp to the beach.

I'm finished engaging with a manifestation that prods at my guilt for still harboring feelings for my brother's fiancé. Dropping onto the sand, I rest my forehead on my knees.

"You said, 'I love you, Tani.'" Her voice is close behind me. "Don't run from me, Rai. You saw me at Miaqua, and then again in the water of the lagoon. If you stopped loving me, I would not be able to come to you then or now."

I grab handfuls of sand. My voice strains past gritted teeth. "Any song of Tani and me finished long before now."

Tani's toes appear to push against mine in the sand. "What if it's not finished?"

My head snaps up to meet her gaze. A frightening notion settles over me. Did the moon send this spirit in the guise of someone I know to ease my own crossover into destiny?

"Are you here to take me with you?" Was I supposed to die the night of the storm? Did the girl with a voice I'll carry in my heart for eternity interrupt the plans of a guardian moon? "Is it my time to take the Cloud Path?"

Tani shakes her head. "No, Rai. It's not your time, and the night of the fire wasn't supposed to be mine."

I fall onto my back and stare at the stars. "What are you?"

She lays next to me. "Tani." Her bitter laugh cuts through the air. "A shadow of myself, but it's still me, Rai."

So many nights we lay together on this beach. I stretch out an arm, trying to touch a memory. When all I feel is sand, hollowness fills me. I ask the being the same question I asked my rescuer. "Are you a dream?"

I wait for a familiar kiss to prove spirit Tani is who she claims to be. It never comes, and my heart relives the break of losing Tani to Piyo and then losing her to the fire.

Movement of shadow and light play across my chest. I prop myself on elbows to watch dream Tani trace the woman on my tattoo. "I'm this. Your heart's fate."

My tension coils until it bursts into a laugh. I'm truly asleep, thank the moon. I'm on the beach, dreaming of lost loves and the lie Juan Estrella Azul's design told of my heart's fate being Tani. There's no need to temper words in a dream. "Fated love doesn't trade you in for your brother."

Dream Tani rises until she's lying above me in the air. Her turquoise dress flows downward, appearing to touch my body. I pretend the breeze is sheer fabric tickling the bare skin of my arms. An urge to relive the real Tani's nakedness against my own kicks off a reaction in my shorts. More proof of a dream. I'm going to wake with morning wood for my brother's fiancé.

She balls her fists and tucks them beneath her chin the way Tani always did when tears were on the way. "My father's script got to me. He'd say, '*Rai's an Orpheus, an eternal wanderer. He'll never put you first, Tanya. He doesn't know how. You feel the truth about him but refuse to believe it. You'll always pale against his music, his pipe dreams.*'"

Tanya. The use of Tani's full name jars me back into questioning mode. I need this to be a dream, nothing more. Nothing says you can't fight in a dream. "Emerson always preferred my level-headed, number-crunching brother." I knew he pressured Tani not to take our relationship seriously. I foolishly believed love was a strong enough shield to prevent outside forces from separating us. "I just didn't think you did."

"I didn't," she hesitates, then continues. "At first."

I sit up and my head goes right through her body. Creepy. "At first?"

She floats to my side and sits. "Those first months we were together, I was your moon and your music, but then you became distant, disappearing into the hunt for fresh tunes and away from us."

Tani knew I had to devote time to my new brand of music, to find the unique sounds to resurrect my flagging career. "I didn't love you any less. Life is a balance." I'm not into indulging my guilt dream any longer. I need something to wake me the hell up. "Kitae," I holler, hoping the real fox will sense dream me.

A sleep-grumpy fox stumbles over and sinks his teeth into the sensitive top of my foot before licking sand off my calf.

"Ouch."

"You're not dreaming, Rai." Tani stares at the moon. "My spirit survived the fire because I'm the woman on your tattoo, your heart's fate, and I'm here to make things right."

I dab a fingertip against the drop of blood on my foot. Fear crackles through me as I whisper, "Dream."

Tani pauses and scans the area around us as if she's afraid we're being spied on. "I'm between life and my Cloud Path." Her form gives a slight flicker before she continues. "Rai, I'm going to tell you a great secret that you must keep to yourself."

Her eyes close as if she's gathering courage.

"There's a chance for me to come back, Rai. If you believe me, if you can love me again, I can return to you."

I smear blood from my finger against my shorts, clinging to my dream theory. You can bleed in dreams. "Dreams are dreams, Tani. You were my dream once."

She slides closer. "Accept me as your heart's fate. I'll do it right this time."

"If you return from the dead?"

"From a place of being half alive."

I fall onto my back. I was raised to believe in fate and the spirits existing alongside us. This is a test of those beliefs. My heart wants Tani to be here in whatever form, saying these things. Rewinding fate might be a beautiful thing. A skeptical drop of acid burns in my gut. If this is truly the spirit of Tani, and fate has sent her to me, I need more than a spirit brimming with apologies and admissions of bad choices. If fate chooses to test me, it'll have to deal with my own test. You can test dreams.

"Help me believe you, Tani. If you are here to guide me to my true fate, help me find the woman who saved me from the sea."

She jerks away as if I've slapped her. "Why?"

"Because I dream of you both. If you want my trust and my belief, shine a light on every path open to me. Until I understand the details of every possibility, how is a choice even possible?"

Tani kicks at the sand. She doesn't disturb a single grain. "You say you love me but attach conditions?"

"You are a mind fuck, Tani. If I say, yes, come back to me, how does it work? Do you walk out of the darkness like the fire never happened? Do you appear in another form? Will you know me? Will I know you?"

"Have you stopped believing the energy of the moon helps you to see truth?"

"No, but what proof can you give me you're that truth?"

The vision paces the sand. If she wasn't translucent, I'd have no doubt it was Tani come back to life. Suddenly, she spins to face me. I notice the sand beneath her feet is smooth and undisturbed. "Why are you so hell bent on finding that woman?"

"I'm almost out of time to keep Cloudpath Music. The woman who saved me sang to me. Her voice is the missing piece to my island rock that will breathe new life into my company, make it relevant again."

Tani's wearing the pout I could never resist kissing away. Damn it, I want this insanityscape to be real. If a fully human Tani walked out from behind a palm and swore there was a terrible mistake and we had a second chance, I'd crush her in my arms and never let go.

I've been taught dreams can also be a path between real and unreal. Am I testing the dream or is the dream testing me? This is an opportunity to embrace my belief in the unseen—or barely seen, in ghost Tani's case—sink into the unknown and take a swim. Why not? Writing off a lucid dream lands me exactly where I already am. Every night for months after Tani left me, I meditated in the presence of the moon. I drank in its energy for strength and wished for Tani to return to me. At the new moon, I wrote my heart into a song and tried to manifest a different outcome than her rejection. One that never came.

If there's a shot I can find my mystery rescuer with supernatural Tani's help, or the less likely chance Tani and I are truly fated and being offered a second chance, I'd be a first-class idiot not to go for it.

Tani is still annoyed. "You search for a wish, not a person."

I lay a hand over my tattoo silhouette. "Or do I search for my true heart's fate?"

Tani shakes her head, her frustration about to blow. "Fine. If that's your price, I'll help you find her to prove she's not the answer to your problems you think she is." She rises once again, a silhouette against the moon, and then she's gone.

Relief swiftly shifts to panic. In this dream reality, I'm reunited with Tani. I'm not ready to leave it. If I wake, will I find her again in dreams? What path should I follow, an image of the Tani I once loved, a mystery woman who sang to me on the beach, or...

My gaze falls on the large, slanted rock in the lagoon.

...to Azure, who ignites a spark in my spirit yearning to dance?

Kitae stretches and yawns, licking the bite marks on my foot. Orchid-colored light begins to bleed over the eastern horizon. There's no awakening for me.

I was never asleep.

I BOTCHED OUR REUNION WITH A BLINKING NEON, CAPITAL B. I SOAR to the top of a bird's-nest-speckled cliff and roar at the open ocean. "Stupid, Tani." I imitate the simpering jerk I surely came off as. *"Oh, Rai, you said you loved me. I love you. Accept me as your future without question. I'm your heart's fate."*

Did I offer any proof? Like a bomb, I dropped the possibility of coming back to him and then argued when he threw down a request to help him believe I was real. Not only that, I deliberately defied Sulaa's edict not to tell Rai about my potential return to the living. I sit at the edge of the cliff and swing my legs to crash against the rock face. Of course, they don't make contact. They sink into the rock.

No doubt Sulaa and Calliwag would enjoy a gut-busting laugh at my attempt to get Rai to accept me. "Ha, ha, the spirit girl actually believes she can convince the living she's real."

Why didn't I ask Sulaa more questions about how to explain what I am and what I still might be to Rai?

Because she forbade me from telling him there was any possibility I could return.

I saw an opportunity, and I took it. I counted on the influence of our commune upbringing rife with Pagan rituals, fire festivals, and reverence for the power of the moon to help him accept me. Did I totally believe Rai would fully buy into my blasted in-between, call it what it is, ghost status? Yes. What a fool.

I go through the motion of smacking my forehead. Why in the name of sanity or insanity should he believe the person who dumped him suddenly is granted the right to offer him a second chance? I didn't even say good-bye or make any kind of plan to see him again. He'll probably wear one of Granny Blossom's crystal amulets to keep the evil Tani spirit away.

I attempt to dig my nails into the rock. The thought of losing Rai sends an ache through my shadow self.

This all bites hard. To have any hope with Rai, I must convince him I'm on board with his mission to find his mystery girl when that babe is the same stinking Azure whom I want far away from him.

Think, Tani. Think.

I imagine moonlight seeping in to illuminate my spirit the way I've been taught since childhood. The best strategy here is to gently coax Rai to trust me and guide him to a place where he'll believe there's hope for us. I'll kiss Sulaa's ass plenty to convince her I'm keeping her up to date of Rai's progress in her game. The sea witch must allow continued visits with my fated love until I've made things right.

"Get it together, Tanya." I punish myself with the name I despise. Time to play nice with sea witches and mermaids so I don't ruin everything with Rai.

There are a few points in the Tani column. Rai loves me. There's work to do to reduce the swelling from the sting of my rejection. At least I know what's in his heart. I'm not proud to admit I'll be able to use his guilt over shattering my urn and screwing up my burial at sea to keep him from easily rejecting the thought of us. The stitch in the vicinity of my non-existent rib cage suggests I still maintain some semblance of a conscience. Guilting Rai is a shit move, but a girl's got to muster all resources available.

I mimic a deep breath. I love the man. I want a second chance to be with him. He is my only connection to return to the life I lost.

The squawk of a mama scrub jay warns intruders away from her nest.

The life I lost.

What calls me back with a louder voice, that life or Rai's love? Am I using him because he's the only path to breath and heartbeat?

I stare at the fresh morning sky. Of course, it's Rai's love. His voice woke me out of nothingness. Granny Blossom was always on about ghosts and unfinished business. Rai is mine. It's madness to think anything else. I am his heart's fate and he's mine. Destiny drives this, not Sulaa, not my desperation.

Dawn fades across the sky. Time to return to Azure. I raise arms to a candy pink cloud. "I'm all yours, destiny."

My gaze drops to the island below, and I scramble backward. Straight down the face of the cliff is the real caliche forest.

I avoided this place in life, and I will damn sure avoid it now. I take a running leap away from the edge and propel my body into the sky between a pair of gulls, away from the killing ground and the stink of omens rising from its ruins before I plunge back into the sea.

10

ISLAND MUSIC

JUAN LUNA ROCKS IN THE HAMMOCK I STRUNG BETWEEN TWO TREES near the lagoon. He pulls a long piece of fiber off the chunk of palm bark in his hands. "You need a deep convo with Tutu or Granny Blossom about Tani."

I use my knife to cut grooves in a hollowed-out oak branch. "I need a convo with sanity." I blow through the wooden tube. The note isn't quite right. I gouge deeper, hoping for a richer tone.

He picks up sandpaper to smooth the edges of the curved bark he's working. "Dude, a closed mind is the road to oblivion."

"You believe I saw Tani?"

Juan Luna closes one eye to check his handywork. "What do you believe, Bro?"

I snatch the bark from his hand. "I believe you are the most annoying third gen hippie in the commune."

He lays three fingers over his heart. "Rad. Lovin' the label."

I hold the bark next to my ear and tap all over it with a smooth, egg-shaped stone. "Damn, listen to this range." I toss it to Juan Luna, who copies my movement.

He wiggles a thumb and pinkie at me. "Nailed it."

I add the bark and stone to the line of other instruments I've crafted out of the natural flotsam of Lalale Island. "I need more high pitch possibilities."

Juan Luna spills out of the hammock to stretch and twist. "I'm due for a moonlight beach walk tonight on the far side of the island. I'll hunt for new shit we can hollow out."

We bump forearms, and he saunters away. At the edge of the tree line, he turns back. "Give Tani my love."

My friend doesn't entertain a single granule of doubt over my Tani encounter. "Better yet. I'll send her your way for a chat."

He opens his arms wide. "Cool idea. Bring it." Juan Luna squints at me. "Do the thing, Rai. Live the now. That's where the magic happens."

I'd like to see Juan Luna keep his cool if a see-through Tani tapped on his shoulder. I laugh. He'd probably ask what took her so long to start hanging with us again.

I strip the leaves off a hardy branch for Juan Luna to work on tomorrow. "*Hoo loo. Hoo loo,*" I sing, stretching my voice to try and reclaim notes puberty stole from my range a decade ago. Try as I might, I hit a vocal wall.

The sun dips behind the tallest peak of the island, a harbinger of sunset and Azure. The thought of her tamps down memories of Tani or lost high notes. I stare at the slanted rock at the far end of the lagoon. Will she slide up and over the edge like yesterday and dive into the water?

I sit with my back to the sunset, close my eyes, and listen to the music of an island settling at the close of a long day.

"Hello, Rai."

When I open my eyes, Azure's shadow stretches along the sand, reaching for the water's edge. I brace an arm to stand, but she presses a hand to my shoulder to hold me in place. Her touch sparks tiny electric shocks across my skin.

"I'll sit with you."

She joins me on the sand, stretching her legs and leaning back. I focus on her nearness and how much I dig it. I admire the light fabric of her one-piece shorts set that clings gracefully to her body and imagine the nearly silent sound it would make sliding across my neck if I kissed my way down past her collarbone. Would it catch on the stubble at the side of my jaw and raise the volume as it scratches across?

Azure bumps my shoulder, lingering in the contact. "Do I get a hello?"

Damn, I can be spacier than Juan Luna after a couple of beers. "Hello." On impulse, I turn and touch my lips to her cheek for a soft kiss. The contact sends a pleasant rush through me.

The corners of her lips tilt up. "Don't you love the way the lagoon changes colors? It was aqua the other day, and now it looks like a splash of lavender tea over a peach."

"*Colors of the Lagoon*. There's a song."

She watches clouds scatter over the breakwater and the sea beyond. "Lavender splashes across a wistful sky."

I pause, waiting for more. When she doesn't continue, I take up the lyrics. "A peachy shade thrown off by a sleepy sun."

Azure turns from the lagoon to watch me as she adds, "Fading trails of saffron hold fast the light to save." She points a barefoot toe at the water.

"Before it's claimed beneath the hush of wild azure waves."

Azure reaches for my hand and twines her fingers through mine. "We made our first song."

I pull our joined hands to my lips and dot hers with a kiss. "We did."

She stares at my lips, and I pull back. Damn, I want to kiss her. The pull I felt between us at Miaqua and then again yesterday amps up. I scared her off once. I'm not going to do it again. I pull her to her feet and drag her to my line of instruments. "Let's see if we can put it to music."

There's subtle resistance from her at the word *music*. "I can't sing above the surface. My mother says it's an air/water-pressure thing. I could strain my vocal cords."

Disappointment zips through me as I recall the voices of The Mermaids from the day at Miaqua. Azure didn't sing a solo. Her voice did contribute to the beautiful sounds that transported me during their concert. I'd love to hear her notes dance with my music.

I nod toward the slanted rock in the lagoon. "Weren't you singing out there yesterday?"

Panic clouds her expression. "No, that was just noise." Azure's right eye flutters. She rubs two fingers against the lid. "There's something in my eye."

After she blinks away the intruder, I gently wrap fingers around her upper arms. Her skin is soft. I want to run my hands to her wrists and back up again. Her surprisingly firm biceps mold to my palms. "I'd never ask you to compromise your instrument." Reluctantly, I release her. "First rule of an artist commune, protect the creative well."

She takes a step closer, relaxing. "I knew I liked you." Eyes a shade lighter than her own azure hair watch me. What is one shade lighter than azure? Does the color have a name, or does it belong exclusively to this woman's eyes? When she blinks, long black lashes, matching the color of her eyebrows, dust her skin. I'm surprised her lashes and brows aren't shades of blue, but the contrast is lovely.

My body continues its campaign to pull her in for a kiss. Restraint warns me to mind my pace. Instead of going full throttle, I slide an arm around her back and gesture to the line of Rai-and-Juan-Luna-made instruments. "Instead of compromising your instrument, care to grab mine?" I hold out a small pine flute, blushing as I register the unintended sexuality of my comment.

She peers through her lashes with a smirk at me as she blows.

The sweet sound flies out of the flute and curls through the air. Azure pulls it from her lips and giggles. "Impressive. You made this?"

"With an assist from Juan Luna, who you met at Miaqua when we visited. I'm the idea man. He's the craftsman."

She picks up a conch the size of Kitae's head. "Do I blow?"

I hand her a strip of oak. "Percussion."

Azure taps a tentative rhythm then explores different sounds the curves and dips in the shell allow.

I hand her several different natural drumsticks. She experiments and hums as she makes music, but never sings a note. We move along the line while she tries out my creations in different combinations. I'm captivated by her intensity. Azure sits on the sand in the middle of a collection of instruments she's chosen for our song.

I can't move, watching her work. Sounds pierce skin and bounce through the resonating chambers in my head. They fill me, lift me. I close my eyes and begin to sing along.

"*Pah, pah, pop. Zhuuu. Talla. Talla. Pop. Cah, cah, crack. Cah, crack, crack, crack. Cahhhhhhh.*"

The rhythm stalls. Azure's hands are frozen mid-strike. Our gazes lock. We both pant, trapped together in the bubble of decaying sound.

I live this music. Its acoustic signature seeps into my bones. Once a note is played, it's gone. Not these. They linger and beg to find life again.

As if reading my thoughts, Azure starts the intro to our new song. I sing and we bring it into the world, once, twice, and then three more times. I fall to the sand in front of her. "This is the core of what I've been trying to find." I pull her to her feet and swing her in a circle. "Do you hear the trees singing?" Crazed with excitement, I grab a stone and an oak flute. As I copy our song on the flute, I rap its pulse against a palm adding new texture to our composition.

Azure laughs, but not at me. It's the joyful release of knowledge we've created something new. Together. She retrieves a pair of broken abalone shells and raps them against one another with just enough pressure to make a new sound, not to chip or crack. Everything she touches adds a layer.

I run onto the beach and throw my arms to the sunset. Shades of scarlet and ginger give my tan skin a ruddy glow. "Island rock. This is island rock," I shout to the fleeing sun.

I stumble up the small rise to Azure's orchestra layout drunk with joy. She switches the pattern of her taps, enhancing the melody. "Let's take it out for a spin. Dance, Rai."

I'm adrift in a creative buzz. I fling my hips, flap my arms, and spin. The music stops.

Azure stares at me wide-eyed. She holds in the laugh for half a second before it bursts free. "What the hell was that?"

I take a few balancing steps. "What do you mean? I'm feeling the music."

"You're twitching like a heron with a bad knee."

The flush across my skin isn't from sunset. "Not feeling my dancing the way I'm feeling your tune?"

She crosses the sand to me. "Let me help." Strong fingers take hold of my hips. "Bend your knees a little. Keep it smooth." Azure guides my hips in a circle. "That's it." Now sing."

My body obeys her touch and glides in arcs and curves as I put voice to our song. The last bit of sun dips beneath the horizon as Azure coaxes my shoulders into a liquid up and down slide.

"Better. Now watch me." Her moves are as fluid as a moon jelly as she bends and swirls. She flips hair over a shoulder and then spins her head to make her locks fly into a blue flare. "Keep singing."

The sight of this beautiful woman, moving to our song in the light of a rising moon steals my breath, my voice.

"Don't stop, Rai. Sing and dance with me."

I grasp the hands she holds out. We sway and circle until her arms slide across my shoulders and stay. She looks up at me, lips slightly parted. My own hands find their way around her. Azure presses her body to mine. Fingers thread beneath my braids, pulling my face to hers. Our dance becomes slower and slower until it stops.

We move at the same time, pressing lips to lips. Our mouths brush and slide to the rhythm of our song. She tastes slightly of the oak flute, a deep earthy flavor. I trace the tip of my tongue over the peaks of her upper lip to lose myself in the way she's become part of my song. She opens to me, and I drink deeper. Azure answers, learning my flavor. Does she taste palm and the sweetness of island cherries?

We move past a tentative beginning and clutch tight to one another. She trails fingers down the sides of my face to my chest while teasing my tongue with hers. I press my own fingertips along her spine, stopping at the top curve of her ass. I breathe fiery breath into her cool mouth as my desire ratchets higher. She grabs my waist and leans back to take in the night air. Her movement presses her hips firmly into mine, leaving no mystery to what the kiss does to me.

I mentally prepare for her to flee from the appreciation in my shorts. Instead, she grabs my waistband, fitting me against her. "Sing to me, Rai. Sing our song." Azure kisses my jaw as I sing. She pulls us into a dance, and my voice fails.

Her long, silky hair slips through my fingers. I pull her to me and claim her lips in a hungry kiss. Our tongues find the dance our bodies—and then our lips—already discovered. I moan her name as she kisses her way across my chest, tasting each star on my tattoo.

"I love making music with you, Rai."

My muscles might as well be made of crumpled paper. I drop onto the sand and pull Azure on top of me. She's done more than make music with me. She obliterated the barrier keeping my island rock from coming alive. This woman summoned the rhythms of the land, the trees, the breeze and infused my vision with its missing pieces. I thought I was searching for a voice I'd only heard once on a dark night. How wrong I was. The creative essence of this artist, this musician, this woman is what I lacked.

I wrap arms around her. "You found the music I've been longing to make." I bury my face against her neck and kiss my way to her temple. "Azure, you have no idea what you've given me." I raise my lips to hers and grace her with a kiss filled with gratitude, tenderness, and the heat of my desire for her.

There's great seduction in the act of making art with someone. If it works, inhibitions peel away, and the raw passion of mutual creation becomes a consuming wave. Azure and I are consumed. I feel a surge of rightness, of beauty, of connection between us more powerful than I've ever experienced. I swear my tattoo expands across my chest as if it too has found the energy to make it sing.

Azure kisses me with a sizzle that only comes with experience. It's a relief. I don't want to take advantage of her sheltered life at Miaqua. As further reassurance, her hand slides into the back of my shorts to tiptoe down my ass.

"Let's see what else we can make beside music," she whispers in my ear.

I sit up in a flash and grasp her thighs to wrap them around my waist. "More dancing?" I nip her shoulder.

"Much more than dancing." She reaches to undo her top button when something sharp rams me from behind.

"What the hell?"

Kitae goes ballistic. He circles, pelting us with sand. When I reach for him, he snaps his teeth. Azure scoots off me to kneel in front of the thing that sliced into my back. Kitae jumps into the middle of an upside-down sea turtle shell, his tongue hanging out as if to say, *"Dude, check out my sweet find."*

I run my hands over the impressive treasure. Kitae yips once and leaps out of the inverted dome, smug as hell. "Good job, partner." I knock on the curve of the shell. "Azure, this'll be a groovy addition to our sound."

When I look up, Azure's gaze is fixed on the shell. Her head snaps up, and she glares. "Don't you dare." She grabs the edge of the shell and tugs it to the water. "It's not for your band. What if someone hunted Kitae to make a whistle of his leg bone?"

Her words chill the air. I scoop my pal into my arms and kiss his head. "Moon, I'm sorry, Azure. I didn't mean to be crass."

She gently pushes the shell into the tide. The current quickly snatches it up. We both watch as it crosses the lagoon and disappears between two of the breakwater rocks.

"It was an intelligent, living creature, Rai. Not a plaything." She storms up the beach. "I should go."

I put Kitae down, and he races into the trees after an unsuspecting lizard. "Please, stay."

She rebuttons her top. "I'm not in a dancing mood."

"Can we just talk?"

Azure crosses her arms and then drops them to her side. "You have to understand. I'm very protective of—"

I lay a finger to her lips. Their moistness makes me regret the possibility of no more dancing. "There's nothing to apologize for. I was callous, only thinking of my music not the cost to the animal."

"You'll always pale against his music, his pipe dreams." The words Tani spoke from her father fly into my head. I see an ugly truth there. If I'd put Tani first, and we'd stayed together, would she be alive now?

Azure's touch shakes me out of the daze. She rubs my arm. "Are you okay, Rai?"

I manage a wimpy smile. "Yeah, sure. Guilt wave."

She looks out to the lagoon and frees a pearl pouch from her pocket. She stares at it for a long moment, then smiles, taking my hand. "Walk me to my shuttle?"

I nod. "Lead the way."

We take the path through a line of palms and into an oak grove.

I wonder where she landed the shuttle. We're not heading toward the sand spit she used before. "Tell me more about your new sound."

What artist doesn't warm right up talking about their vision? I squeeze her hand. "I call it island rock."

Azure's brows furrow.

I hold a hand up. "Stop. I see Yacht Rock written all over your face."

She laughs. "Sorry. I'm having a margarita, deck shoe moment."

"You heard what we made. It's more primal, natural. I want the sounds and the rhythms to come from the island."

"Isn't that what Cloudpath Music is?"

I puff my cheeks and blow. "For moon's sake, no. My parents were into soundscapes. New age, calming stuff. Like an app you use to fall asleep to. They took it to a whole new level before anyone else and built the company." I grunt out a laugh. "Big hit on submarines."

She pouts. "You're sour."

"Their soundscapes went sour." I shake my head. "No, stale. The sound got stale."

Azure stops and turns to me. "Then why are so many people hot to buy your company?"

"Our artists. We've got frickin' genius musicians under contract. They're totally underutilized. If I can score some collaborations, my new sound could be crazy great."

"You don't want to sell your company?"

I press my lips together. "It might be out of my hands."

She grabs my T-shirt and pulls me in for a delicious kiss. "I want to help."

I smooth her hair. "You already have. May I see you again tomorrow? How about a picnic lunch at the lagoon? I'd love to work on more music with you."

She flashes me a smile that makes it nearly impossible not to push her against the nearest tree trunk. "I'd like another dance." She blows me a kiss and skips down the path to the shore.

"Noon," I call after her and watch until she slips behind the tower of shoreline boulders hiding her shuttle. My fingertips play against swollen lips, sending a lustful surge to my groin. I use my new dance skills to bust a couple of turns up the path until I come face-to-face with my past and nearly fall backward onto the rocks.

Standing in my way with a scowl to freeze lust is Tani.

11

OPEN YOUR EYES

MY RAGE IS THE FROTHY TOP OF A POT ABOUT TO BOIL OVER. I seethed watching it all, the noise they call music, the dancing, the groping. I was seconds away from calling Sulaa to drive her sex wedge between them when Azure bailed.

Curse Azure. The merwitch threw herself at Rai, my Rai. Here's news for you, babe. You're nothing but a loaner until Sulaa helps me claim my rightful place as his heart's fate.

Curse Sulaa too. I'm sure Ms. shades-of-blue-paint-chip hair is basking in the sickening attraction I'll report between Azure and Rai. The lovesick fools play right into the sorceress's conniving hands.

I don't give a flying gull if the deceitful mermaid's heart gets pounded. I do care about Rai's. It's imperative I extricate him from his pit of romantasy goo before he's out of reach. Luckily, I possess the perfect bomb to set him free.

Azure's fishy little secret is about to blow wide open.

I must tread lightly. Rai's artistic sensibility works both ways. It sends him into monumental highs or plunges him into a cocoon of isolation. I swear the man can disappear when he's standing right in front of you when his black moods prevail. Will I send him spiraling into the unreachable place if I slap him across the face with Azure's truth? I'm banking on the possibility of us having a second chance being enough to keep him on the light side of the moon.

One factor is solid. Azure is an obstacle on my path back to Rai. The thing growing between the two can't go further. It's time for a preemptive strike.

I smooth my hair and dress as if anything I do improves my looks.

"Treat Rai like the brittle shell he can be."

My voice sounds birdlike here on the island, as if it's trying to blend into the breeze and shush of waves. Is that what Rai hears?

I watch the mermaid dive under the surface, leaving Rai alone on the path. Shoreline boulders block the view of her transformation. This is risky. Sulaa already has my eternity pinned to the wall. My instructions are to stick to Azure, not clock unsanctioned time with Rai. A flash of a Calliwag lionfish head on my body sends a tremor through me. If the sorceress discovers I'm working against Rai and Azure and ignoring her rules, will I decimate my destiny? I'll be cautious with an extra shot of sneaky.

I may be playing with sea-witch fire, but Rai Cloud deserves to know everything. I'll be quick and then catch up with Azure.

Carefully, I drift toward Rai. The T-shirt stuffed into his back pocket flaps behind him as he climbs the path. He'd prowl the island naked in only flip-flops if he could. My fingers tingle at memories of tracing the contours of his smooth, sun-warmed chest. I love this man. I'll awaken the *mana*, the fate, Juan Estrella created in Rai's tattoo. That fate is me.

Keeping enough distance not to frighten him, I curve to block his way.

"Hey, Tani. Everything cool?"

My eyes snap wide. "What? You're not opening with 'are you a dream' talk?"

Rai settles on a large smooth rock next to the path, never taking his eyes off me. It's the way he stares at the movement of a palm frond or the swish of the tide when it covers the sand. He's writing me into his head like a song. Hey, whatever works to convince him I'm in his life as more than a fleeting vision.

I float to sit next to him. "And here I thought I needed to drag Juan Luna here by his ponytail to verify I'm real." I shrug. "Well, as much I can be for now."

Rai taps his head. "Consider my mind officially opened." His gaze finds the moon. "After you..." He wiggles fingers at the sky, indicating my less than amicable retreat from our last meeting. "I thought about how disappointed my mother would be for dismissing the gift of seeing you again." He grimaces. "I semi-panicked that I'd blown everything with my asshattery, so I told Juan Luna about you."

"What was the phrase Corinne always used to say?" I ask, tapping my bottom lip. It comes to me as Rai starts to speak, and we say it at the same time.

"See the unseen. Sense the unknown. Suspend the common belief."

Rai's voice breaks on the last word. The loss of his family is still fresh sorrow hanging over him.

Brittle shell. I remind myself.

He searches for the moon. When he finds it, I see a thread of blue-white light stretch from its face to the moon on his chest. It's beautiful. Is this an actual perk of being between life and death, seeing such wonders? Am I witness to *mana*? I'm about to ask Rai if he can see the thread or sense its energy when he reaches for me.

"All my life, I've waited for a clear sign of the moon's power. I never thought it would be through you."

"It makes sense, Rai. We were in love. That's the part we got right." It's my turn to study the moon. "People fuck up."

He pulls away. I imagine the warmth of his body being snatched from me. Even though I can't feel it, I remember it. I want it.

"And lose trust. I see you as Tani. It's hard to separate your now from our then." He rubs his lips together. "I am sorry I was harsh with you before. It was an unfair ask to insist you prove yourself by finding the woman who saved me the night of the storm. Juan Luna helped me understand I'm a total loser if I don't appreciate you with no strings attached." He's silent for a beat as he assesses me with intensity I recognize as his truth-seeking stare. "Do you get my soul was altered when you ended us?"

I wish I was a being sent by a moon deity from one of Corinne Cloud's tales instead of a lost spirit stumbling between past and present. Maybe then guilt wouldn't fray what feeble form I still possess.

Rai stands and stares into a cluster of oaks on the hillside. "I did believe Tani was my heart's fate." His palm rests on the tattoo silhouette. "Even as I held her urn to the sea, part of me still believed it."

His words circle through my thoughts. *I love you, Tani.*

"Saying good-bye to her...to you..." He stammers. "...was supposed to be my closure."

I glide around to face him. "There's a reason fate refused you closure. Do you still love me?"

He reaches out, seeking as if to grasp my hands. When he doesn't make contact, his arms drop to his sides, and he says nothing.

"I believe you do, and I still love you, Rai. That's why you see me, and why fate is giving us this second chance to love. There is more to life than mistakes, regrets, and even death. I've seen it from my side."

Instead of answering, Rai begins to sing.

"Tani breeze, sliding through my hair
Smoothing, taming
Tani breeze, brush across my skin
Wandering, wanting

Tani breeze, sighing in the night
Loving, giving
Tani breeze, watch the rising sun
Needing, staying

Always in my laugh
Always in my arms
Always in my soul

Tani breeze, blow through endless years
Soaring, brightening
Tani breeze, etched upon my heart
Deepening, piercing

Tani breeze, spirits claim our way
Knowing, seeing
Tani breeze, as one we do fly
Loving, trusting

Always in my laugh
Always in my arms
Always in my soul"

It's the song he was working on the day I left him. His expression is full of regret that seems to flow into me, pinning me to the earth where I long to stay.

"I never finished the song." Rai wipes a hand down his face and cuts his gaze to me like the slice of a blade. "It doesn't matter if I still love you. I'm on this side and you are..." He flings an arm at the moon. "... gone."

"It does matter because your love can call me back." I'm saying what I believe even if it's not to the letter of the cosmic plan that brought me here. I wait for him to react, to ask questions, to let in the smallest sliver of hope. He might as well be part of the stone cliffs. I wish I could shake him. "What if I hadn't died in the fire? Would you give me another chance?"

Rai's body jerks. He raises a hand to me. "Stop."

I fly around him so fast I'm a yellowish blur. "Would we have another chance?"

He drops into a squat, covering his ears. I stop my frenzied circle and give him space. Slowly, his hands slide to his knees. His voice is raspy, a branch against rock. "Yes, damn it. If you'd left Piyo and come back to me, I'd give us a second chance." He jabs a finger at the silhouette on his chest. "This was supposed to be you, Tani." He raises his voice. It echoes off the cliff behind us. "It was supposed to be you."

He weeps, artist's tears, lover's tears. My spirit grows brighter. He notices and gapes at the new shimmer.

"I am your heart's fate, Rai. I will find a way back if you swear our love hasn't died. If you will truly wait on your side for me, it can happen."

Rai straightens and grinds a rock under his flip-flop. His voice is laden with misery. "If I wait—if I swear. You're laying a shit ton of responsibility on me."

I move closer to him and lower my voice to a soothing whisper. "Not responsibility, possibility."

Rai tears at his hair and destroys one of his braids. He catches the small wooden whistle freed from his twisted strands and squeezes it in his hand. "You want me to commit to a dream." He looks straight at me. "I get this isn't a dream now. You want to hear about dreams? You giving us a second chance after you dumped me is the dream I couldn't shake for a long damn time." He jams the whistle into his pocket and jabs a finger at his tattoo. "Even if she was you once, she can't be anymore." His eyes fill with a new layer of tears. "I truly believe fate can be about second chances, Tani. I do, but not for us."

Rai rubs his lips together again, the nervous twitch I used to stop with a kiss. Oh moon, I miss his kisses, the way we'd lay naked on his hammock while he relearned my body every time we made love. His musician's fingers strumming and stroking until my skin crackled with a fire only Rai could quench.

I never felt incendiary with Piyo. Steady Piyo. Predictable Piyo.

Rai backs away. "I thought destiny gave me a second chance, a new heart's fate with the woman who saved me from the storm." He shakes his head. "But she is as lost to me as you are. Letting go is fucking hard for me." He wrings his hands. "I accept now, neither you nor that woman were my heart's fate."

I'm losing him. I know what's coming next. Once he says it, I know what I must do to keep any possibility of Rai and me alive.

His voice takes on a gentle timbre. "Because I've found the one who is."

Both his palms press over the woman painted over his heart, and I die all over again.

"Deep in my gut, I knew music would lead me to my heart's fate. When I tried to write a song for you, I waited for a sign we were fated." His eyes clear. "Instead, you chose Piyo. Not the sign I expected."

He stares at the sea. "It wasn't until her music found me tonight I knew my search was over."

"Azure."

Rai is legit stunned. His eyes are wild, his mouth unable to form words.

"Perks of this," I say and fan my hands down my body. "I see more than I wish I did."

He frowns and sits on the rock. For moon's sake, Rai admits he loves me. Why isn't that enough for him to wait for me? Okay, sans specifics, it's a stretch for him to commit. I get it, but a leap of faith instead of a tiny hop would be appreciated. If he hadn't decisively traded me in for Azure as his heart's fate, I'd never hit play on my next move.

Anger sends a flush across his face and chest, turning his bright white moon tattoo pink. "Is spying on me part of your new reality?"

Oh, this is getting ugly fast. Panic launches words right past my lips. "Azure can't be your heart's fate."

He crosses his arms. "Because my life is supposed to stop moving forward to gamble a magical living version of Tani will reappear?"

My brain screams at me not to shatter the first glimmer of happiness Rai's been given in the soul-sucking months since he lost everything but Cloudpath Music, which will soon fall away as well. If I back off now, we may lose our chance to be together.

"Because Azure's a mermaid."

Rai's neck juts forward. He gawks at me.

"All Sulaa's daughters are sea freaks. Azure's a mermaid. Her sisters have fins or gills or full-body scales."

He recovers and shoots to his feet. "You're lying. Azure's no freak." His arms wave wildly. If I were solid, he'd have popped me one. "Her sisters are every bit as human as she is. I've been in the same room with The Mermaids..." His voice trails off as he says the word.

"It's all an illusion, Rai. Sulaa's doing. Every rumor you've ever heard about the sea witch is true. Granny Blossom warned us to watch out for Sulaa Kylock, and she was right. Azure's mother is a sorceress, and not a very nice one."

"How do you..." His eyes circle as he works out a new reality. Finally, they settle on me and narrow. "Sulaa is the one feeding you this crock of shit, saying you can return to me, isn't she?" Rai's voice is laced with toxic hate.

My gaze falls to the path. "It's truth, Rai. I sort of lent her my soul in exchange for the chance to return to life, to you."

Rai's intake of breath snaps through the air. "You didn't." He's quiet for a long moment. "Fuck, Tani. Did I do this to you by saying I loved you the night of the storm?"

In his eyes, I see shades of gentleness and love to give me hope.

Thank moon, he doesn't see me as the villain here. "Sulaa found my lost spirit in the sea. And yes, I believe that there is a way to fix my mistakes and be with you again."

Rai reaches out for me, only to be disappointed. "Oh, Tani, I doomed you when I said I loved you." He pounds a fist against the nearest tree. "My words drove you to bargain with the sea witch."

"What's done is done," I say and attempt to pull off a smile. "You need to hear it all, Rai." I go through the motion of a deep, fortifying breath and look him straight in the eye. "Azure is a mermaid." I wait for him to speak. All I get is goggle eyes and a full-face flush as if he's choking, so I plunge ahead. "Think about it. Has she ever asked you to walk her to the shuttle she supposedly takes here from Miaqua?"

He opens and closes his mouth trying to land on a response. I push on. "Mermaids don't need shuttles. Azure swims to the island."

Rai stares at the rocks where he assumed Azure hid her ride to Miaqua.

"If she's seriously into you, haven't you wondered why her visits aren't much more than a flyby? Her time on Lalale is finite before she needs to hit the water. It has something to do with the scales she keeps in a pearl pouch drying up."

His hand drifts to the place on his hip where Azure keeps the pouch on hers. "That makes no sense. Miaqua is underwater but not in the water. Why don't the scales dry there?"

I shrug. "Sulaa's magic? Sea proximity?"

Rai leans on a tree next to the path and stares out over the ocean. "This can't be true."

"Ask her." A thought darts into my head. "And watch her eye. It twitches when she's lying."

Rai rests his head on his forearm.

I can't back down now. "You believe I'm real." I take the downward thrust of his chin as a nod. "It's an if-then, Rai. You can't pick and choose your truths. If you accept me, then you must accept Azure is a mermaid."

Rai turns his face toward me. His expression burns the space where my heart once beat. There's longing surrounded with deep sadness. I start to glide closer to him but stop. Who is the longing for? Who is the sadness for? If only my new reality came with mind reading.

His silence doesn't feel like a tick in the Tani column. "I know I have a steep path to climb to win your trust, Rai. I love you. Please, let's start from there and rebuild."

He makes an X with his forearms across his chest, pressing fists to the underside of his jaw, gaze fixed on the path. When I start to speak, he holds up a hand to stop me. "If I could take you in my arms, feel the way we used to fit together like a single note, a single beat, I might see a way this is possible." He flicks a finger to me and then at him.

I fly close enough for our bodies to appear to be touching and ghost grip his shoulders. We stare into each other's eyes. "Do you feel anything? Energy? Adrenaline?"

He steps back as his gaze rakes my hands, my body, and lands on my face. Rai shakes his head, and his two remaining braids whip across one another. "Why did you bring Azure into this?" He moves away, suspicion clouding his eyes. "You're afraid she may be my heart's fate instead of you."

"Yes, I am afraid, but not out of jealousy. It's because without you and I being in love again, there's no reason for me to come back. Do you get that?"

Rai stares at the open sea and mumbles. "I get it."

"A mermaid will never be able to give you the life you deserve, the love you want. I can if I return."

He focuses on my face. "If. You're asking me to choose my fate based on *if.*"

As much as I hate to keep dumping on Rai, he needs to see the traps being set for him. "Believing in us is not the only reason to back off from Azure. You're going to get screwed."

Rai chuffs out a dry, emotionless laugh. "More screwed than deciding if a mermaid or a ghost is destined to be my heart's fate?"

"I'm going lay more on you, Rai. You're not going to like it."

He avoids looking at me and spins his hand in a *get on with it* circle. Shadows grow under his eyes. I hesitate. Does talking to me suck his energy or cause other strange effects? Will my next bit of truth knock him flat? I'm powerless to help him if it does. Rai deserves to know he's in the middle of a sea witch storm.

"Sulaa is manipulating Azure to get Cloudpath Music. She wants you to fall for Azure so she can pull the plug on letting her little mermaid come to the island as blackmail until you sell the witch your company."

"That's despicable." His thick, dark brows pull together over squinted eyes. "Does Azure know?"

I should say no. Azure has no clue Mama plays her like a toy guitar. I've already harpooned Azure over the mermaid thing, but Rai is at a tipping point. He must tip my way for us to have our second chance. I can't paint Azure with any pretty colors.

Rai takes my silence as acquiescence. Unshed tears, pooling in his eyes, reflect moonlight. This is my moment, the opening to help him accept there is still a chance for me to be his heart's fate. I slowly approach and float my hand over the silhouette on his chest. "I'm right here, Rai, waiting for you."

He covers my phantom hand with his. "I can't unpack everything right now."

Do I see hope replace his hopelessness or is it a trick of my vacant heart? Before I can strengthen my case, lightning cracks through my brain. I grab my head in my hands and unleash a cry of pain that makes the leaves of the oak shudder once but doesn't disturb a single loose strand of Rai's raven hair.

Oh, moon. Sulaa's heard me. Does she know I've broken rules?

Rai reaches for me. "Tani, what's happening?"

The witch's voice pierces my body like a shower of knife points. *To Azure.*

I pray this gamble isn't my ruin, and that Sulaa believes my only transgression is leaving Azure's side. I'm ripped from the path, from Rai. As I plunge headfirst into a black, churning sea, I hear him call my name.

12

DEEP BLUES

I STEP OUT OF THE SHOWER AND SCRATCH A TOWEL THROUGH MY HAIR. Falling asleep on the beach under the moon last night gave me headful of sand and zero insight. Sand finds a way into everything, even the spaces between toes. I twist my hair into its trio of braids, carefully securing the abalone and whistle to their respective ends. When I pinch the moonstone disc between thumb and index finger, resurrections and realizations flood my brain.

If one of my mom's moon entities is truly guiding my destiny, it's doing a crap job of painting a clear path. My heart pumps in large, sloppy beats. I always believed the fated mate inked onto my chest would clearly reveal herself. It made sense for Tani to be my heart's fate. I rest my palm over the silhouette. We shared the life of growing up in our unconventional artist commune. Our world view was built from the creative freedom of paint splatters and soul-seeking poetry. The two of us and Piyo were adventurers seeking out every mystery of the island, usually in bare feet. Tani was the spice to my sugar, a source of equilibrium between Earth's spheres, until she wasn't.

Now, this supernatural version of Tani asks for a place back in my life. A place that feels simultaneously right and wrong.

In all the stories Juan Luna's grandmother, Tutu, spun for us, she never mentioned scorned lovers reuniting after death while one still inhabited the here and now. They became constellations, stardust, or traveled to otherworldly realms to hang together.

Does Sulaa Kylock possess magical talent of enough magnitude to bring Tani back?

And then there is Azure. I press my lifeline against the tattoo of my heart's fate.

Making music with her stretched my creative essence beyond a limit I hadn't realized existed until she obliterated it. My want for her drives me in a way it never did with Tani. She was a constant, our romance a gradual and welcome extension of deep friendship. Azure is the splash of moonlight illuminating sensations and emotions with untapped intensity. Heat flares beneath my palm as if my ink were on fire. I yank my hand away to find skin glowing the bright red of being too close to a fire. Which woman makes my skin burn?

Shaking my hand to cool it, I call out the window, imagining the position of the moon in the daytime sky. "Selene, Artemis, Chang'e, if that was your sign, it's as clear as mud."

I weave the moonstone disc into my braid. The choice between Tani and Azure isn't the loudest racket between my ears. Getting to the truth of Tani's *"Azure is a mermaid"* revelation is. An ominous minor key buzzes in my bones. Was Tani being truthful about Azure using me so Sulaa gained an edge on a Cloudpath Music deal? Who the moon can I trust anymore? Mermaids own the unfortunate rep of being duplicitous sirens who loiter on sea rocks to lure sailors to their doom. It isn't as if spirit Tani is without an agenda with her ask for a commitment from me to give her a second shot at life.

When did the edges of reality become so undefined?

I tap a tentative fingertip to the moon on my chest. In momentary insanity, I hope the gesture will summon Tani. I have more questions than answers from her visits. The tattoo's previous heatwave is gone.

My cell phone buzzes from the kitchenette counter in the main room of my tiny house. A few years ago, my mom and stepdad had the groovy idea of building a village of tiny houses to attract new blood to the commune who weren't as into rustic as the core group. Lalale Village also needed to house non-bohemian musicians coming out to the island to record for Cloudpath Music.

Piyo and I got first dibs on the digs. I chose the one set farthest apart from the rest, nestled on the top of a small rise at the edge of the palm grove with a killer view of the channel and distant mainland. My front window angles away from the marina and Cloudpath HQ, giving the illusion Kitae and me live alone on the island.

Emerson's ringtone plays. I debate for a half-sec whether to ignore him, but I don't want my noon convo with Azure to be interrupted.

"Hey, Em."

"Any material ready to record yet?" says Mr. Cut-to-the-Chase in peppery tones.

"Close."

His huff is a wind gust through the phone. "A new nibble came in from a rising conglomerate on the block, Dark Vinyl Artists."

"Never heard of them. What's their brand?" With a toe, I work my flip-flops out from under the pull-out couch.

"I'm guessing edgy."

"They'd better be with a name like that." There's a stitch in my side. This Dark Vinyl Artists might be the antithesis to my vision of island rock and its connection to the natural and life affirming. Selling off the family company to what could be the polar opposite of my parents' mission statement is rank betrayal.

"Shall I set up a meeting?"

The metaphoric bag of rocks hanging around my neck doubles

in weight. Tani, Azure, Cloudpath Music—I am not designed to juggle this many flaming chainsaws at once.

"Give me a week. I'm in creative mode, not biz mode."

Emerson mutters something about me never being in biz mode. He means for me to hear it. I want to be pissed, but the dude has my back on all things biz. I nearly slip and ask if he's had any recent Tani moments. I bite my tongue in time. Would he tell me? Dropping any hint I've been with her to a grieving father who hasn't is heartless.

"I'll keep you posted, Em." I end the call before he drags me down a path to further complicate my overly munched mind.

I throw bananas, lentil crackers, and hummus into a string bag, not a gourmet picnic. If fate sends my impending confrontation with Azure south, neither of us will have an appetite. I cram down a protein bar and guzzle coconut water since I haven't eaten since lunch yesterday. When I open the front door, Kitae bites the strap of my flip-flop and growls.

I raise my knee to extricate footwear from fox teeth. "If you can't be a gentleman, buzz off."

He gives me a vulpine smile and takes off toward the lagoon. Is my fur bro a clairvoyant mammalian GPS, or am I that predicable?

Azure beat me to the sand. Like a coward, I hide behind a curtain of sago palm fronds to study her for signs of a tail. She sits cross-legged, not cross-finned, on the sand, strumming a guitar in her lap. Kitae's muzzle rests on her knee. Both instrument and woman are bone dry. Are mermaids equipped with a quick-dry setting?

Azure picks out a song. She only voices single notes with long intervals between. It's as odd as it is mesmerizing. A longing to encourage her to string the sound together into the gorgeous composition they'd create flushes me out of hiding.

Kitae's eyes dart to me. Deciding the pillow of Azure's leg is superior to his loyalty to me, he doesn't move. She's wearing denim capri pants and a coral-colored, sleeveless blouse that perfectly complements the loose blue waves flowing down her back. Did she stash the outfit behind a rock earlier to slide into after a naked tail swim from Miaqua? Oh moon, I'm an ass clown for imposing secretive mermaid tactics to a woman I've fallen hard for without giving her a chance to call me out on my insanity.

I'm about to shout a greeting when my gaze falls to her hip and the pearly pouch at her side. Tani's explanation about Azure's drying scales kills my words as I walk mute across the sand. Kitae, resentful of my intrusion on his date with Azure, yips at me to get lost. When she turns, a smile to knock me off my feet brightens her face.

"Rai." She nudges Kitae aside to stand. "I brought you a present." Azure holds out a stunningly beautiful guitar. Its body is covered in a thin layer of abalone shell that catches the light to reflect delicate, multi-colored beams. "My sister, Lapis, makes these. She designs them to play sea tones that a land-made guitar can't duplicate. It's the abalone. They give the notes an underwater quality."

Underwater quality? Could her gift be a precursor to truth telling?

"You bagged on me when I wanted to make the turtle shell an instrument, but you're giving me a guitar made from abalone?"

Azure's cheeks redden. "I may have overreacted, and I'm sorry. Sea turtles are a very personal subject with me. Lapis collects broken chips of abalone shells. She'd never harm a living creature for parts. I know you wouldn't either."

Azure's gaze digs deep, letting me know she sees who I am.

"Her guitars allow the beauty of the abalone's shell never to lose their shine."

When I don't answer right away, she steps closer to pass the instrument over. "It's a cool addition to your island orchestra."

I give her an opening. "Is there any other message here?" Moon, this would be much easier if she offers her revelation before I'm forced to ask.

She tilts her head and smirks at me. "Maybe I'm entertaining the possibility of an enthusiastic thank you."

I drop the string bag with the meager picnic onto the sand. "I'm sorry, Azure. It's a bitchin' instrument. It truly is." My fingers itch to play it and discover what sea tones are. Until the mermaid question is resolved, it's not cool to let her give it to me. "I don't know if I can accept it."

Azure's forehead creases, and she hugs the guitar to her chest. "I thought we were into making music together." Her gaze falls to the guitar. "This is my contribution."

Words, fears, anticipation all jumble inside. I want to make music with Azure. I ache to keep this woman in my life. Why did Tani fall out of the clouds at the same time Azure reawakens inspiration and the direction for my music I feared I'd never find?

"Shit." I kick the sand.

Azure backs toward the water. "What is it, Rai?"

If Tani is wrong about her, Azure will think I'm a whack job and run as fast and far from me as she can. If Tani is right, and Azure's been lying to me, how can I believe what I thought we were building isn't a scheme to get her family's fins on Cloudpath Music? The truth buzzer goes off in my head. It's time to go balls-out.

The blue of her eyes is the perfect blend of sky and sea. I stare at her bare toes as I blurt. "Are you a mermaid?" As soon as the words leave me, I hear how ludicrous they are. I spin away and clutch my head. "Moon, I'm sorry, Azure. I'm a jackass." I should have waited and asked Tani for solid proof instead of dumping this on Azure.

Her touch on my shoulder is gentle, forgiving. I turn and grab her hands, now free of the guitar. "Can we pretend that didn't come out of my mouth?"

Azure shakes her head. "No, we can't." I expect her to pull away, but she steps in. We stare into each other's eyes.

"Please, Azure. I can't explain why I asked. All I can say is I bought into something someone told me—"

She lays her hand over my mouth. The pressure and heat of her fingers undo me. I want to wrap my arms around her and kiss my ridiculous words out of her memory.

"We can't pretend because..." Her breath hitches. "I don't want to pretend with you."

My body is a fuzzy, out of focus picture. I want to shout at her not to speak because, moon, strike me, I know what she's going to say so I say it first. "You are a mermaid."

Her mouth puckers as she nods her head. No flutter or twitch stirs in her eyes. I hate myself for even checking. Damn Tani for making me doubt Azure's honesty.

I rest my forehead against hers, adrift in a moment of realization I am completely unprepared for. "Mermaids are real?"

"Mermaids are real," she whispers, her breath sliding over my lips.

I close my eyes. This isn't the answer I wanted. Are we even the same species? I can't deal. I also can't move. I wait for shock or the flight reflex to make the decision for me, rip me from her arms, and send me running through the trees.

Instead, peaceful acceptance flows through me. Beliefs from deep in my core quench any doubt. My mother's voice resonates in my heart.

"See the unseen. Sense the unknown. Suspend the common belief."

Azure's voice is quiet enough to mimic a breeze. "Do you want me to go?"

Here's my out. The problem is, I don't want out. I want Azure. There is still one burning question between us. It's my turn to whisper. "Are you working with your mother to coerce me into selling Cloudpath Music to her?"

Azure takes a step back, eyes wide. "What?"

I didn't think this through. How am I going to explain I get my intel from the spirit of an ex-girlfriend who's straddling the fence between life and death? If there's anything ten shades crazier than Azure being a mermaid, it's that. We are quite the pair.

"I wish I could give more specifics. I've been told Sulaa wants to meddle with us to use you to manipulate me into selling her my company."

Azure's pale apricot skin blanches to cloud white. Her gaze darts around the lagoon as if a different truth than what I've just revealed is written on a palm frond. She collapses onto the sand. A hand presses to her mouth. "I think I'm going to be sick."

She didn't know. I'm so relieved I want to crumple onto the sand next to her. I grab a water bottle out of the string bag, unscrew the lid, and kneel, resting a hand on her back. "Here. Sip."

Azure raises a shaky hand to take the bottle. I don't let go as she raises it to her lips. She hands it to me. "I don't want it to be true."

I rub a gentle circle between her shoulder blades. "Neither do I, but do you think it could be?"

"My mother is far from transparent." Her voice breaks. She lets out a mew like a forlorn kitten and buries her face against my shoulder.

I wrap both arms around her. "I had to ask about the mermaid thing and the scheming thing. A dude's gotta know where he stands."

Azure sits and lays her hands on my chest. "Here's where I stand. I fell for you the first time I saw you. I knew I shouldn't. Anything between us is mega complicated."

The side of my lip curls up. "You fell for me playing peek-a-boo at Miaqua? Am I that magnetic?"

"Before—" She cuts herself off. A flush brings a sweet baby pink color to her cheeks. Damn, every new shade of this woman digs my hole deeper. "I mean, yes, that day." If it was there, it's gone so quickly I can't be sure if I saw her eye twitch.

I cover her hands with mine. "Before? Don't tell me you put my poster up in your bedroom after I won the *You've Got a Gift* show five years back. Wow, that's some serious unrequited pining. Do you want me to bust out *Fire Capped Waves* for you? I'll work your name into it."

Azure gives me a gentle shove but doesn't remove her hands. "It's a signed poster. You were hot."

"Were?"

"Stop fishing."

I release my highest-octane smile. "I'm messing with you." I dip my chin to drop a kiss on her fingertip. "I was hooked that day at Miaqua too." Shit, should I say "hooked" to a mermaid? "I'm the one who blew up the phone trying to get a hold of you."

Her gaze pierces my own. Her long lashes flutter in the sea breeze. "Would you blow it up now, knowing the truth about me?"

I shift to sit beside her and lean back on my forearms to take in the sky. I could really use a full moon right now to give me energy.

She stands, staring down at me. "I get it if this is too weird."

"Weird doesn't begin to cover it."

"Please keep the guitar. It'll make beautiful music for you." Azure forces a smile devoid of a single drop of happiness or joy.

Her expression nearly breaks me, and my decision is made. In a quick sweep, I sit up, pulling her into my lap and settling her knees on either side of my hips. "You mean the beautiful music we'll make together. Tell me, Mermaid, how does weird work?" I want today to be a beginning, not an ending. My hands slide to the sides of her heart-shaped face, and I bring my mouth to hers. Our kiss is fragile like our new reality. We don't break apart until we've thoroughly kissed away the slight dusting of salt the sea breeze leaves across our lips.

"That's a start," says Azure, voice raw. Her arms snake around my neck as she takes her turn to kiss me. Her lips part, inviting me to chase and tease. I return the favor, taking my time to learn a mermaid's kiss. I run a hand down her side, over her hip, and along the leg of her capri until I touch skin. It's warm, smooth, and completely human.

Azure softly ends the kiss and twines her fingers through the hand exploring her leg. "Are you looking for my tail?"

It's my turn to rock a fluster. "I'd be lying if I said I didn't have a million questions."

She guides my hand under her shirt to her bare waist. Her silky skin and position on my lap disintegrate my million questions. "My tail technically starts here and ends at my toes." Azure shifts to stretch across my lap into a textbook *mermaid on the rocks* position. More than my leg presses against her thigh. "But there's more. It's a whole-body shift."

"You go full dolphin?"

Azure laughs. "I can outswim any dolphin, and have." She nestles between my legs and leans back against my chest not looking at me. "Before we go forward, I want you to know everything."

I run my hands down her arms. "I want to hear it."

She takes a huge swimmer's breath. Mermaid breath?

"My father is a selkie." She twists to look at me. "Do you know what that is?"

"Oh, I didn't realize Prospero was Scottish," I tease. "Legends, myths, fairy tales, it's how an artist commune rolls. Yes, I know what a seal man is."

She settles against me. "Daughter of a selkie and a sea witch. One plus one equals mermaid."

"You," I say and kiss the place where her neck meets shoulder. "You're a miracle."

She tilts her head to kiss me again, deeper, with more wanting. I return the favor, running the tip of my tongue along hers until it curls around mine. My heart and groin join in syncopated desire. Her hand finds its way under my T-shirt, stroking, caressing. If this gets any hotter, we're going to melt the sand beneath us into glass.

Azure breaks the kiss and reaches to stroke the side of my face. "No one outside my parents and sisters know the truth."

Sisters. Do I mention what Tani told me about their strangeness? I take a pass on the topic for now.

She sighs. "Lifelong warnings about being hunted or studied in a lab freaked me the hell out and kept me from sharing my truth with boyfriends or lovers."

Boyfriends? Lovers? Now I have another million questions. All I ask though is, "Why me?"

Azure whispers two words. "Music and fate."

She doesn't need to say anything else. I pull her body against my chest, against the tattoo of my heart's fate.

See the unseen. Sense the unknown. Suspend the common belief.

I add to my mother's mantra. *Get out of fate's way.*

Okay, Mom, I, Rai Cloud, hereby own that I speak with the dead spirit of my former girlfriend and am falling in love with a mermaid.

13

UNDERWATER

AZURE SWIVELS IN MY ARMS TO NIP THE UNDERSIDE OF MY JAW. HER hands clamp onto my thighs as she takes my bottom lip gently between her teeth in a languorous slide I much prefer to Kitae's love bites.

"May I suggest we take this to my hammock," I half-speak, half-moan, nodding at the cluster of palms.

She leaps to her feet, pulling me with her. "I have a better idea." Azure backs toward the water lapping at the edge of the lagoon and brings me along. She peels her blouse over her head. It flutters to the sand just out of the water's reach. Her denim capris follow, leaving her only in bra and panties.

I'm not allowed a moment to take in her sinuous curves before she flicks a wrist in my direction. "Board shorts, shirt, off."

I turn away to strip since there will be no hiding my enthusiasm for her near naked body once boxer briefs are my entire ensemble. She didn't specify full nude, so I opt for minimal coverage. When I face the water, a bright lime bra hits me in the chest, followed by matching panties. Azure's head is the only part of her above water. Her hair seeps across the surface of the lagoon like watercolor across wet paper.

I fight the urge to enjoy the scent of her delicates and set them on the pile with the rest of her ensemble. A quick sprint past the lazy waves takes me far enough out to dive into the lagoon, hoping the drop in temperature will tame my inconvenient arousal. When I'm arm's length away from Azure, I tread water.

"What's about to happen might freak you out," says Azure, staring into my eyes. "Promise you will trust me completely and do exactly what I say. Understood?"

The way she sinks her top teeth into her bottom lip encourages me to promise her anything.

"Rai? Do you promise?" she says, voice insistent.

I return her stare, throwing in an extra dose of intensity. "Yes, Rainn Cloud trusts you completely."

Azure barks out a laugh. Do I hear a slight hint of sexy, come-hither seal tone?

"Your name is Raincloud?"

"No, it's Rainn, two n's, pause, Cloud."

Azure slaps the water, giggling. "Nice try Raincloud."

I swipe the splash from my eye. "My brother, Piyo, got the uber cool name. Picasso plus Yo Yo Ma equals Piyo."

She flicks a thin stream of water at me. "And you got stuck with angry skies. What a loud-mouthed baby you must have been."

I capture her hand before she blinds me with a saltwater sting to the eye. "Rainn was my grandfather's name."

"Ah, you're Raincloud Junior. How did your dad dodge the name?"

I drop her hand. Our parents never kept the Cloud family origin story from Piyo and me. We were encouraged to treat past rejections as insignificant. What matters is the family we made, not the circumstances that created it. "Long story. Now show me what requires minimal clothing."

Azure moves closer. "I want to hear the story, Rai. I want to know everything about you."

My skin warms at her touch. "My biological father was a musician from south Texas who chose touring with his crap-level band over mom and me. My very pregnant mother heard about the Lalale Island commune and decided it was the life she wanted for us. She's a bitchin' painter." My throat jams closed. "Was..."

Azure reaches into the water to take both my hands.

I swallow hard so I can get this out. I want Azure to know me, even the rough parts. "Mom met Lucas Cloud who had newborn Piyo slung in a pack across his chest. Piyo's mom hit her limit with the commune and split as soon as he was born. My parents connected and decided to give the blended family thing a go out of mutual survival at first, then it stuck. Soulmate stuck. Created Cloudpath Music together stuck. It's all good."

Azure trains a stray wisp of hair out of my eyes. "You realize that's a beautiful story, right?"

Memories of family crash into me. Dad teaching me how to make a wood whistle. Mom making Piyo and I sit longer than two rowdy boys were capable while she painted us. The thousands of adventures my brother and I invented in the wilds of Lalale Island. The pain of missing all three drives a spear through my heart. Tears drip off my chin.

Azure catches a tear on her fingertip. She marvels at it. "Mermaids can't shed tears."

I bring her finger and my tear to my lips and kiss them. "You can have all of mine."

"Thank you, Rainn, two n's, pause, Cloud."

I burn to pull her to me and almost do until I remember she's completely naked. Azure's drawn me into the water and asked for trust. I won't spoil her plans by indulging in the feel of her sliding against me in the water and the taste of her kisses. "Stormbringer's daughter and Rainn Cloud. There's fate for you."

Her eyes mirror the teal of the lagoon as her lips dance into a smile. "I believe it is."

Sometimes the way she looks at me reminds me of the woman who sang to me on the sand. I shake off the sensation. Drawing a connection between two generous souls isn't so out there. My heart swore my rescuer was my fate, just like it swore Tani was my fate. Moon knows, I searched my ass off for the voice I heard in the moonlight. I prayed she sought me with a desire to match my own. The truth is neither my savior nor my dead friend are part of my real life. Azure is. She brings joy and music and yearning to make our tomorrow a path of possibility.

I squeeze a fist to squirt a stream of water. "Now, about my obedience and trust...

Azure nods past the series of rocks jutting between the lagoon and the open sea. "I'll be different, changed out there, but it's still me." Her voice quavers.

My imagination goes straight to a sexy, form-fitting, seal-shaped wetsuit. For her sake, I vow to handle whatever I see out there without a meltdown.

Azure lifts her pearl pouch, the only thing she's wearing, above the surface and opens it. Lovingly she lifts two iridescent pale ovals, the size of my palm, that shimmer with a blend of emerald and sapphire in the sunlight. They remind me of bubbles, light and delicate.

"These are my scales. Keep them safe in your hand while we're beneath the surface. They'll allow you to share my breath." She places both against my palm and closes my fingers around the pair. "Do not let go."

A sudden whoosh like water being shot through every one of my cells with a cannon sets off a full-body shudder. A lovely internal breeze follows, hollowing out my insides in a sensation of absolute calm. I expect her scales to be slimy and fishy. They are far from it, silky and substantial.

She takes my hand and clamps it to her hip. "You must keep contact here. Think of it as a spare air tank. It will also allow you to travel with me when I speed up." A blush runs across her face. "Your hand is inside the top of my tail."

I nod, flushing my mind of what else might be inside her tail. My palm touches skin, while the back of my hand brushes against a thick, spongy barrier forming the top rim of her mermaid tail. I put the temptation to explore more of Azure's mermaid body on immediate lockdown.

Azure squeezes my shoulders. "Ready?"

I smile. "Ready."

With a swift jerk and twist, Azure locks me against her back, double-checking my hand is clamped onto her hip. "Hold tight."

The sky disappears. We plunge below the surface and surge forward with force greater than the breakers crashing against the wild western shores of Lalale Island.

My first impulse to hold my breath morphs into terror at the realization I never took a deep breath before the dive. I have no oxygen stored in my lungs.

Sensing my panic, Azure squeezes my fist holding the scales. Her words *share my breath* remind my body not to fight. As soon as I suspend my human definition of breathing, I feel the rhythm of Azure's. It doesn't draw a straight line from lungs to air. It flows between cells in my body and the sea, in and out, in and out. My heartbeat mimics the pattern.

Shh, swah, Shh, swah.

My clarity of sight is another blast. It's as if I'm wearing a diving mask with magnification cranked to superhuman max. Sunlight piercing the water from above divides into individual droplets, golden rain sinking into the blue. We're moving unnaturally fast. Nothing swims near us, which is a slight surprise. I always assumed mermaids and fish shared a watery synergy. Ah, but selkies do enjoy a hardy seafood platter.

Azure reaches to stroke my hair. It snakes loosely through the water, freed from braids in our lighting strike away from the lagoon.

Her fingers slide from the crown of my head to my neck. Panic interrupts the momentary calm from her touch. My talismans! Have I lost the moonstone, the abalone, and the whistle? I nearly drop her scales combing through the post braid-crimped, inky strands of my hair.

Once again, Azure's hand clamps over mine in warning not to let go of the scales. Her fingers guide my chin to look at her pearl pouch. She points to my hair and then pats the pouch to tell me my treasures are safe in her care.

As my adrenaline spike of freak-out dissipates, I slowly become aware of the woman, the mermaid my body fits against. I nuzzle my cheek against her neck, and she presses into me. I relish the length of her upper back, the dip of her lower back, and her sweetly rounded ass pressing against the front of my briefs. Before that point of contact has a chance to summon the lion's share of my blood flow, my legs brush against—a tail. I gently run my toes along its length, stretching to explore the fluke at its end.

My scaleless hand lies in the space created between the small outward flare at the beginning of her tail and her hipbone. When I use the knuckles of my scale-filled hand to gently caress the circumference of the top of Azure's tail, she arches and twirls, holding me slightly away. One hand fans the length of her body as if to say,"Take it all in."

Her mermaid form is splendid, flawless. She's covered from face to tail in a soft spring green shimmer, a lithe pearlescent body suit, sparkling underwater the way her scales did in sunlight. It mimics the bioluminescence that sometimes graces a nighttime sea. Azure is a rare gem mined from undiscovered depths.

Her mermaid skin is a close copy of what I believed to be her exotic wetsuit at our first meeting on Lalale Island. I'm awed as my gaze learns the swimmer's muscles of her arms that end in tiny, webbed fingers. The features of her face are slightly shrouded with a green veil molded to her skin. I still know those eyes, lips. I reach out to trail my knuckles down her long, elegant neck, between gorgeous breasts barely hidden beneath her watery silk. When my travels stop at the edge of the flair where her tail begins, she quivers beneath my touch.

Emboldened by her reaction, I coil an arm around her and pull her flush against me, face-to-face. My mouth covers hers, pulling in pure aquatic radiance. To my delight, an eager tongue easily slides across mine, her mermaid skin not a hindrance. The sensation of the sea rushing through our kiss is beyond hot. I greedily scrape my tongue over her teeth, which, to my relief, are wonderfully human. Her tail fluke flicks between my legs again and again, teasing, as we deepen the kiss. I want to free both hands to explore every nuance of this exquisite mermaid, but one is trapped between her hip and tail, and the other must keep hold of her scales.

My knuckles stray upwards to graze her breasts and are rewarded with raised nipples, assurance she's enjoying our watery encounter as much as me. I slide to her navel. The moment I try to dip further between her tail and body, Azure grabs my wandering hand and breaks the kiss. She shakes her head.

I'm disappointed I don't rate high enough for inside-the-tail action. Before I wonder if I've broken a rule, Azure slides me onto her back again and takes off. Her body undulates through the water as smoothly as a dolphin. The curves of her ass slip purposefully up and down the front of my briefs, obliterating any chance of my dick not hardening like a tower of coral. When her hand circles around to grab my ass and press me closer, I give into our sexy underwater foreplay. Crimping an arm around her waist, I answer every alluring sway with a grind against this luscious mermaid.

My eyes close, sight unnecessary to the language of our bodies. I long to flip her face-to-face, kiss and caress until we bring each other to...

To what? Trying to imagine the mechanics of fulfillment only succeed in dousing my rising need. My payoff would be obvious, but what about hers? How does one make a mermaid climax?

Brightness blasts outside my eyelids, demanding my attention.

Azure swims out from under me until we're side by side, my hand still firmly tucked inside the top of her tail. She studies my face as I take in the view.

A great, underwater plain stretches before us. At least a dozen striations of bright blues, bluish purple blends, and deep mulberries stripe the water from the surface high above us to the seabed. I wait for the shades to bleed together and mix into new hues as flares of one color invade the boundaries of another. These vibrant forays merely tease their neighbors, and the bands maintain their original core color. A myriad of deep aquamarine, buttercup, and ruby sea flowers flutter in the current to dot rolling underwater hills. In the surreal seascape, smatterings of vividly colored fish flit through towers of wavering kelp clusters and around coral sculptures. The sand could be made of finely ground cobalt glass beads. Even this far down, they manage to reflect the faraway sun's rays.

In hundreds of dives, I've never encountered this place. The water is bathwater warm. We've got to be somewhere in the unique tropical current that detours around Lalale Island.

Azure presses a hand over her heart and stares into my eyes, waiting for my reaction to her paradise. I touch my fist to her cheek and smile. Words will come when we're back on land. For now, I speak the language of wonder with my eyes.

We skim low over flower beds. Azure collects one of each different colored flower into a rainbow bouquet. At the edge of the coral formations is a natural arch of green and gold. She guides us downward until my feet crunch on the gemstone sand. As we near the shadows of the arch, movement within catches my eye. I tug at the top of Azure's tail to stop her from going any further. She flashes me the *okay* sign and keeps us moving.

When we cross the shadows, Azure carefully lowers herself, the mermaid version of taking a knee. I swing around next to her and suck in a breath. That action normally promises a mouthful of salty water, but Azure's version of scuba keeps the pipes clear.

Settled into the crystalline sand is a behemoth of a sea turtle. Its mottled gray head projects the air of an ancient being. One at a time, Azure feeds the old fellow flowers she's picked. I laugh as it gobbles certain colors and spits out others. The turtle reminds me of Tutu at a potluck. The old gal never pulls any punches of what she finds delicious or inedible.

When the creature finishes the last of its lunch, Azure moves aside and gestures to me. The turtle's bulging eye flicks around, scrutinizing the dude she's brought home to meet the family. I swear the frown line on its mouth intensifies. I'm clearly being judged. Moving like an arthritic, one massive, speckled flipper strains through the water. I don't dare move so as not to startle the sea turtle. It would be my luck to gain admittance to this magical place and then give its chief a reptilian stroke.

Pressure against my spine tells me Azure wants me closer to her friend. It wants to touch me. Scooting within its reach, I pause. The sea turtle closes its eyes, and the tip of a flipper grazes the tattoo on my chest. Azure stretches out an arm so the creature can rest its head on her palm and kisses its wizened brow. We carefully glide away from the sleeping turtle.

Once we're back among Azure's playground, we bob in the water. Her gaze meets mine, and I see a light of pure happiness in her eyes behind the aquatic veil separating mermaid from woman. I feel as if I've passed some test, and I'm glad of it.

In a rush of guilt, I understand her distress when I tried to repurpose a sea turtle shell for an instrument. She was thinking of this creature she lovingly attends. I need to reframe my sensibilities about all things below the surface with Azure in my life.

She dots a quick kiss to my lips. I marvel her mermaid skin doesn't buffer any sensation. Kissing her here is just as wondrous as kissing her on the island. The soft joy on her face is replaced with a twinkle in her eye and a quirk of her lip. She drags me toward a tawny rock formation roughly the size of an upturned yacht coated in lacy mint lichen. Azure jabs a thumb to where the base of the rocks meet sand, and I see a series of small alcoves. She thrusts a hand behind my knee and lifts my foot then gestures to the dark holes. When I shake my head, she repeats the movement, and her meaning sinks in. Lift my leg, got it. I smile and execute the desired leg lift.

With mermaid super speed, we dive to the base of the rock. She raises one finger, then two, and finally three to count us down. We zip in front of the little caves. As we pass each one, an eel explodes from the shadows, making a beeline for my bare feet. I jerk my knees up to avoid the sting of the beasties. When we reach the end of the row, Azure is laughing her ass off over my terrorized reaction to the impromptu game of eel tag. Streams of bubbles escape her kiss-swollen lips.

Instead of getting pissy from my close eel encounter, I pull her mouth to mine, effectively quelling her laughter. After a kiss for each dodged eel, I float at her side, fingers locked inside the top of her tail, marveling at this realm Azure belongs in and her desire to share it with me. To be a mermaid is truly a wonder. Why ever surface when you belong here?

Azure lives in two worlds. Unbidden, my thoughts fill with Tani. Azure has the choice to shift between one reality and the other. Tani is at the mercy of a sea witch's whim. A sea witch who is Azure's mother. Lost in monkey-mind, I loosen my grip on the scales. One slips through my fingers. Azure grabs it, but my lungs constrict as they search for badly needed oxygen.

As dizziness sets in, Azure flings me on her back, and we soar upwards at a diagonal. In moments, my head breaks the surface. I gulp and gasp for air. We're not far from the lagoon.

Fingers pry their way into my fist and Azure reclaims her scales. She dunks underwater for a second and then reappears.

"I'm sorry," I sputter. "I blew it."

She swims close and kisses my cheek. "No, I kept you too long. Between being on shore then using my scales to let you play with me underwater, I pushed them to their limits." Her mermaid sheen covers her face even above the surface.

"Are they ruined?" My heart thumps loud enough to attract every shark in a ten-mile radius.

"No, they just need serious tail time to refresh."

She laughs when I blush at *tail time.*

"Not that kind of tail time, Rai. Get your mind out of the eel cave." A splash covers my face. "I replace them on my tail for a...recharge."

She grabs my hand and tucks it into the space between tail and hip. "That's the reason your hand must keep contact with my tail, in case the scales failed."

"A scale fail, huh?" It's my turn to laugh. "Can't you swap out for fresh scales?"

"No, any new scales need to be spelled before I go to the surface."

I seethe at this reminder of Sulaa's disingenuous control.

Azure's expression turns serious. "Thank you for taking the risk with me."

I kick my legs to stay afloat and grab her hands. "I'll take any risk with you, Azure." I kiss her pearly green lips.

"Even if what you said about my mother using me to get Cloudpath is true?"

I'm suddenly aware of the ocean's chill. I hold back very unsexy teeth chattering and nod. "Even then."

Azure juts her chin toward Miaqua. "My mother and I need to have a discussion."

Fear plus the cold water take me down, and my entire body starts to shiver. "Is that the best move given her...powers and all?"

"She's my mother, Rai. She loves me. I'm perfectly safe." Her brows knit, and a tiny dimple forms between them. "If I don't like what I hear, I'll consider consulting my father as a last resort."

"Prospero?"

"The only father I've got."

The sparkle of Azure's mermaid skin begins to fade. If a mermaid is capable of stumbling in the water, she does.

"Azure, what's wrong?"

"I have to go, Rai. Recharge time. Thank you."

"Moon, Azure. Thank you for showing me your beautiful world."

With a soft smile, she's under. I feel the gentle brush of her tail against my legs. I dunk under to watch her swim away. She's already out of sight.

Surfacing, I swallow a mouthful of salt water. As if my reality isn't complicated enough. The clock is ticking on the release of my first island rock song, thanks to some cosmic blip, Tani's future landed on my head, and now I've sent Azure for a smackdown with her magical mom.

Bitchin'.

Above, a gull scolds. When it swoops in for a second admonition, a single feather escapes its tail. I snag it before it gets waterlogged and sinks beneath the surface to tickle the snout of Azure's eels. Twirling the feather between thumb and forefinger, I study the way light reflects differently off each of its parts. A soft, diffused blur blends individual lines of the vane while a stronger glow bounces off the central shaft. It's so simple yet complex a creation...like Azure. She's both mermaid and human, a musician without a voice on land, a generous spirit who's managed to smooth the ragged edges of my heart-rending losses.

As much as part of me longs to find the woman who snatched me from the greedy waves and sang with the perfect voice to fill the void in my island rock, it's time to let go of any foolish remnants of finding her. The granite truth is, if I mattered, she would have found me.

For a fleeting moment, I imagine Azure's face as my savior. Who else but a mermaid would defy a storm-tossed sea to drag my ass to the sand? I slap the water. Wouldn't that tie my life up in a neat little bow? It was a woman, not a mermaid, my friends saw on the beach with me. A woman who bolted and let them pound the seawater out of my lungs.

Of all the muddle in my life, there is one beautiful note of clarity. I will do anything the woman encased in a bioluminescent mermaid skin asks of me.

14

TANI'S DARK DREAM

I PEER THROUGH WARPED INDIGO GLASS. SHAPES ON THE OTHER SIDE of this demented fun house mirror are distant, distorted, and so out of proportion they're unidentifiable. Wherever I try to move, I hit resistance. Twisting my body fails to conform successfully to this prison.

"Sulaa," I scream. No sound. My body of mist and gauzy nothing throbs with a full-body charley horse.

Obviously, I'm being punished. Does Sulaa know of my rule-breaking? Has she been tipped off I spent extra time with Rai and slacked off at my post as Azure's shadow last night? Shit, she's monitoring me more closely than I realized.

After Sulaa called me back to Miaqua, I watched Azure sleep and then left her at what was supposed to be an all-day recording session with her sisters. I thought I could steal some me-time under the waves to figure out my next steps with Rai without Sulaa cluing into my absence.

Serious misstep.

Moon, did Azure slip out of rehearsal while I shirked mermaid-sitting and do something stupid with Rai, and Sulaa found out? Curse me for entertaining too low a dose of healthy fear for the sea witch. Such a fuck up could ruin my chances for the future I yearn for. If Azure clocked sexy time with Rai and I didn't warn Sulaa to stop it, I'm terminally screwed.

Fresh pain pounds in the space where my heart should be. Did I risk Sulaa's wrath only to have Rai not believe me about Azure's truth? I ache for him to accept that the heart's fate tattoo Juan Estrella burned on his chest is me, not the fish girl. For moon's sake, I've got to split them up before Rai learns Azure was his savior. If he ever makes the connection, my chance to rewind my life with him dies.

I push against my cage, and new swells of pain rip through my body. They could be together right now, sharing secrets, sharing their bodies. I gotta get out of here and back on duty.

On the other side of the glass, a kid wails. What the hell is a kid doing here in Sulaa's freaky garden? I strain to match sound to its source. Although everything is tainted indigo, the eerie shapes of the caliche forest become clear. It's enough to make anyone cry. I make out the hazy shape of a woman holding a small child as she comes near.

She settles the weeping kid on her hip as a second wavering figure approaches. It's a man, a full head taller than the woman. "I'm not your damn nanny," she snaps at him.

His voice is an oil slick. "Ah, but no one makes the child cry harder than you, my sweet Rubata."

Rubata? I squint and press against the glass. Damn, it is Rubata Lear. What is the reality TV star/influencer doing in Sulaa's caliche wasteland?

"Tending to the child is an insignificant price for your sanctuary, hmm?" His voice is not the only darkness. The man is a smudge of black. Based on his outline, he's wearing a suit. Never took Sulaa's dress code as formal. His presence gives off a large-and-in-charge vibe. I swear he soaks up light.

They're very close now. I'm able to see dark dude sidle next to Rubata and press something glassy against the sobbing child's cheek. In moments, golden light fills what looks like a perfume bottle. The man raises it to examine every angle. "Tears of a child," he coos, then the timbre of his voice frays at the edges until it's raw and hungry. "Tears of power."

This is the same voice I heard giving Sulaa props just before I flew off to find Rai. It's oddly familiar beyond that. Who is he? I search for a spot where the indigo tint is nearly clear.

The man touches the small bottle to his lips and throws back the contents. Recognition sends a shock through me. I attempt to retreat and smack against something sharp. My thrashing draws the attention of the pair.

Grant Gothel, former president of Rampion Records and current felon, lowers his face to study mine. He sneers. "Ah, Sulaa's disobedient spirit."

They see me. Sulaa wants them to see me. Why? If Sulaa is bad news, Gothel is worse. Dude's a legit criminal who deserves to be ditched in a jail cell, not in Miaqua with Sulaa, Rubata Lear, and a wailing kid.

The kid stands on the ground now and pushes past him to stare at me. "Papa, who's the lady in Ms. Sulaa's throne?"

Papa?

Gothel swings her around and sets her down in front of Rubata, using his body to shield her from me. "No one, my angel. Now go practice your opus with Auntie Rubata."

If a chill can run through a ghost, one blows through me. Standing in front of me is the fiend outed last year on the Summer Number One live broadcast as Rai and I watched. The truth of the Svengali power Gothel held over Zeli, the chart-topping pop diva of Rampion Records, hit the news cycle with an even louder bang. Apparently, the Pres of Rampion Records had controlled her since childhood with enchanted toxic tea and a tower-high list of lies. She called him *Papa,* and he called her *my angel* just like he's doing with this kid. To dig Gothel's grave even deeper, Zeli unleashed bizarre accusations that he used her tears to fuel some freaky fiery magic in his hands.

Now, here he stands in Sulaa's garden instead of prison, pulling the same shit. Oh, moon, could this child be the dark bastard's Zeli 2.0? If only I had any freakin' way to help the kid.

Rubata's voice is acid. "Not—the—nanny. Grant, we agreed I need free time to tweak the social media blitz Dark Vinyl Artists will rock the world with. It's got to be supe amaze."

Gothel's hands begin to glow.

Sometimes you can believe everything you read.

Rubata backs away from the licks of flame now dancing across Gothel's palms, then pivots with legendary Lear sister haughtiness as she drags the kid away.

So, it's Sulaa's throne holding me captive. Is this how the witch gets her kicks, banishing spirits into self-aggrandizing furniture?

I startle when I realize the throne heats as Gothel sits on it. I push through pain and slither into an arm of Sulaa's pompous seat to stare at his face instead of the ass of his black suit pants.

Gothel twirls his fingers, making circles of sparks in the air as he tilts his chin to meet my gaze. "Let me guess, naughty spirit. You're making all the wrong assumptions about the child because of Justin Time and Zeli's insane accusations. Allow me to enlighten you." He snaps and his fire fingers fade out. "That child is my future. Young Maisie possesses talent that defies description." He thumps the arm of the chair near my face. "I will rebuild my legacy through her."

Gothel and Sulaa colleagues with a side dish of Rubata Lear? I'll ask Rai to fill in the blanks of how Gothel is back in circulation with a Lear sister in the mix. You miss shit when you're dead.

"Comfy?" purrs Sulaa, materializing in front of her throne. The opalescent gems on her shoulders pulse with light.

"Quite," says Gothel, rising with a gesture for her to take his place. "I've been chatting with your latest acquisition."

Sulaa assumes throne with a flourish. "It's time we all chat."

I'm a pebble being forced through the eye of a needle as I explode from my indigo jail into the spirit form I'm getting far too used to. Blurs of black, white, and gray spin in clockwise and counterclockwise circles until they finally settle back into the familiar landscape of dead trees and boulders with the one exception of Sulaa's polished coral throne. Since Gothel's not turned to driftwood, we must be surrounded by air instead of stagnant caliche forest water.

I'm a few feet from Gothel and Sulaa. The sea witch leans a forearm on her knee and pierces me with a sorceress glare. "In a rather unpleasant chat after I discovered Azure left rehearsal to go see Mr. Cloud, I was blindsided with probing questions about my strategy to buy Cloudpath Music."

Damn Azure for bailing on rehearsal. Double damn her for bringing up taboo topics with Sulaa. I should have been more on guard and not missed her visit to Rai. That explains being stuffed into the throne. The witch is clearly pissed she wasn't tipped off about an interrogation by Azure about the Cloudpath sale. My filmy muscles clench. How many details did Rai spill to Azure? Does the mermaid know about the emo blackmail her loving mother has planned with her as bait? She can't be fool enough to broach that subject.

Moon, on top of that, if the sorceress catches wind I blabbed to Rai about Azure's mermaidiness, on a *you're screwed* scale from one to ten, I could be in triple digits.

The density of my shitstorm intensifies as Sulaa waves an arm and a handful of trees disintegrate into rubble, a sign she's all business. Neither the surroundings nor destruction faze Gothel. Bleak and ominous fit his brand.

Sulaa's voice booms across depression central. "Calliwag." The *flop flop* of her lionfish-headed minion echoes behind me.

"No need to bellow." He pats his gills in the vicinity of an ear. "I'm always streaming *The Sulaa Channel*."

Gothel glares at Calliwag. "Such a level of insubordination in my underlings would not go unpunished."

Calliwag raises his arms as if pleading to the gods. "Poor Calliwag, deformed, defamed, and disrespected." He levels his gaze at Gothel. "I serve your every beck and call and present you with the ultimate of local cuisine, yet you chastise me. Poor Calliwag."

Gothel rubs his hands as if sharpening a knife. "Variations on fish stew are not my idea of ultimate anything."

Calliwag backs off from the heat waves pouring off Gothel's hands. Once a safe distance away, the fishman crosses his arms and sniffs. "I suppose the crab cake souffle also offended you?"

The longer they bicker, the longer the spotlight stays off me.

Sulaa roars. "Enough, Fish Fool. Did you bring the message?"

Calliwag unleashes a combination of fishy slurps and human snorts. The sound alone nauseates me like a belly of raw fish. When he brandishes a crumpled note from his raggedy pocket with a moonstone disc attached, I gasp. It's the talisman from Rai's braid, the one that honors the lunar energy that's supposed to connect him to the tattoo of his heart's fate—to me. If Calliwag has it in Miaqua, Rai sent it to Azure.

Sulaa reads the note aloud.

Azure,

Take this moonstone as a sign of my devotion. Meet me at the Moon's Eye Lighthouse at dusk to figure out the mess with your mother and Cloudpath. I'll be waiting.

All yours,

Rai

My feet scrape across the rough ground as Sulaa's magic drags me to her. The level of fury contorting her features is in equal part to the invisible pressure squeezing my head. "*Figure out the mess, is it?* Hardly a lover's message." She crushes the moonstone in her fist. Tiny white particles fall like dust motes through a shaft of light.

She couldn't be more wrong. Moon's Eye Lighthouse is romance central, a hot spot for parties and intimate encounters. Piyo took me there the first time we made love, and again on the night he proposed. Visions of champagne bubbles and sunset trickle through my memory. If Rai is taking Azure to the lighthouse, I'm ninety-nine-point-nine percent sure it's to woo her into his bed for a memorable first time.

The sea witch raises me off the sand until we're eye to eye. Her fingernails puncture skin. She's popped me into a form she can damage. "Your negligence blinds me. It seems I'm missing vital pieces of the intimate progression between Rai Cloud and my daughter."

Gothel clears his throat. "And, Ghost Girl, we're not convinced you haven't purposefully botched my esteemed colleague's flawless plan to acquire Cloudpath Music by leaking forbidden bits of information to Mr. Cloud."

Relief bursts inside me like a water balloon against a palm trunk. They don't know how much I've told Rai. Their threats only speculate. Thank the moon. Maybe an eternity stuffed inside Sulaa's coral throne can still be avoided.

"I believe they've fallen in love," I blurt.

Gothel leans casually against a petrified caliche trunk. "Ah, love. How do we classify such passion between Rai and Azure, affection, adoration, or culmination?"

Sulaa's bruise-colored stare digs into me. "If your negligence has failed me—"

Gothel nods. "Do elaborate, Spirit. Carnality is the clear tell your bleeding-heart musician and save-the-drowning-man mermaid entered water deep enough for us to manipulate."

I don't know what disgusts me more, the thought of Rai and Azure tangled in a naked love romp or the way Gothel and Sulaa refer to them as pawns instead of people. I've been out of commission, but I'd still put money on Rai's compulsion for over-the-top romantic gestures like lighthouse loving. "People go to the lighthouse to make memories. Rai would invite Azure there so the first time they *culminate*"—I toss a sour look at Gothel—"is special."

Sulaa purses her lips as if she's bit into a rotten piece of fruit.

"Speaking of drowning men," says Gothel in his sticky spiderweb voice. "Why not remove your spell and allow your youngest to sing to her fool? Instant fated bond. You'll have your leverage to make Rai Cloud dance at the end of your strings for the chance to reunite with his rescuer. Quick and easy." He strikes his hands together.

"The strength of a true fated bond could destroy our whole plan. My daughter mustn't invoke such a connection with the half-witted, shell-banging, spawn of Lucas and Corinne Cloud. She's destined to find a proper selkie to mate with and perpetuate the mermaid line I've carefully curated."

This convo devolves from despicable to fucking wrong. Sulaa's talking about the sick breeding program Bluebell and Azure alluded to. Does the witch subscribe to a hotline of seal men sperm donors? I thought I'd lost my sense of taste, but I swear bile coats my tongue.

"Their coupling sweetens the bait for Rai Cloud," says Gothel. "Can't you spell Azure to prevent her dalliance from sullying your family tree but permit him to take her to his bed? Dark Vinyl Artists cannot advance to our next phase until we acquire Cloudpath Music, and we need that fool on his knees begging to sell for the chance to crawl back to his lover."

"I agree. Since Tani created blind spots for us, it's time to seize control while we also eliminate whatever *plan* Rai Cloud and my daughter brew that could possibly thwart our forward motion." Sulaa's gaze locks on me. "It's your lucky day, Tani."

With no warning, the sea witch stabs me in the heart with a pearl blade she pulls from the folds of her gown. I slap useless hands over the wound. Ribbons of black liquid spill between my transparent fingers to float in the air.

Gothel moves closer. "Is this *the* legendary obsidian blood?"

Sulaa's smile is sly and satisfied. "Yes, *the* obsidian blood filling a soul between life and death."

He reaches out a finger. "May I taste?"

The sea witch smacks his hand. "Not unless you choose to join Tani's spirit in its cage." She raises a small nautilus shell, and with a flick of her finger, thin rivulets of my dark blood flow into it.

Sulaa balances the nautilus on an open palm. Sparks flare in her irises, and the shell begins to spin. The sea witch's voice fills the caliche forest as plum-colored mist drifts from her mouth to encase the spinning nautilus.

"Of tides and tears,
Flow fast the years.
Match voice to voice,
And love to choice.
This vessel holds,
A soul to mold.
Release the one,
Back to the sun.
Her guise affix,
'Til passion's quick,
Falls silent."

The shell stills, dark tendrils seeping from its opening. Sulaa holds it to me. "Drink."

"Why?" I prepare for a new strike of pain from the sorceress for my question. She only smiles.

"Good, girl. Like I tell my daughters, don't accept a random drink at a party." She sets the nautilus in my hand. "Nothing random about this. Drink, and you, Tani, will once again be able to make love with your heart's fate. Exactly what I promised."

I grip the shell. What does my father always say, "*If it's too good to be true...*"

Disbelief and mistrust salsa dance in my gut. "You implied I have to jump through tons of hoops before you help me." I peek inside the mouth of the shell and see only shadow. "Your secret recipe will give me my life back?"

"Ummm," hums Sulaa. "Loans you a life. I allow you to borrow Azure's voice and body to seal the deal with Rai Cloud. The intimacy will ripen his vulnerability without damaging the real Azure. Men are delectably pliable in the afterglow." She grunts. "That clears the way for me to insist if he refuses to sell me Cloudpath, he will never see his dearest, darling Azure again." Sulaa shoots me a leer. "Consider your little tryst this evening as a preview of what you will regain once you've faithfully fulfilled our agreement, and Rai Cloud sells his company to me."

Gothel clears his throat. "Technically to Dark Vinyl Artists." He circles me. "Allow me to add fine print. Fail to convince him you are Azure or work against our interests in any way..." He runs a perfectly manicured finger along the arm of Sulaa's polished coral throne. A dark gaze locks on me through narrowed eyes. "There are plenty more spirits in the sea to serve our purpose."

Gothel's vibe is as ashy as a charred tree in the caliche forest. Sulaa's plan is vile, but the possibility to feel Rai touch me, kiss me, makes me ache with desire. As Azure, Sulaa expects me to make love with him, but I want to love him as Tani. That's not the choice they're offering. If I do what they want, once this is over and Sulaa and Gothel dig their nails into Cloudpath Music, it will be Rai loving the real me instead of my spirit masked by Azure's form.

Black mist thickens near the mouth of the shell. It should wear a tag that says *Do Not Drink*. Banishing good sense, I raise the nautilus to my lips. Viscous, scalding liquid worms its way down my throat as Gothel hisses in a breath. I half expect him to start chanting, "*Chug it, chug it.*"

At first, I taste nothing, then the brew erupts with the taste of melted tar or highway asphalt. It's so filthy it takes total concentration not to spit it out.

This is your only road to Rai.

When the last drop slithers past my lips, I lower the shell. Like cracks in glass that start as a single line and then expand into a web, my form shatters from scalp to toes. Black goo closes in on me from all sides, encasing me in what could be a stink bug carapace. I try to hold onto thoughts, but they fade.

Smell hits me first. An acrid scent of charred wood burns my sinuses. My fingers sift through chalky powder and a breeze slides across my bare shoulders. I blink to find I'm sitting on a bed of white ash. When I lift my head, I let go of a throat-ripping scream.

A caliche forest surrounds me, not the foul imitation of Sulaa's demented garden. I'm on Lalale Island, sitting in the middle of real cursed ground. Echoes of terror and agony course through the fissures in my brain, dulling my sight except for fragmented shadows that writhe and break on all sides. I leap to my feet and push off to fly. I'm earthbound.

Run.

I stumble over scrabbly ground to escape this place of death cries and the sensation of tortured spirits rasping across my skin.

Sulaa's sick message is loud and clear. She controls my strings and maintains her power to put me wherever she wishes.

I burst out of the caliche forest and onto a winding path up to an oak grove. Before I reach the top, I'm out of breath.

Breath.

I hold a hand to my mouth and feel the sweet exhale of life. Fresh scents of oak and salt-infused sea breeze seep into my soul. I smell them as clearly as I did the stench of the caliche forest below.

Dimensions of my existence expand with the return of my senses. I run a hand over bark on the nearest tree. It's scratchy and perfect. A fat, black bug lands on my arm and bites. "Ouch." I stare at the arm and the rising red welt. Flesh. Living flesh. I gaze over the sea and delight in the sound of waves, slamming into grand boulders offshore. Tears gush from my eyes. I lick the salty ambrosia as it reaches my lips.

I am alive.

A gust of wind whistles through the nearby canyon to blow strands of hair across my face. I snatch them in my fist and stare, not quite believing. My fingers spring open as if burned. A heart that radiated joy moments before splits.

Instead of the white shades of my spirit self, or the maple tresses from a living Tani, my hair shines azure in the fading light.

15

A MAN CLAIMED BY THE SEA

I RACE TO THE TOP OF THE CLIFF AS IF I CAN OUTRUN AZURE'S BODY.

"I'm Tani, not Azure." I slap hands over my mouth. The mermaid's voice flies past my lips. I grab at my body, searching for anything to prove I'm me.

"No."

My current physical mind can't embrace the sea witch's plan my spirit mind agreed to. I knew I'd be Azure. Desire to be Tani battles within the form I'm stuck with. I want to be alive as me, not her. Rai should be with all of me, spirit and body.

Collapsing onto a flat rock surrounded with scrubby yellow flowers, I drop chin to chest. The world spins like a hangover morning after the commune's annual summer festival where I always intend to stick to two drinks and end up doubling that. Those delicious cocktails Tutu experiments with at her Palm Bliss booth defy self-control.

I do the same thing I do to push through the festival hangover. *Inhale for three. Hold for three. Exhale for three. Hold for three. Inhale...*

Thirst blindsides me. The breathing pattern calms me enough to get my bearing. I hear it—the waterfall. Its heavenly sound of tumbling water soothes. All at once, the joy I felt moments ago as I relearned life returns and spreads like warm honey through my bones.

I stop fighting. Thirst is magnificent. Breathing is magnificent. Who cares if I'm in Azure's body? I've been gifted the perfection of being alive again. A chance to be with Rai, to touch him again, is the best gift of all.

I dodge granite slabs and prickly pears to reach the waterfall. Cupping my hands, I capture and drink the mother's milk of Lalale Island, crisp, cool fresh water.

I park close to the waterfall and let mist kiss my skin. Is staying moist a mermaid thing? Does Azure's body naturally seek water? This thing I am—how much is me and how much is her?

The sun takes a drastic dip toward the horizon. From my pocket, I grab the note from Rai and the moonstone that Sulaa restored. Here, on the other side of panic, I feel weirdly acclimated to wearing Azure like a costume. It would have been nice for Sulaa to prep me for the sensory overload. Nice and Sulaa aren't a working team.

Slapping the flat rock next to the water, I stand. "I'm coming, Rai."

To every eye, I am Azure. The spirit inside the shell is pure Tani. My goals are clear cut. Azure/me is hot for Rai and needs to seduce him into selling Mommy Sea Witch his company. Tani/me must draw a path, however crooked, for Rai's heart to return to what we once had.

I pick my way down to the beach and around the cove. For courage, I take advantage of Azure's voice and sing the song Rai wrote for me when we were in love.

"Tani breeze, sliding through my hair
Smoothing, taming
Tani breeze, brush across my skin
Wandering, wanting

Always in my laugh
Always in my arms
Always in my soul

Damn. Azure's voice is a mix of gorgeous and bizarre. It's filled
with tones and shadings beyond a human range as if the whine of
sea breeze and rumble of waves underscore each note. I'd never be
able to make these sounds. No one could. The mermaid is one of a
kind.

Was Sulaa careless? Did the Witch put a lockdown on the real
Azure's singing voice but forgot to do the same for the Tani
takeover version? A knot lodges in my throat when the Moon's Eye
Lighthouse appears in the distance.

Sulaa is lots of things, calculating, conniving, condescending,
but never careless. The flare of realization scorches. I rip an oval
leaf off a coastal live oak, ignoring its barbed edges. "You witch."
The sea hag hides motives wrapped in tainted seaweed. She lied to
me and Gothel about keeping Azure's voice a secret. Sulaa wants
me to sing and out Azure as Rai's storm savior.

I tear the leaf into bits as its tiny thorns scratch my skin. My
soul screams. Once he discovers the truth, Azure is the mystery
voice he's been searching for, Rai will give the sorceress everything,
Cloudpath Music, his body, his heart, to be with his mermaid. He
will be reduced to a pliable plaything for Sulaa.

When I dump him as Azure, will there be enough left of Rai for
this Tani to win back?

A chill having nothing to do with the waning day ripples
through me. I'm terrified *Tani returned* will be reduced to a flashing
reminder of heart break and dead hope for Rai. I know him. My
previous betrayal coupled with the loss of his parents, Piyo, the
mystery savior woman, and Azure may decimate the last of his
spirit. The man will never trust again.

Where does that leave me? Resurrected and alone, rejected by
my heart's fate.

As shadows grow, so does my hatred of Sulaa. Everything about her disgusts me: the damage she inflicted, trying to breed mermaid daughters, Calliwag's curse, the cabal with Gothel and Rubata Lear. Her vilest move is luring Rai to bang it out with me in an Azure shell to keep the real mermaid ripe to spawn Sulaa's next generation of freaks. The sea witch makes us all dance to her despicable music.

I don't want to dance, but any attempt to leave the party is a guarantee of losing Rai and a second chance at life. The late afternoon wind cues a change in the tune of the island. Trees whisper and scratch against rocks. Small creatures skitter and squeak. Birds cry their evening song as they wing to nests. The sea raises its volume of hisses and slaps. This is Rai's island music, the core of the new sound he wants to share with the world. It's home. It's peace. It's Rai.

I hesitate before stepping clear of the oak grove to mount the steps. High above me, Rai grips the rail around the gallery deck surrounding the lantern room. He's clad only in bright red board shorts that flutter in the rising breeze. A final beam of daylight adds dimension to the well-drawn muscles of bare chest and arms. Wind bounces his triple braids with the two remaining talismans against his back. My fingers move in phantom memory of undoing those braids until his shining hair tickled my bare skin as we made love. I grasp a low branch with one hand and sway, eyes closed, remembering the path of Rai's lips from my throat to my breasts, my thighs, and the delicious pleasure between them. Azure's hand slides down the throat we share and trickles across her breasts. I open my eyes to lock onto Rai as Azure's hand lifts the hem of our dress to cup the hot and wanting space beneath.

Who owns this rush of lust? Azure's flesh? My spirit? Or a communion of both?

I pull the hand away. Currents of need course through this body, each more powerful than the last. My conscience screams at me to hold back and consider what I'm about to do to Rai. I silence it. The yearning of this body for Rai to take me with the force of passion that's been building between Azure and him is my master. As Tani, I need Rai's love, the reminder of what it is to be human and to join with my heart's fate. If I don't follow through, Sulaa will have taken everything from me.

Tonight is destiny's wish. I believe fate will send a storm more powerful than the one that brought Rai and Azure together to tear the two apart. A sorceress's magic will fulfill the future designed for Rai and me.

Rai moves to the sea side of the gallery. Only his profile is visible. I abandon the arms of the oak and climb the first step. Before I take another, I hear the strum of a guitar. Its notes are odd, ethereal, and organic like—Azure's voice.

I stumble back into the oak's protection as Rai sings. His voice resonates with newfound richness as it blends with the guitar. He owns the sound he's chased through palm, shell, and wave. Rai is island music.

> *A man was claimed by greedy, stormy seas*
> *The waves did swallow life's last destiny*
> *It gave no time for cries or sounds of grief*
> *A watery end was all left to believe*
>
> *Until a soul through currents did appear*
> *A second chance to save his life shone clear*
> *Bright spirit swam to halt the theft below*
> *This newfound fate was gifted to the soul*
>
> *Upon the beach his eyes did find a light*
> *His savior sang the words to end his plight*
> *Together notes from lips did blend in song*
> *Loves sweet first kiss was lost before the dawn*
>
> *The man alive did wander through the mist*

His heart to search for blessed lips to kiss
When fate denied the gift of finding her
Instead, a spark of hope inside did stir

A new heart's fate made songs to chase despair
Fortune's light swore promises to the pair
Bringing fresh beams of love to light his way
This joy defined fresh destiny that day

A man was claimed by greedy, stormy seas
Yet fate can change if love does life appease
In moonlight's claim, a heart's fate can be saved
By you, my love, beneath wild Azure waves

A clutch of pain seizes my borrowed heart. There's no mention of me in his love song. Tears course down Azure's face and continue falling until they soak into the ground. I hear what I'm loathe to belief. Rai loves Azure with feelings stronger than his fantasy of the mystery woman who saved him or the spirit of a lost love returned. To him, the mermaid is the one who broke his grief to show him the beauty of being alive and making music again.

I crushed him. Azure saved him twice.

I don't deserve Rai. Azure does.

I love Rai Cloud. That love forbids me to manipulate him with Azure's body. Slowly, I melt into shadow to mourn. Failing to follow Sulaa's orders may truly be my eternal death sentence, but this deception, this betrayal is beyond what I can force myself to do.

Through oak boughs, I see Rai pace the gallery, searching for Azure. I know what must be done. Before Sulaa catches me, I must get word to Azure that Rai waits for her.

How in the name of the moon will I pull that off?

Rai sits and hangs his legs over the edge of the gallery walk. He picks at the guitar and experiments with notes. The instrument reflects spectral streaks of the setting sun. I'm mesmerized as Rai sings Azure's name, sustaining each note until the wind steals it from his lips.

He's calling her.

I snap my fingers. Calling her. That's it. I take a trio of deep breaths, burst from the trees, and power up the steps.

Rai stands when he sees Azure running toward him. His face glows with relief and then happiness so powerful it tears my heart into tiny pieces like the oak leaf I destroyed moments before.

"Close your eyes," I holler.

Rai looks baffled. "Close my eyes?"

I almost yell *shut 'em, Buster*. It's too Tani, not Azure. Until I have the means to connect with the real Azure, Rai must believe I'm her. He'll do whatever she asks. "Please close your eyes and give me your cell."

Rai rests his guitar against the wall of the lantern house and follows Azure's directions.

I'm winded from the climb as I snatch his phone. "Listen closely, Rai. You are not seeing what you think you're seeing. I'm not Azure." His eyelids wobble. "Don't open your eyes. You did not see Azure. Stay here."

I move to the opposite side of the gallery walk and search for Azure's contact number. It's odd to touch the phone with human fingers.

She answers immediately. "Rai, hi."

I spill out words as fast as I can in case Sulaa figures out what I'm doing and slurps me into her underwater caliche forest. "I can't explain who this is, but please listen. Rai is waiting at the Moon's Eye Lighthouse on Lalale Island for you. He sent you a message and a moonstone. You'll find them at the bottom of the stairs. Get here fast and on the down-low so your mother doesn't know you're coming."

Azure starts to make a sound. I cut her off.

"Just get your ass over here." I end the call.

When I look up, Rai stares at me.

"Tani?"

I stare at my body, still Azure. "How do you know?"

"I feel you."

Fragments of my heart slam back together. "Feel me?"

He shakes his head. "I can't explain it except to say your essence speaks to me."

I want to shake Rai and get him to admit that's proof we are each other's heart's fate, but I must bamboozle a sea witch to protect him.

Rai narrows his gaze. "Why do you look like Azure?"

I hand him the phone. "Sulaa did this to me. She ordered me to boo hoo to you as Azure to inform you that if you don't sell Cloudpath to Miaqua Music, you'll never see your lover again." I grip his rock-hard biceps. Thank goodness he figured out who I truly am before I touched him. Contact sends thirsty waves through Azure's body.

"Rai, be careful, Sulaa Kylock is every bit the witch we were always warned about. Time for me to go. Your mermaid will be here any minute. If Azure sees me, there's danger she might slip up to the sea witch that I'm involved, and then I'm cooked."

I spin toward the stairs. Rai grabs my arm. "Thank you for watching over us, Tani. You are a true friend." He pulls me in and kisses me gently on the lips.

The sweetness of his mouth on mine nearly blows every circuit of my good intentions. Before I launch myself at him, I push away without another word and blast down the steps. Azure's body wants to respond to the warmth of his breath across its skin. My spirit wants to take the kiss deeper. I can't be trusted around Rai.

I tear through the trees and back to the waterfall. Azure will go to Rai. It's too painful to be near what I suspect will happen at the lighthouse. Sulaa gave me a ticking clock to carry out her deed. I'll wait here long enough for her to believe I've carried out her disgusting plan. In the meantime, I'll rehearse lying my ass off.

One microscopic spark lights my hollow soul. Rai kissed Tani.

He knew it was me. My heart's fate recognized my spirit. I wanted him so badly, but I'm at peace with what I've done. I'll never have to face confessing deception to Rai because I chose honesty. My spirit within Azure's body warms with renewed hope that at the end of this sea witch generated nightmare, Rai and I will find our way back to one another.

16

MOONSTONE

CURSE THE SEA WITCH AND HER UGLY SCHEME TO USE HER DAUGHTER for blackmail. That horror will not touch my family's legacy. I retrieve the moonstone disc and note I sent to Azure from where Tani dropped them on the step.

Azure,
Take this moonstone as a sign of my devotion. Meet me at the Moon's Eye Lighthouse at dusk to figure out the mess with your mother and Cloudpath. I'll be waiting.
All yours,
Rai

Instead of sending a note, I should have called Azure and not given Sulaa the chance to intercept my message. Tani's warning takes root in my gut. We are dealing with a sea witch. Azure could get hurt.

"Okay, Rai. My ass is here." Azure stands a few feet in front of me.

I'm so relieved I don't register her anger right away until I see the crease between her eyebrows and her mouth pulled into a tight line. "Who was the woman on the phone?"

How much do I tell Azure? I'm protective of Tani, but my friend voluntarily smacked herself in the middle of my business, and Azure deserves to know everything. I grab the railing to steady myself. "It's out there. Very far out there."

Azure crosses her arms.

Moon willing, a mermaid will understand there are other forces in the world. "It was my friend, Tani." I stammer. "Not a human Tani, her essence, a spirit form."

"Spirit forms can use cell phones?"

This is getting sticky. "Can we sit?" I collapse onto a step.

Azure is clearly pissed but joins me, leaving distance between us.

My mind races, searching for a place to start the explanation. How do you tell the person you're falling in love with the spirit of your ex-girlfriend is using her body to deliver a warning that your mother is using bad magic to acquire your almost lover's music label? The answer: in small, digestible pieces.

I hold the note and moonstone to Azure. After a beat of hesitation, she takes it and reads. The tension in her face melts and those lagoon blue eyes widen. She pinches the moonstone disc and reaches for my braids. "It's your talisman, the connection to your moon energy."

I close her fingers around it. "Yours, all yours. Azure, I truly believe a moon spirit brought you to me. My mother believed in moon goddesses that champion creativity and love. There is no one else. The woman on the phone, Tani, is a friend to both of us."

"Tani? The name is familiar."

I swallow hard. "She was my brother's fiancé who died in the fire with him and my parents."

Azure's mouth forms an O. Her eyes are sad, and she lays a

hand on my arm. "I want to believe what you're saying about Tani is true, Rai."

There will be time to tell Azure the story of Tani and me. Right now, we need to deal with the news Tani dropped in my lap. "What did your mother say when you mentioned the Cloudpath Music sale?"

Azure studies the dirt path below the steps. "It put her in a super foul mood. Basically, she blew me off as soon as I hinted at a connection between us and Cloudpath. I didn't get a chance to dig any deeper or accuse her of anything."

Obviously, Sulaa did not think Azure's poking around was nothing, or she wouldn't send Tani to deceive me. I hesitate to be the wedge between mother and daughter, but there's some shadowy shit going down, and I don't want Azure caught in the middle.

"There's more, Azure."

She stiffens.

"Did you recognize anything about the voice on the phone?"

Her head bobs. "It was familiar in an unsettling way."

"It was your voice. Tani's spirit came to me as you. Sulaa sent her to mess with my head and put me in a position where she could give me an ultimatum. I sell Cloudpath to Miaqua Music or risk never seeing you again."

Azure springs to her feet. "My mother controlling a spirit? That's crazy."

I gently grab her wrist. "Please, Azure. Think about it. Am I wrong about Sulaa being a sea witch?"

Azure's shoulders slump. She shakes her head.

"Do you believe she may be capable of more than what you've seen?"

Azure stares at the ground and nods. There's a hitch in her breathing. "My father tries to tell me about things she's done. I always cut him off and chalk up his attempts to the bitterness between them."

I guide her to sit on the step next to me. "Could Sulaa's power control a spirit?"

Azure stares out over the water. "I've never seen any evidence of her doing such a despicable thing." She takes a deep breath. "But I'm afraid it might be possible."

"I hate being the one to confirm that is exactly the shit your mom is pulling."

She slides over until our hips touch. "You're the only one I can believe. You know that, right?" A kiss is the last thing I expect from her. It's short but purposeful. Azure hands me the moonstone disc.

My chest sizzles with fear. Is she giving it back?

"Braid your stone into my hair. I want my mother to see we're together on our terms. She can't use me to steal Cloudpath Music from you."

I free a strand of hair next to her face and twist it into a thin braid, weaving the talisman into the end. "Tell me the truth, Azure. Could your mother keep you away from me?"

Her hands fall to the pearly clamshell pouch holding her scales, and I have my answer.

"Sulaa spells your pouch to keep your scales wet, doesn't she?" Sorrow is a shadow across Azure's face. "She has the power to ruin your ability to be on land."

"She wouldn't."

I bite my tongue to keep from cursing Sulaa to Azure's face. My sweet mermaid loves her mother. It's a crack through the soul to realize someone you love has trapped you in a cage. Hate is not an emotion I have much experience with until now. It slithers through my veins. I hate Sulaa.

"What about your father?" I'm dying to specifically ask about his magical chops but hold back.

Azure trembles. I put an arm around her. "My father is a hard man to know. He's very closed off. When he speaks of my mother, he gets very worked up and..." She points to the clouds. "The skies suffer."

There's the proof. Prospero Tempesta's nickname, Stormbringer, is literal then, not a popular commentary on his business persona. The dude is a bonified sorcerer. I don't know much about selkies. I wonder if messing with the weather is their thing or an added sorcerer perk.

Azure buries her face against my chest. "Getting in the middle of their power struggle is a frightening prospect. Maybe it's better if you and I cool it until you decide who to sell Cloudpath Music to. That takes away her leverage."

My parents were the most loving human beings I've ever met. Not just to Piyo and I, but to everyone. Generosity of spirit was their operating system. I can't imagine being raised by parents one click away from dark, destructive agendas.

I stroke her hair. "I'll come with you to talk to your father." Azure's head pops up. "If he's as powerful as your mother, we'll ask for his help to counter her scheming."

She stands and clutches her head. Lines stretch across her forehead and at the corners of her mouth as if stitches holding her together unravel. "I need to think." Azure taps up the steps to the gallery.

I start to follow and pause. She deserves think time. I wish for a dose of Juan Luna mellow. The adrenaline bubbling in my core repels mellow. I thump my chest to interrupt the whirlwind inside. What happened to the Rai who could cop a chill anyplace, anytime? My gaze locks on the blue-haired woman at the lighthouse rail.

He fell in love.

I ache to run to her and swear I will force a sea witch to behave, but I'm powerless.

A drop of sweat sneaks down the side of my face as urgency tightens in my chest. That's not entirely true. Music is my power. I've brought a song to give Azure tonight. The time to play it for her is now before her gut tells her to pull away from me and tackle her family issues on her own.

I climb the stairs slowly, so she doesn't think I intend to interrupt her. She slides farther along the rail, sending me a clear message to back the hell off. Luckily, it positions her farther from the lantern room door. I slip inside. The old cut glass, Fresnel lens that used to direct a mighty beam to ships at sea reflects the golden ruby sunset. The nearly twelve-foot-high glasswork is an art piece with its series of clear steps. There's been talk of removing the massive lens ever since the lighthouse was decommissioned in favor of a pair of LED light stations placed at strategic points on the open ocean side of Lalale Island. The commune fought for the eye of Moon's Eye to remain in its historic home.

I zip over to the sound console installed here for beach parties or folks renting out the old lighthouse as an Airbnb. After a last check of levels and reverb, I hit play.

The song begins with a rhythm mix of shell on shell, rock on tree, paddle on water. It's the blend of beat and peace only natural island instruments can produce. The guitar sneaks in next. Not any guitar, the abalone guitar Azure gave me. Its strings sing of tides and currents. Now, the hum of my voice feathers into the composition, adding a new tone to make way for abstract to shift into lyrics. From the recording, I sing.

"A man was claimed by greedy, stormy seas."

As my song drifts through speakers around the gallery, I stay inside and watch Azure through the windows. She's startled at first, then begins to sway to the intro. When the lyrics begin, her hands grip the rail. Shoulders move, and Azure drops her head for a few bars until the words:

"His savior sang the song to end his plight."

Her body syncs with the music in twirls, dips, and undulations. My darling mermaid dances with the same graceful swirls she rocks beneath the waves. The song ends. Azure straightens and searches the gallery walk. Her mouth forms my name.

I dash to the door, suck in a deep breath, and ease out of the lantern house. Her eyes shine as bright as the beam the lighthouse used to guide ships safely into port. I take a first tentative step toward her as the song begins again.

"Sorry, I hit loop. I'll turn it off."

Azure shakes her head. "Don't." She closes her eyes and hugs herself as hips sway to the song. Her feet stamp in half-steps as she spins.

I mimic her moves, forcing my body to flow with music the way Azure taught me to do on the beach. My turns bring me close enough to spread my fingers across her hips. She continues to dance in my arms, carrying me with her into every sweep and dip. I sink into our lighthouse pas de deux. Azure's hair brushes across my arms, my cheeks. Everywhere it touches, I savor the contact.

My body simmers at the edge of a boil. Losing myself in the song gives me the strength to hold back from kissing her. This dance and the next steps between us are Azure's to lead. She's the one barreling toward a collision with a sea witch because of me.

"A new heart's fate sang songs to chase despair."

In a graceful move, she slides her hand up my chest and presses against the silhouette. Her face is a lovely mix of question and hope.

I cover my hand with hers. "It's you. You are my heart's fate, my fresh morning even in dark night. The very instant I saw you, my heart flew to yours." I dismiss a fleeting wisp of guilt. Once upon a heartache, I called Tani my fate. My soul settles into peace as I finally understand. She gave me a gift by leaving me for Piyo. It cleared the way for my spirit to find Azure.

Her smile opens like the white, night-blooming petals of cereus cacti on the north side of the island. She twines her fingers with mine. "Here's my hand, and with it, my heart."

While the first song of my island rock plays on repeat to trees, flowers, and the waves battering the rocks, I gather Azure in an embrace. My hand travels up her back to thread into the hair at the nape of her delicate neck. Scrunching a handful of blue between my fingers, I angle her head to share breath. She's salt and sea, surrounded by the scent of jasmine. Azure is everything I want.

"I love you, Azure."

Our mouths collide. Lips and tongues mirror the rhythm of music and dance. Our bodies answer, sliding against one another to the heartbeat of the song. As my fingers trace her shape, the skin beneath my tattoo tingles in approval.

Below, sounds of surf change from a major to a minor key. The sun, low on the horizon, hides behind a dense gray layer. As I slide the sleeve of Azure's slinky floral shift off her shoulder to run my tongue across her collarbone, a few drops tickle my arms. There's barely an interval of drizzle before rain claims the sky. Wind follows, using the space between trees to raise a low howl.

Azure backs against the window of the lantern room, dragging me with her as she kisses the space between shoulder and neck. The thin overhang of the lighthouse cap doesn't give much relief from the downpour.

"Inside," I breathe before running my tongue along the shell of her ear. Taking her hand, I pull her through the door. As soon as it closes, she grabs my waist to spin me around and practically slams me against the wall. Azure curves and slides her body against me. Breasts drag along my chest, and hips skirt mine. She pulls away before repeating the move once, twice... It's as if we're back underwater, swimming upright while our bodies find the perfect way to bend and flow against one another. Each pass is a delicious flame to my crotch, providing her a larger target to skim. Tonight, there is no tail to hide the beauty of her body below the waist.

She continues our sexy, vertical strokes as her hand slips below my navel, making its way to the waistband of my shorts. I buck my hips against her hand to emphasize my approval before I speak. "Let's go below."

In one swift movement, Azure lifts a toe to the top of my shorts and slips them down my legs to the floor. Her fingers tease my length. "Is this below enough?"

"There too." I moan and gently remove her wandering hand. "But first..." I nod to the spiral stairs. My low and growly voice inspires Azure to scrape her body against mine with another sexy undulation. I chase a sigh of pleasure with, "I'll go first." I don't want her to go ahead of me and flash my bare ass and primed balls in her face. "We go down backwards."

"Sounds promising," she says with a naughty twinkle in her eye.

"Seriously, the steps are too twisty and narrow to go face first."

"Umm, face first." Azure licks her lips.

"You're one saucy mermaid." I yank her against me and devour her mouth.

I break mid-kiss, leaving her panting, and stumble to the narrow steps, obeying the sign *Descend Stairs Backward*. My feet hit the huge rag rug on the floor of the former living quarters of the lighthouse keeper. Brick walls encircle a cozy space with an overstuffed couch that hugs the curves of the room beneath a bank of windows to the ocean. On the ceiling above, huge blown glass pieces in myriad shades of blue, green, and gold appear to float in the air. They're backed with tiny white lights, stars showing through a sculpted sea. Off to the side, ceramic logs in the repurposed, old-fashioned potbellied stove ooze warmth.

Azure tentatively picks her way down the spiral steps, giving me time to light the dozen mismatched candles on the round table hugging the white support pillar at the center of the room, the spine of the lighthouse. I grin at the thought mermaids lack experience with lighthouses. Her poky progress presents a view to make my southern real estate become even more eager.

Moving to the bottom of the steps, I reach up to grab Azure by the waist and whisk her to the floor. Her squeal turns to a gasp as she takes in the ceiling. She lifts a hand to touch, but the smooth glass is out of reach. I gesture for her to jump onto my back. From there, I offer my hands as steps. She slides her toes across my palms and straightens her legs to stand. Twisting my neck, I watch her touch the sculpture.

"It's beautiful."

The sun flashes once more through the clouds before dipping beneath the horizon. The room is bathed in the glow of candles, fake fire, and twinkle lights.

Azure grips my shoulders to lower herself, sliding her body down my bare back until legs wrap around my waist. A soft, warm cheek rests against my neck. I revel in her touch for a beat before I coax her knees down so she stands. With a quick move, I spin her so we're face-to-face. Hands cup the sides of my neck as she dives into a kiss as only a mermaid can. Her tongue travels in tiny flicks against the length of mine, a pebble skipping across a pond.

I back into the curved couch and sit hard. Azure bounces onto my lap and laughs. She arches and straightens her body over and over to slide against my arousal until I plead for mercy. Azure bends to kiss around the outside of my moon tattoo then licks each star, whispering a new flavor for each. Finally, she traces the silhouette with the tip of her tongue. My entire body pulses as she languishes between my bare knees.

"I've loved you from our first moment on the beach, Rai." Her hands stroke my face, my shoulders, the sides of my body, hips, thighs, and stop just shy of my cock, which pulses in disappointment. "I've longed to touch you, to believe you're real. To believe we can be real."

This is the song of a heart's fate I've yearned to hear. Every word, every touch from Azure ignites its mate in my soul. What a fool to think a mystery girl on a stormy beach could ever fill me with the love and the want this mermaid does.

I slide Azure's dress to puddle on the floor. To my delight she's braless. I drag my tongue from her throat to draw a wide circle around one breast, moving in closer and closer until I steal a taste of her blush-colored nipple. Slowly, I tug on it with my teeth until it slips free. Her moan is long, low, and luscious as I repeat my curvy design on her other full, round breast. There's music in her pleasure.

Azure grabs my hair to pull me closer. Emboldened by her permission, I bite and suck until quick, squeaky screams bounce off the brick walls. I swivel her sideways, lifting her onto the cushions. Continuing to use my tongue as a paint brush, I draw a wet line from between her breasts to the top of lavender satin panties. Gazing at her face, I grin. "These aren't blue or green."

She smacks my head. "There's no rule mermaids have to wear sea colors."

I hook fingers inside her panties and feel something thin and metallic. I trace its path to her hip and the small pearl pouch resting there.

Azure sits to face me. "It's okay, Rai."

A bubble of panic rises in my chest. "Does what we're doing mess with your scales?"

She cups my face. "As long as they don't dry out, I'll be fine." Azure raises her hips, inviting me to slip panties down her long legs and over adorable toes.

I rise onto my knees to admire the flow of every curve. In the scant light of the room, her skin has the tiniest hint of bioluminescence. "You're glowing."

Her hand reaches up to stroke my shaft. "And you're as hard as coral."

"Oh and ohhhh," I say as her fingers play with my tip. "You glow when you're—"

I capture her hands and hold them in one of mine above her head. My fingers dance across the top of her thigh and between her legs to sneak into her folds. Her liquid heat is silkier than her panties and a thousand degrees hotter. I repeat my circle motif over all her beautifully swollen places. When I discover the spot that makes her writhe and press against my hand, I increase the pressure. "Are your scales this wet?"

"More, Rai." She frees one hand and guides my circles until her cry drowns out the sound of the surf below.

I slide up her body to enjoy the pounding of her heart and the rise and fall of her breasts against my skin as she pants. Tiny tremors of pleasure course through her sex, pattering like raindrops against my cock. I release a slow groan of delight.

Azure wraps legs around me, her body rolling under mine in increasingly wild waves. Her hand sneaks between us, stroking my arousal in harmony with her movements. She pushes me off her with those lean, serious swimmer arm muscles and forces me onto my back. My sizzling mermaid straddles me backward and takes me in her hotter mouth. Eager dampness slides against my chest as she continues to rock to the beat of my song that still plays in the lantern house above us.

My cock relishes the long slow drawl of Azure's tongue from tip to root and reaches the last of its patience. "Azure." I coax her shoulders back toward my chest as her teeth gently retrace the path of her tongue. "Oh, fucking moon, Azure. I'm close."

She slides to the floor and pulls me to my feet. "Wait for me, Rai. I want to watch the waves with you inside me." Azure grips the back of the couch and leans forward, her body a siren's call.

I grab one of the condoms I hid behind a huge decorative scallop shell in a bout of wishful thinking and roll it on. I ease in behind Azure, pressing her forward onto the cushions as I raise her hips and gorgeous ass to a tantalizing angle. It takes all my restraint not to immediately slide into her. Instead, I lower myself to my knees and kiss my way up her inner thigh until I reach the perfect position to taste her readiness with a deep kiss, my tongue exploring every hidden flavor. Lusty pulses answer my questioning lips, and my restraint shifts from reality to an abstract concept. Finding a way back my feet, I curve around the sinuous body of this gorgeous mermaid, my chest molding to the contours of her back. Instead of kisses, a much more determined part of me pushes inside the alluring slickness and heat of her. Colors and music yet to be written explode through my mind as I enter my heart's fate.

Azure sings a single note, then pauses and sings another in her strange, fragmented song cadence with each new thrust. I force my pace to slow to offer her as shattering an experience as the one I'm having. I travel deeper with each approach and then retreat, rocking my own pattern of waves into her flesh. Azure reaches with one hand to thread fingers through mine as she presses firmly back against me. I sink the rest of the way into her, relishing every inch. When I hit the spot inside waiting for me to find, she sings a note so high window glass rattles. Nails dig into my hand.

She tightens around me, and I pump harder. As much as I long to tantalize and tease, desire wins. I grab a handful of her hair, and with a sharp rock of my hips, plunge. Together, our cries drown out the crash of waves as heart fates celebrate the joining of their destinies for the first time.

I dig my chin into her shoulder as we ride the aftermath of release. Sliding out of her leaves me lonely even as we collapse in a tangle onto the couch.

Azure nuzzles my neck. "I knew we'd be incredible, Rai."

"Did you?" I kiss her forehead and squeeze her tighter.

"We're supposed to be."

I rub my palms over her solid back muscles. "Yes, we are."

Her finger lazily traces my tattoo. "It's true. You find when you stop looking."

I tense. I was looking. Longing with all my being for the woman who saved me. The soul I completely believed was my destiny. Azure deserves to know there was a void in my heart when we met. Has she listened to the words of my song closely enough to hear the truth I gave up on finding my savior when I met her? Is it enough for her to believe how deeply I believe in us? My song starts over again.

"I should go turn the music off." I roll her onto the cushions and stand.

Azure brushes fingers across the dip in my lower back. "No. I'll never get enough of it." She shifts to kneel behind me. "Your braids are falling apart." Loving fingers play through my hair as they free my two talismans and comb out the twists in all three braids. She drapes long strands over my shoulders. "I thought your hair would be smooth and straight, but it's thick and wavy."

I tilt my head back to look at her. "And always in my way, hence the braids. Are you disappointed?"

"Nothing about you disappoints, Rai." Azure leans over me for a quick upside-down kiss. "Except...oh, never mind." She drapes herself over my shoulder and taps my lips. "Kiss puff looks good on you."

I flip her over my shoulder, settling her in my lap. "Except?"

Azure's fingers continue to mess with my hair. "What's the name of the song?"

I bury my nose behind her ear as new heat builds between our naked bodies. "Wild Azure Waves."

"Aha," she says, giving my chest a playful slap.

I catch her hand. "What?"

"You stole our line."

Pulling back, I tilt my head to the side, feigning innocence. "I did?"

"Colors of the Lagoon? The first song we wrote together?"

I peek into her ear. "I don't think so. You must have kelp on the brain."

Azure squeezes my cheeks with long fingers and locks her gaze on mine. "Lavender splashes across a wistful sky. A peachy shade thrown off a sleepy sun. Fading trails of saffron hold fast the light to save. Before it's claimed beneath night's wild azure waves."

"Oh, that song." She pinches my thigh. "Ouch." I toss her onto the cushions and ease my body on top of her. "It was the perfect line to steal for my first island rock single."

Azure wraps arms around me. "A perfect line for a perfect song. It'll be a hit, Rai. I feel it in my—"

"Scales?" I reach around to pinch her ass.

She opens her mouth to scold, but I steal her lips with mine until the rumble of thunder shakes the windows.

I rise on elbows to look out the window as lightning slices through the cloud bank.

Azure wraps her legs around mine and traces my brow with a pinkie. "Rai, you're trembling."

Forcing a shaky smile, I switch my focus to her eyes. "Not a fan of storms." The night of breaking Tani's urn and being dragged into the sea blazes through my mind. If I share my story with Azure, I'll be forced to confess my obsession with the woman on the beach. Not tonight. Not with the echo of lovemaking trilling across our skin.

Azure wiggles out from under me to perch on the windowsill behind the couch with her back to the glass. She's nearly a silhouette against the darkening sky.

I lean my forearms on her thighs. "I take it you are a fan of storms."

"Let me teach you the best part of storms." Her toe seeks out the part of me unbothered by a little thunder and lightning, and it's my turn to squeak. A spicy smile twists her plumped lips. "Give me your hands. Keep looking out the window and appreciate the glorious clouds."

I obey my sultry mermaid. She circles my calloused palms over her nipples until they rise to my touch. My cock goes from interested to invested.

"Azure, your scales?"

She reaches into her pouch. Lifting one of her oval iridescent beauties to my mouth, she whispers, "Kiss."

I press my lips to her scale, delighted to find it warm and still moist.

"We have time." Azure tucks the scale inside its pearly home. She places my hands on her knees and coaxes me to spread her legs. Circling one of my wrists with her thumb and forefinger, she invites my hand inside her slippery mound. Rocking to the song I wrote for her, she urges my fingers to set her ablaze.

Pulling her body toward me, I find the perfect position to lose myself again with my heart's fate. Before I erase even inch of distance between our bodies, Azure curves a hand around my throat and takes my mouth in a deep kiss. Slowly leaning back to welcome me in, she growls. "It's your turn to watch the waves."

17

MAN TO SELKIE

THE MOST BLISSED OUT STRETCH OF MY EXISTENCE WRAPPED UP IN Azure is followed by seven days of pure agony. I play with the moonstone disc woven once again to the end of my braid. Azure spooked me when she insisted I keep it for now. Her only explanation was Sulaa shouldn't get a hold of anything belonging to me. My bucketful of questions over dark magical possibilities remained unanswered as did Azure's commitment to seek advice from her father. We parted at the Moon's Eye Lighthouse with my reluctant promise to be patient and let her decide on the next moves with her paranormal parents.

Oh, our glorious night. My fingers tingle with the memory of Azure's velvety soft skin and the adventure in her lovemaking. Beneath moonlight punching through lingering storm clouds, we strolled to the water's edge, pausing every few steps to kiss. Azure allowed me to watch her strip off her clothes, attach them to her pearl pouch, and dive into a frothy, storm-weary sea. With a graceful leap to assure me the mermaid was on duty, her luminescent form arched through the air before dipping under the waves. A final flip of her bright tail was the last good-bye.

My insides glow as much as her electrified mermaid sheen with the knowledge her luminosity cranks higher with her desire for me. When she left, I lingered on the rocky beach, staring at the water, hand flat against my tattoo. After a thousand thanks to the moon for Azure, I trudged back up the stairs to finish the night alone in the lighthouse. Falling asleep with my heart fate's scent lingering in the air was a perfect brand of magic.

That was a week ago. A week since the lighthouse. A week since I've held Azure in my arms and made love to her. A week since I've heard squat from her except a one-word text.

Patience.

A week of silence from Tani. A week since I released *Wild Azure Waves*. Even though it's garnered decent traction and interest, I don't know if it's enough. There've been a few interview offers and a smattering of *comeback* mentions online. Social media clamors for a video. I need to whip up visuals to match the mood of the song. Kitae, and possibly Juan Luna with his groovy vibe, can co-star. Who can resist a hippie and the cuteness that is an island fox? A chuckle breaks through my murky mood at the thought my two besties will define my new brand.

The sand in my hourglass to reinvent Cloudpath Music is running out fast. I followed the new release with *Colors of the Lagoon* and a remix of my former hit, *Fire Capped Waves* to whet the appetite for more island rock. My manager awoke from hibernation to field a few requests at minor mainland venues for live performances. I've found distraction from Azure's absence by experimenting with ways to reproduce the acoustic resonance of my island ambiance onstage.

Overall, calm illudes me. I'm so round-the-clock agitated even Kitae, the prince of agitation himself, won't hang with me. Juan Luna insists I should get high to mellow my shit. My shit will remain tragically unmellowed until I hear from Azure and know the sea witch isn't behind our separation.

I kick sand, and it peppers my face. What do I have to lose if I hand Cloudpath Music over to Sulaa? I'll negotiate giving island rock a lifeline with her label as part of the deal. Despite sun spanking my bare chest, I shiver, remembering Tani's warnings about Sulaa. I can't risk a Faustian deal with a loose cannon sea witch. My gut tells me losing my leverage to Sulaa Kylock won't do Azure and I any favors.

I check my cell. Nothing from Azure. A text blips in from Emerson.

Less than three weeks.

Screw you, Emerson. I am well aware.

Rampion Records, Caliwood Inc., Golden Pipes Records, Dark Vinyl Artists, and Tempest Tunes must be lighting Emerson's ass on fire to figure out where they stand with acquiring Rai Cloud's company.

Tempest Tunes.

I face palm hard, and pinpricks of light dance behind my eyelids. I'm an idiot. Here I am batting around the ridiculous notion of making a deal with Sulaa to guarantee my island rock a home when proposing the same arrangement is my ticket to getting a face-to-face with Prospero Tempesta. Unless he already hates me because he knows about Azure, me, and the whole mess with Sulaa. He might be as opposed to our union as the sea witch and would rather hit me with a Stormbringer lighting strike than hear me out.

I can't shake the hairs on the back of my neck feeling that Azure needs me to do something. She is my heart's fate. We're connected. I can't ignore instinct, and if I'm forced to attempt chill for one more day waiting for Azure to make a move, I'll go completely bat shit. I dash off a text to Emerson.

Set up a meeting with Prospero Tempesta.

I swear the three dots on my phone blink faster than normal.

We decided not to pursue his offer.

My thumbs fly across the screen.

He doesn't know that. I want to propose an addendum. See if he bites with a better package.

The dots flash and disappear at least a half-dozen times before Emerson calls. I come in hot and determined. "Em, I want to discuss Tempest Tunes absorbing my island rock label."

"You're not seriously revisiting the Tempest Tunes offer? It's shit."

When it comes to Cloudpath, I've never lied to Emerson. For my future with Azure and the future of my family's company, I've got to push through the bile in my throat and rip off a whopper.

"I've been listening to his catalogue. Let's lean into a reconsideration." The combo of an unrelenting sun and deception soaks the front of my T-shirt.

"Tempest was our bottom offer, Rainn."

"Noted. So, let's troll for something sweeter." I flap the moist fabric away from sticky skin.

Emerson *harrumphs* into the phone. "You're serious?"

I give up and peel the shirt off over my head. "I am."

"This is lunacy, Rainn."

Lunacy is right. If Emerson only knew how deeply the moon and my heart's fate are involved.

He growls. "Meet me in the offices in an hour so I can dissuade you."

Good old Em. I'm a giant thorn in his ass, but he's still loyal to the last remaining Cloud.

"Or to write a revised proposal. I'll be there." I fling my damp tee onto the sand. Bounding out of the tree line, Kitae leaps onto the shirt like it's a hapless mouse and starts licking it. "And Em, I want to meet with Prospero Tempesta no later than tomorrow."

I hear Emerson attempt to cover a choke. "Tomorrow?" His voice lowers an octave. "What aren't you telling me, Rainn?"

Where do I start? I need a man-to-man, or man-to-selkie, meeting that breaks my word to Azure because I can't wait this out any longer. A week of silence is too long and my imagination of Sulaa's potential control tactics too vivid. I've found my heart's fate, and I'll do anything to protect our future, even if it means stacking the deck against a sea witch with a selkie on my team. Hell, Prospero may even greenlight our proposal to house island rock with Tempest Tunes. Dangling Cloudpath Music in front of his selkie snout is my only channel to enlist his help to get to Azure.

"The bonfire is coming up fast, and I plan to announce the sale at the event. I'll see you in an hour." I end the call, lob my phone onto my shirt, kick off my sandals, and dive into the lagoon.

I MADE A DEAL WITH MYSELF: I'D ONLY TELL AZURE ABOUT MY MEET up with Prospero if she initiates contact before the event. I don't want to give Sulaa any advantage by attempting a message that could get intercepted. Azure's silence continues. Even this morning, as Emerson and I cross the channel to meet with Prospero, my internal battle rages on whether to try to connect with Azure. There's a reason my texts have gone unanswered. It's not a ghosting sitch. We parted as lovers with shared visions of a future together. The deep pang of fear from Tani's warning twists my gut.

"Rai, you've got to be careful. She's every bit the witch we were always warned about."

For all I know, her mother hexed Azure's phone and is laughing her witchy ass off at my pathetic, lovesick texts. I can't risk Sulaa catching wind of my session with Prospero. The nagging sensation over going back on my word to Azure sharpens to a point between my ribs. I promised patience, and here I am about to knock on the door of her father's multi-level, steel and glass brick, beachside mini mansion.

After seven days of silence from Azure, this is the move I've got to make or lose my mind. My soul aches, worrying about my beloved mermaid. Did she confront Sulaa, and things went south? What if the witch took Azure's pearl pouch away so the mermaid is banished to Miaqua? I nearly bolted to the old research station a dozen times to demand to see my heart's fate. Panic of something even worse happening if I showed up and surprised Sulaa is the only thing that kept my feet on the island.

An executive assistant type in slacks and a slate gray button down answers the door. His black, shiny, slicked hair makes me wonder if he's a selkie. It makes sense for Prospero to surround himself with folks who are savvy to his unique lifestyle.

"I'm Antonio. Mr. Tempesta is ready for you." He ushers us up two levels into a wide room with a glass wall facing the sea. Behind his desk of thick aqua sea glass, a giant of a man sits with his back to us.

"Mr. Emerson and Mr. Cloud," Antonio announces before descending the stairs.

As if propelled by a personal gust of wind, Prospero Tempesta spins in his high-backed leather chair to face us. His shoulders are broad enough to skateboard across. Waves of black hair with stripes of gray chase around his head. The dude's brow is prominent, nearly overshadowing navy eyes. Every bone on his face is sharp and almost too pronounced to be human. I've been called brawny, but Azure's pop elevates toned bulk to a whole new level.

Dude is a selkie. Being not completely human is part of his jam.

Even cocky Emerson is cowed when Prospero rises and swoops around the desk with an outstretched hand. We are forced to look up to meet the gaze of the Tempest Tunes president.

"Prospero Tempesta. I'm delighted to finally speak with you both in person." While he gives Em's hand a perfunctory shake, he prolongs the grip on mine. "Mr. Cloud, I'd like to take the opportunity to personally extend my deepest sympathies for the tragic loss of your family."

"Thank you, sir." The genuine tone of his words moves me. Maybe talking to him about Azure won't be as terrifying as I imagine.

With a final squeeze, he releases my hand and perches on the edge of his desk. I'm surprised it doesn't tip over. With the wave of an arm barely contained within the sleeve of his suit jacket, Azure's father gestures for us to sit in a pair of gray leather chairs. He strokes his pointed chin with an oversized hand.

My heart stutters. Azure's chin tapers to a point in a similar but beautifully feminine way.

When Prospero aims a smile at me, I try not to stare at his overly sharp canines. Does Emerson notice the man's not-quite-human features?

"So, Mr. Cloud—"

I wipe a hand through the air. "Rai." Might as well start off cozy since I'm about to take a can opener to his family secrets.

Prospero nods. "Rai. Illuminate your vision of island rock for me."

Emerson puffs out a barely audible breath. He'd prefer the discussion stay contained between business types, not the air-headed musician who has a failing record company to unload.

"An organic pulse exists as the spirit of my new sound. The music will be a fusion of wind, tree, and tides with human emotion embedded in every melody, every lyric. I want my audience not just to hear the songs. The notes will resonate in their soul."

Prospero circles his hand for me to continue.

"I'm experimenting with a unique acoustic shadow for each song. A fingerprint, so to speak, that sets it apart from everything else."

Tempesta crosses his arms. "Lofty."

"Necessary, or I'm rehashing what's come before." Prospero's eyes begin to take on glazed boredom. I wonder if Azure's inability to shed tears comes from her selkie side. "Close your eyes."

His gaze snaps into focus.

Emerson clears his throat. "Rai, I'm sure Mr. Tempesta has heard *Wild Azure Waves.* There's no need—"

At the mention of *Azure,* Prospero narrows his eyes at me. Did she mention us to her father? I'm coming in blind here. The mogul raises a hand to quiet Emerson. He rounds his desk, settles onto his throne-sized chair, and closes his eyes.

I walk to the window. Below is a stretch of sand bookended by two very jagged, sea-battered rock formations. I imagine them as the gateway to Prospero's selkie kingdom. I close my eyes and tune in to the surf below. "What do the waves say when they speak to you?"

Prospero claps his hands twice. The sound is loud, and I jump. Emerson lets out a startled grunt. The mogul pauses and claps twice again, perfectly timing his percussion with the interval between breaking waves.

I answer his claps and then rub my hands against one another to mimic the sound of the water returning to the sea. He adds a slap to his thighs as a new cluster of waves rushes to shore. I tap my fingertips against his desktop, adding a new dimension to our symphony. Prospero counters with a hiss. I respond with a barely-there falsetto howl to wake the sound of wind skipping across the water.

Slaaaaap, hoooo, shh, shh, crack.

We jam for another minute or so, then Prospero is quiet. We stare at each other, the wavering veil of comradery between music makers connects us. Slowly, he nods. "Extraordinary. I heard an undertone to *Wild Azure Waves* I couldn't quite put my finger on. This is it."

Emerson pipes up. "Rainn would like to propose the possibility of absorbing his new island music label under the Tempest Tunes umbrella if we sell Cloudpath Music to you.

I lock my gaze onto Prospero's. "My instruments are mostly crafted from natural island resources. In *Wild Azure Waves,* I've encountered a whole new dimension of sound through a unique instrument that's recently been gifted to me—a guitar crafted of abalone."

Prospero startles, recovering in less than a beat to stare me down. Heat flares in my chest. My own stare stays locked on his. He knows the instrument. Azure must have played one for him.

"Emerson, I need a private word with Mr. Cloud."

"I don't feel it's—" stammers Emerson as Prospero's intense blue-black glare targets him.

"Antonio," bellows Prospero. His assistant appears at the top of the stairs before Emerson can protest further. "Show Mr. Emerson to the patio. We will join him momentarily for refreshments."

Emerson exits, clearly nonplussed by Prospero's darkening mood. The top of Antonio's head has barely disappeared down the steps before Azure's father whips around the desk to grab the front of my polo shirt.

"You have exactly sixty seconds to explain yourself."

I yank his hand off my shirt. "I'm in love with your daughter."

I didn't mean to lead with emotional truth, but sixty seconds doesn't give me much time for a slow intro.

I don't know what Prospero thought I'd say. Judging from the shock on his face, it wasn't about my feelings for Azure. He takes a few steps backward until his legs hit the edge of his desk. This answers my question about whether she mentioned me to her father. That's a big fat negative. If I can't convince him we're legit, he'll give zero shits about anything else I say.

"Azure is the soul of my island rock. It totally gelled once we made music together and then she gave me the abalone guitar." I can't read the dude's concrete mask, so I go all in. "We're both truly in love."

It hits the target. Prospero recovers and closes in. "Impossible."

I swallow hard, stand my ground, and spill the rest as fast as I can before he throws me through his plate glass wall. "Sir, I know Azure's a mermaid, and the only way she can survive above the surface is keeping her scales safe in the pouch Sulaa spells for her."

Prospero takes my words in for a beat without comment, then flicks a wrist at me. "You're a fool, boy, if you imagine a future for you and my daughter."

"That's exactly what I imagine. I'm not blind to the obstacles. Azure told me you have ideas for"—I almost say spells but hold back—"ways to keep her safely out of the sea for more than a few hours."

Prospero's robust eyebrows knit together, not in anger, in contemplation. Time to hit him with my big play. "Our differences do not jeopardize our future. Sulaa does. She's using Azure as leverage against me to force the sale of Cloudpath Music to her."

Stormbringer hits me with the full force of his stare.

This is for Azure, Rai. You can't fail.

"Sulaa encouraged Azure to be with me so I'd fall for her. Well, I did, but it goes beyond a simple crush or infatuation. It's love for both of us. If I don't sell Cloudpath to Miaqua Music, Sulaa will stop spelling Azure's scales to keep us apart. You know, without that insurance, it's impossible for Azure to thrive above the surface."

Prospero spins to face the windows and thrusts a fist at the sky. His roar shakes the room. Outside, the clouds triple, shifting in a blink from white to dove gray. Dude is definitely not totally human. He whirls to face me. "How dare she!"

I square my shoulders and step closer to Prospero. "Sir, I haven't heard from Azure in a week, and I'm pissed scared." Passion for my heart's fate fuels my courage. "I will risk or give anything to be with her. I don't care if it means a life beneath the waves and never seeing Lalale Island again. If it means selling you my company to earn your support for us to be together, it's yours." Here comes the finale. If it fails, I fail. Pulling my shirt up, I expose the tattoo of the moon and the silhouette of a woman. A sense memory of Juan Estrella drawing this lifepath flares across my skin as I press a fist to my chest. "Azure is my heart's fate, and there is nothing you, Stormbringer the Selkie, or The Sea Witch can do to erase our destiny."

These last words confirm I'm privy to all the family skeletons. I hope I don't regret the reveal.

Prospero points a long, thick finger at my ink. A pencil-width line of gray fog stretches between his fingertip and my chest. The wisp trickles across my skin as his eyes roll up until only white shows.

"There's *mana* at work here," he whispers.

I feel as if he laid a boulder on my chest. It's a trial to draw even the smallest breath. My vision begins to darken and then, with a snap of Prospero's fingers, the pressure evaporates. I gulp a lungful of air. Black thunderclouds flow through his bluish charcoal eyes.

Here is the crossroad. It's Stormbringer's call to either kill me or help me.

Help us.

18

STORMBRINGER

I'M ALONE IN SULAA'S CORAL GARDEN. IT'S BEEN SEVEN SUNRISES AND sunsets since she interrogated me about sleeping with Rai. It tore me up to recount precious memories of the days Rai and I did make love as lies to assuage the witch. The fact I'm not stuffed into her indigo throne is a good sign I pulled off the deception.

Azure must be sticking close to home if Sulaa has me tethered in her garden instead of glued to the mermaid's side. A nervous buzz tickles my insides. Did I plant the right amount of doubt in Rai to be wary of Sulaa and make him question Azure's part in the witch's scheme? The buzz escalates to a stress ball. Or did I go too far? Personally, I want the two of them to cool it to make space for me in Rai's heart. I vow to do anything it takes to reclaim the life that was taken from me, but if I opened too great a rift between Rai and Azure, Sulaa's shot at grabbing Cloudpath Music may have been damaged. That does not work in my favor.

There's no choice but to wait and see what my actions triggered. I am subject to a tyrant, a sorceress, that, by her cunning, has cheated me from either moving back to life or forward to what lies beyond death.

I hear the distant rumble first, then the ground begins to shake.

The sea churns like rocks in a blender beyond the transparent shell. Air inside the garden swirls like the onset of a storm. Sulaa keeps the garden habitable for Gothel or her other guests that may venture outside their place inside the rock wall. A great wave slams into the barrier, and the seabed quakes beneath my feet. The tops of a few tall coral stacks snap off and lodge in the sand. Metallic creaks and moans from the research station echo around the garden. Miaqua sounds ready to pop its rivets.

I duck behind a huge formation of coral as if it would be any defense from this freakish storm. The undersea hurricane batters the boundary of Sulaa's domain. What the hell is going on? I expect a battalion of killer sharks to advance on Miaqua.

A shadow grows larger and more menacing as it approaches. The sea boils around it in a turbulent shield. I make out a shiny black body, and...flippers? The face of the thing presses up against the sheen of the barrier and I gasp. Massive black eyes stare above a snout filled with overlarge, pointed teeth. A monster bent on destruction has erupted from a deep-sea trench.

As the beast molds itself to Sulaa's barricade, a flash of lightning cuts through the water from above and blinds me. When my vision clears, the beast and sea storm are gone, and a very imposing naked man strides through the garden gate. His skin is the leathery tan of a dedicated sunbather. My gaze trails from the top of his storm –tangled, black-and-gray hair down his muscled torso to what lies south of the dark line of hair beneath his navel. Everything about the man is overlarge. He's equal parts terrifying and magnificent.

"Sulaa!" he roars.

I shrink farther behind the coral stack as the sea witch strolls out from between two vibrant trees.

"Hello, lover," the sorceress purrs.

The man balls his hands into fists and thrusts them at the

ground. My coral hiding place crumbles into sour-apple-colored dust along with several other towers in his zap zone. I dash for new cover.

"Never again," growls the man through gritted teeth.

Sulaa flashes him a lecherous smile. "So, this says." She touches a finger to her mouth. "But..." Her finger swishes in the direction of the agitated appendage between her visitor's legs. "That says something else," she says with a throaty laugh.

With a wave of his hand, the man appears to conjure a slick, shiny black covering akin to a wetsuit to cover himself.

Sulaa clucks her tongue as she saunters over to the man and dances a finger across his shoulder. "And here, my darling Stormbringer, I thought your selkie rage was born of overwhelming need for a tryst with the best you've ever had."

Stormbringer? Shit, this is Prospero Tempesta.

Prospero stares at Sulaa's hand on his shoulder as if it's an annoying beetle before he grabs her wrist to remove her teasing fingers.

"I'm not here to throw you onto the sand and have you."

Sulaa twirls into Prospero as if they're dancing. "Pity. Those were some good times."

Ugh, what a vile pair. How did these two make someone as sweet as Azure?

Prospero backs away. "Where is my daughter?"

Sulaa's expression hardens. "She's in no mood for daddy time."

He moves to glower down at her. Prospero may be the only being taller than Sulaa. "What have you done?"

The sea witch feigns surprise, laying a hand over her heart. "Me?"

Whirlwinds of sand circle Prospero's hands as his face reddens. "To Azure and Rai Cloud."

There's a slight twitch between Sulaa's shoulder blades Prospero can't see. Someone got caught sticking her magical nose in her adult daughter's love life. No wonder I haven't been on Azure spy duty. Whatever Sulaa set in motion hasn't required my supernatural skill set.

"Direct your question to Rai Cloud, the breaker of Azure's heart. The fool promised her a life above the waves, which we both know is impossible, then at the first sign of difficulty, set her adrift. She vows to avoid the surface altogether." Sulaa's concerned mommy act is gag worthy.

Prospero growls, "Liar," in a duet with the same word zipping through my mind.

Rai is incapable of such hard-hearted cruelty.

Sulaa straightens to full, legendary Amazonian stature. "Ask Azure." She whispers something into her golden trident necklace.

How in the name of the moon did this happen? I left Rai at the lighthouse to get closer to Azure, not break up with her. A faint buzz of joy vibrates through me at the thought of Rai free from his Azure love haze. It dies quickly imagining the consequences of his broken heart. Devastation. Isolation. How could he make any pledge to me in such a state? If Rai can't give me his love as my touchstone back to life, what becomes of me?

Azure appears from behind a line of twisting fuchsia coral next to the silver sand path. "What, Mama?" Her gaze darts to Prospero. "Dad?"

I shudder as Azure walks right through me to where her parents face off. Azure's a hot mess. Greasy, blue hair clumps over her shoulders. Her puffy face looks like she collided with a jellyfish. The girl clocked serious weepy time. She needs a facial recovery mask from Rubata Lear's trendy cosmetic line.

I run a finger under my eye as if I could touch the soft skin there. Will I ever feel the tingle of Rubata Lear's anti-wrinkle products again?

Prospero rushes to Azure and pulls her close. "My darling."

Ah, the crusty bastard has a soft spot for the mermaid. He's so damn tall he kneels for an eye to eye. "What put you in such a state?"

The mermaid moves to sit on a coral pedestal. "I got involved with someone on the island instead of someone in Miaqua. I knew it was risky, but I believed I found my heart's fate."

Prospero stands. His bass resonates throughout the coral garden. "Rai Cloud."

Azure jerks at the sound of Rai's name. "How did you know?

Prospero raises a finger. "Your mother claims he ended the liaison."

Azure crosses her arms. "Spare me the lecture on how losing him is for the best, and I'm only supposed to care about people who've committed to live beneath the surface."

Daddy closes the gap between them, stooping to thread an arm around baby girl's shoulders. "Azure, will you explain the means with which Rai Cloud broke off your association?"

Association? Boy this family is all about the warm fuzzies.

She wiggles out of his grasp. "It's private."

"Azure." Prospero's voice deepens even more with an authority I doubt few dare to question. "Trust me."

I swear the air around the not-so-happy family begins to fog.

While father and daughter stare at one another, Sulaa clears her throat. "Being devoid of a heart, Prospero, you don't understand the pain when one breaks. Give our daughter the space she needs to work through her sorrow without making her relive it to satisfy your curiosity." The opalescent discs on Sulaa's shoulder begin to flicker when she's ignored by both sorcerer and mermaid.

Tacit understanding blooms between Azure and Prospero, and their expressions soften. From the pearl pouch on her hip, she pulls a moonstone disc with a note identical to the one I gave Rai at the lighthouse and hands it to her father.

He reads it. "Interesting." With a quick swipe, he tears the note in half. "And complete bullshit." Prospero waves a hand over the disc. It morphs into a bubble which he pops by smacking his hands together.

Azure grabs for the former moonstone. "No."

Sulaa tenses.

"I just came from Rai Cloud. He tells a very different story." Prospero narrows his focus, aiming it straight at Sulaa. "One of ultimatums and deception." A softer gaze meets Azure's. "And love."

Sulaa digs fingernails into Prospero's arm. "Separating them is for the best. They have no future."

He bats her hand away. "Your poisonous note dims the noontide sun. You dare use our daughter to force Rai Cloud into selling you Cloudpath Music. Such rough and heartless magic dishonors our art."

Azure sucks in a breath and stares at Sulaa. "Tell me you didn't conjure Rai's note."

If only I could shout "*she hella did*" and get away with it. I cringe knowing this family feud has a direct effect on my afterlife. I'm screwed if Sulaa blames me somehow for being called out on her nasty plan. Shit, who else knew what she was up to? I float behind a coral stack further away from the sea witch.

Prospero slides his hand to Sulaa's throat. For a moment, I think he's going to squeeze. Holy moon, if she's offed, do I vaporize? The woman holds my soul in a literal knot. Should I ghost swoop in between them to give Sulaa the impression I'm on her side?

His hands cup her neck but do not tighten. "You will disentangle your influence from Azure's personal business and allow her to see Rai Cloud. You will not concoct mischief with her pearl pouch or her scales. The manipulation ends here, Sulaa."

Sulaa sends a magic whammy that distorts the air with a lavender glow, and Prospero stumbles backward. "You do not command me, Stormbringer."

Azure is the one to step into the fray. "Stop it." She turns to Sulaa. "You've lost my trust."

The sea witch modulates her voice into a soothing coo. "Baby, I knew that man would break your heart eventually. I was trying to save you before things got too serious."

Lying witch. She wants Azure and Rai in as deep as the bottom of the ocean to force Rai's hand.

Azure glares at both parents with her combo genetics of selkie rage and sea witch viciousness. "Stop treating me like a helpless fool you battle to control. Isn't it enough I'm forced to live with what you two created? You both claim to understand what I am. You don't." She flares her fingers around her face. "I am the first of my kind. My entire life will be about testing limitations. Maybe I'll be successful and maybe I'll fail, but I'll do it without any more interference from you." She turns and power walks through the garden gate.

Sulaa's voice is low and deadly. "What have you done, Prospero? Her obsession with Rai Cloud could kill her."

Prospero stares after Azure. "Rai Cloud is her destiny. I've felt it."

The sorceress practically spits at him. "You don't believe that any more than I do. What's in it for you to champion the Cloud idiot?"

A smile stretches across Prospero's face, revealing freaky seal teeth.

Sulaa's teak brown skin blanches. "You bastard. He sold you Cloudpath Music, didn't he?"

The wetsuity covering on Stormbringer's body begins to liquify and reform into sleek, black seal skin. His shape rounds, and flippers sprout. His head is last to transform to full selkie. Before it does, a threatening bark rings through the air before his words. "The new owner of Cloudpath Music will be announced at the annual Lalale Island Bonfire. Save the date." Prospero vaults through the air and bursts through the transparent curtain between Sulaa's garden and the wild sea. With a final flick of shining flippers, he blends into the current.

A heat signature wafts off Sulaa's body. Her eyes spark with fury. The coral garden melts around us like crayons in an oven, and the colorless caliche forest spikes into being. Gray water fills the space from fetid sand up through layers of silt.

I've nothing to hide behind. I need to be smart and pretend to partner with this woman who holds my eternity between her flashing fingernails.

"What can I do, Sulaa?" I drop to my knees and go full supplicant. If I'm humble and pliable, maybe I can keep my betrayal with Rai under wraps. My gut tells me submission, however faked, is my last hope to possibly have a future outside her indigo coral throne. "I will continue to give loyal service, tell no lies, make no mistakes, serve without grumbling to earn the promises you made to me." My statement teeters on truth with a dash of painting a pretty picture of my intentions.

The sorceress's nails bite through the air in the strike of a cobra. I shriek as three vertical gashes open along my torso. The pain is fire burning from within. Obsidian blood seeps into the water. She knows. All this time she ignored me, I'd thought my lies had worked. She's not going to imprison me. Sulaa will tear me into strips of shredded spirit and feed me to Calliwag.

"Only fools and corpses try the patience of my power," she bellows. "Rai Cloud is one, and you, malignant thing, are the other." Invisible hands press on either side of my head, reducing thoughts into nothingness. "I searched for the stink of Rai Cloud on your useless spirit and found nothing. You wasted the gift of Azure's body and did not take the man as a lover. For what? To doom your soul?"

Sulaa tears the shadow of my spirit from the folds of her gown and reties the knot with an agonizing yank that sends me to my knees.

I am both fool and corpse. Fool to believe she wouldn't find out I'd compromised her plan. I did it for Rai as much as for myself.

As quickly as it arrived, Sulaa's incendiary anger vanishes. With a wave of her hand, the damage to my form knits together. Not a single drop of my half-dead blood floats around us.

The sorceress's eyes, nails, and freaky skin discs flash in turmoil as she stashes my shadow away. "If I didn't need your connection with Rai Cloud, you'd be food for sea beasts that manifest in the darkest of dreams."

Her message is unchanged. Do what the sea witch commands. I allowed my conscience to muddle Sulaa's directives by not using Azure's body to seduce Rai. I must stop dancing around the fact that betraying Rai is my only path back to him. I betrayed him in life when I left him for Piyo, I hate that I must do it again in this half life. I have no other choice.

A gut feeling tells me not to dissolve in front of Sulaa despite the terror seeping through my spirit. I must be obedient while still maintaining enough strength to appear useful, not defeated. Gathering my nerve, I ask, "If I obey, you'll still keep your promises?"

To my surprise, Sulaa lets loose a guttural laugh. "Ah, Tani. I admire your survival instincts. Another reason I haven't destroyed you yet." She drums her fingers on my shoulder. "We made a bargain. A life for a record company. The game hasn't ended until Rai Cloud signs over Cloudpath Records."

"To you, Grant Gothel, and Rubata."

Pupils take over her plum irises as she pins my soul to the sand with a glare. "Yes, if he sells to Miaqua Music or Dark Vinyl Artists, we both win."

It's a relief when she shifts her focus to fuss with the peacock strand in her collection of blue hair.

Win.

She said we could both still win. I need to invest in the witch's game in earnest, no more self-serving detours. I will help Sulaa break Rai's heart and pray the promise of being with me again is enough to super glue him back together.

Sulaa clucks me under the chin too hard to be considered playful or affectionate. It still freaks me out I feel her touch when anything I reach out to fades through the ether of my body.

"It's time to best a sorcerer. You, Tani, will be going to a bonfire."

19

AT THIS TIME, I WILL TELL NO TALES

THE NOTES OF THE ABALONE GUITAR BENEATH MY STRUMMING FINGERS sound as bummed out as I am. Prospero sent me packing with the caveat to be patient. I tried patience with Azure, and it resulted in heartsickness, fear, and the leading edge of despair.

Lying in the hammock, I watch scrub jays squabble over strings on palm leaves in the dimming light. Sunset reminds me of Azure. It's my favorite time to connect with her and watch scarlet slashes melt into the golden pool of sky. Every sunset from here on out will be filled with thoughts of my love.

"Oh Moon, I'm begging for a lifetime of sunsets with Azure."

I hug Azure's gift to my chest and gently rock the hammock. Closing my eyes, I drift through every moment I've been gifted with Azure. Weight on the hammock near my knees disturbs the rhythm of my sway. The scent of sand and grass wafts over me. I raise a knee to encourage Kitae to jump down before he starts to ruin my revery with licks and nips.

Instead of fur, my knee brushes against slinky fabric and then bare skin. I bolt to sitting, twisting the hammock mid-rock. Azure falls across my chest to prevent getting dumped onto the grassy patch below us.

In one swift motion, I slide the guitar aside and throw my arms around my heart's fate, pulling her fully on top of me.

"You're here. What happened? Where—"

"Kiss me, Rai."

My mouth finds hers in a frenzy of relief and happiness, shoving questions and wonderings aside. She thrusts her tongue past my lips, diving deep into the kiss. Enthusiasm makes us sloppy. It takes a few beats to rediscover the way our mouths fit together.

Azure scrapes her hands into my hair, pulling my mouth roughly against hers. We kiss and bite as if the world shatters around us and this is the last breath we'll ever take. I pull away, hands on either side of her face, to meet her gaze and prove to myself she is not a dream.

"Azure. Oh moon, Azure." I bury my face against her neck. Tears that can only be mine dampen her skin.

"It's okay, my love. Happy cry for me too," she whispers, nestling her head on my shoulder. "As long as you keep touching me."

With a sloshy, guttural sound, I ravage her mouth. Her dress rucks up to her waist, and I become acutely aware there's nothing between my raging erection and her nakedness except the thin nylon of swim trunks.

"I want you, Rai. Now." She grinds against me. "Show me we're real."

"Exquisite mermaid," I breathe and then moan as she reaches around to slip her hands beneath my waistband to dig her nails into my ass.

I take the opportunity to yank her dress over her head and kiss my way down her neck until my lips find one breast and then the other to savor. She tastes like the fresh morning air before the day's heat sullies it. I crave more, sucking and biting as if at any moment we'll be ripped apart. Her hand finds its way between us. She rips the Velcro of my fly open, twisting to yank my shorts to my knees. I kick them the rest of the way off as Azure shifts to settle onto her side facing me. She encourages me to face her.

"Azure, I was terrified you'd never come back."

She presses her palm to my tattoo. "I never left." Her lips brush against mine in a gentle promise. "I never will."

The long, slender fingers of her other hand stroke me, gripping tighter with every journey along my length. Through lusty panting, I force words. "I don't have anything."

Azure moans in my ear. "I've taken care of it."

I pull her leg over my hip and skim my fingers between her thighs to discover every slick and deliciously ready place. I ease her leg higher and slip inside. I mean to make this last. I pair every drive deeper into Azure with a fresh kiss suffused with the scalding desire flowing between us. I long to freeze time as we join, relishing every sensation, worshipping every place we connect.

Azure's body ripples against mine the way it does underwater, claiming all of me. The hammock rocks with each thrust until the blur of sky, palm, and the taste of Azure's skin against my lips sends a blaze through my core. Before the series of shocks from my release subsides, she guides my guitar-calloused fingers between our hips. Her skin radiates the delicious, faint glow of longing as she shimmies against my hand. I play a rapid flutter of notes against her sweet little nub, raising a delightful shudder through her body. My mermaid's cry joins the island's song.

We lie naked in each other's arms except for Azure's ever present pearl pouch. The thing is so thin and pliable it's like part of her skin. I sling one leg over the side of the hammock to rock us as we downshift from ecstasy into satisfaction.

I twirl a piece of bright blue hair around my finger. "I've fantasized about making love to you in this hammock since the first day you showed up in the lagoon."

Azure says nothing.

I release her hair. "It's a compliment, not a horny insult. I wanted all of you. Your laughter, your kindness. You seduced me when you elevated my music from concept to relevance."

Her silence begins to unnerve me, so I gush. "By seduced, I mean fell for you, in a real way."

"Shut up, Rai."

By the tension in her body and the fact she stopped dancing fingers across my tattoo, I know it's not an affectionate *stop blathering and kiss me* shut up. It's a *don't speak because you're pissing me off* shut up.

I stop rocking the hammock. Her body temperature spikes beside me. Not the gradual rise of a turn-on. Thermometer busting anger.

Azure pushes against me to launch herself out of the hammock. The sudden shift in equilibrium dumps me on my bare ass on top of a hidden pebble pile in the grass. "What?" I say, brushing grit off my behind.

Azure's skin has shifted from a hint of bioluminescence to sunburn apricot. She entertains no qualms about her nakedness as she paces back and forth where grass meets the sand. My dick twitches appreciatively, unable to read the room the way my brain does. I approach with caution, pulling on my trunks to hide the insensitivity of my anatomy.

"What's wrong, Azure?"

"It was not my plan to jump you. I intended to talk first, then I saw you lying there with your damn ink and those unfair chocolate syrup eyes." She stops pacing to glare at me. "Damn it. I love you, Rai. I thought you'd broken up with me."

"What!"

She doesn't explain. "I ached for you, and I thought we were never going to—" Her arm arcs through the air in the direction of the hammock.

I grip her adorably muscular biceps and restrain from rubbing my chest against her equally adorable breasts. "You're mad we made love?"

Azure pulls out of my grip. "Yes. No." She launches herself into my arms, pulls my braids, and savagely kisses me, wielding her tongue like a weapon. Her hands slap my chest, and she pushes me away. Her temper reminds me of Prospero without the kissing.

I rub my smarting scalp. "I know it's the ultimate disrespect to go caveman on you, but if you don't stop attacking me, I'll throw you over my shoulder and take you back to the hammock."

She growls at me. "Absolutely not."

Despite my best efforts, the primal response sends my gaze skimming down her naked body. "I ached for you too. I still do."

"Damn it, Rai." Azure storms past me to swipe her dress from the ground and pull it over her head.

I sit on the sand and pinch my thigh to focus on whatever issue has her in a rage.

She plants herself between the water and me. I have a horrible suspicion she's giving herself a straight shot to escape. "I'm sick of fighting for control of my life. I never thought you'd put me in that position too."

I've clearly screwed up.

"You went to my father when I specifically asked you not to."

I start breathing hard. "This is what you're pissed about?"

"Yes, Rai. I asked you for patience. After you went to see him, he confronted my mother. It set a very volatile dynamic in motion with you in the middle of it. I'm afraid for you."

I spring to my feet. "I was afraid for you. Shutting me out for a week was not part of the patience deal. I was out of my frigging mind with panic."

Azure's breathing so hard I worry she'll pass out. "Are you listening to my side? I thought you'd ended things with me. My mother gave me the moonstone with a note from you saying how impossible we were. I needed time to piece myself together before I involved my father. You took that from me."

"Focus on my perspective for a sec." I thump the side of my head. "I was clueless you thought I broke it off. When I didn't hear squat from you, and knowing what your mother might be capable of, I did what I felt I had to do. Prospero was my only conduit to find out what the fuck was truly up."

We stare at one other. I see my agitation mirrored in her eyes. I'm first to crumple. "I can't wrap my head around you believing I'd blow you off in a note."

Azure presses fingers to the corners of her eyes as if stopping tears that will never come. "My mother is a master at misdirection. My entire life has been about bouncing back and forth between my parents' manipulations. Mother conjuring a fake note was just the latest intrusion. Too many times to count, I've wanted to swim away from it all." She drops her hands, breathing deeper than human breath. "But I couldn't leave my sisters. They're bigger casualties of my mother's game than me." Azure pounds a fist against her thigh. "The note was very believable. It picked at every fragile thread holding us together."

An unpleasant suspicion makes a muscle in my jaw tick. If Sulaa was desperate enough to orchestrate a breakup, she knows too much information about Azure and me and what we might suspect her of. Other than some sorceress trick, I can think of only once source. Tani. She's been warning me about Sulaa, but how much is she telling the witch? Did Tani betray us and tell Sulaa that Azure and I, not Tani and I, were together at Moon's Eye? "Does your mother know you came to me at the lighthouse?"

"Of course not. She only knows I've been seeing a lot of you." The apricot of Azure's skin deepens another shade.

"What did the note say?"

Azure's throat ripples as she swallows hard. "It claimed you mistook attraction for love. You confessed you were carried away, exploring your curiosity about me being a mermaid. Finally, you broke things off, insisting we happened too quickly to be real." She stills her breathing. "The last part is true."

I grab her hands. "Screw quickly. I believe I've been waiting a lifetime for you. I love you, Azure. When we make music together, when I touch you, it's timeless. I believe with all my heart our connection is fated and unbreakable." I press both her palms against my tattoo. "When Juan Estrella Azul burned this story into my flesh, it was our story, a promise from the moon that you are the one. You are a sacred promise made real."

My skin heats beneath her touch, an unnatural heat as if the *mana* embedded in my ink attempts to sear her hands to my chest.

"Do you feel it, Azure?" She nods. "The force drawing us together is bigger than questioning the speed of our bond. Your life is surrounded by magic. Can't you believe there is magic between us?"

She replaces her hands with a lingering kiss. "I do believe, Rai, for more reasons than I can share."

I pull her close. "Then why are we fighting?"

Azure backs off enough to meet my gaze. "Because you sold your company to my father. You gave away your dreams because my mother used our relationship to trick us both. The fact it backfired doesn't matter. You still lost Cloudpath Music because of us."

I shake my head. "Not lost. Gave willingly. I told your father I'd sell my company to him if he helps us be together." I attempt a reassuring smile. "He promised Tempest Tunes will offer a home to my island rock music." My lips find the corner of her mouth. "Our island rock music." Turning toward the water, I watch waves erupt over the rock circle at the far end of the lagoon. "I may be letting my parents and Piyo down, but this is the best I can do."

"Oh, Rai." She drops the top of her head to my chest. "I'm sorry you couldn't keep your family's legacy." Azure can't cry tears, but her body shakes with sobs.

I sigh. "Me too. At least it's still mine until the annual Lalale Island bonfire when I officially announce the sale to your father." I kiss her forehead. "All the prospective buyers, Rampion Records, Golden Pipes, Dark Vinyl Artists, Caliwood Inc., and your parents will be there like every year. Your mother can't make a fuss in front of that many witnesses."

"Not like every year. My mother has never been invited before."

I cringe. She's right. Sulaa was never on the guest list while my parents were alive. I change the key. "Don't worry. It'll be a good night, a fitting farewell to Cloudpath Music. You're going to love it. Justin Time and Zeli are going to sing, so are Chorda and Midas Lear."

"Chartbusters and a reality star. Big ticket talent."

I smile. "Friends. They wanted to come and make tonight a belated memorial to my folks and brother."

She shifts to lean back against me, and we enjoy the peace of the waning day in silence for a few precious moments.

"Azure, will you sing with me at the bonfire?"

She shakes her head. "I can't sing, but I will make music with you."

I rest my chin on top of her gorgeous blue hair. "Will you sing with me someday?"

Azure tilts her head to give me a gentle kiss. "Someday." Sadness in her tone derails my tranquility.

"I promise to share all those somedays with you." Tension thrums through her body. "You're still freaking."

She swivels in my arms so we're face-to-face. "Selling Cloudpath Music to my father goes beyond losing your company, Rai." Azure's voice is thin. "You've started a war between my parents."

20

PRE-SHOW JITTERS

I KNEW TODAY WOULD BE BITTERSWEET. THIS YEAR'S ANNUAL LALALE Island Arts Festival and Bonfire Night is the first opportunity for most of my folks' associates in the music biz to shower me with sympathetic looks and hugs. It's tougher than I anticipated. I power through with a few tears and a clenched throat.

Each time someone gushes over my parents and brother, guilt drives a fist into my gut at the memory of Tani. She should be included in their misery roll call. I'm glad I kissed her at the lighthouse even if she was in Azure's borrowed form. She knows there is a place in my heart that will always be hers.

Since Tani hasn't appeared to me since, I fear I've lost her again. Visions of her shattered urn bum me deep. Her belief she is my fate and I her way back to life wear on my soul. I'm convinced Sulaa played her the way she did Azure and me. Was the promise of a life restored false bait or the real deal? I can't bear the thought of Tani's spirit trapped by the sea witch.

Is Sulaa the reason Tani is gone, or did my surety Azure is my heart's fate break the bond with my beloved friend forever?

I make my way behind the collection of vendor booths where

commune members display a year's worth of effort. Leaning against a raspy palm trunk, I stare at the bright blue, cloudless sky.

"You are a dude with a 'tude," says Juan Luna, shuffling up to me in flip-flops covered with plastic flowers.

I nod to his feet. "Nice kicks."

He holds out a drink filled with blue liquid with a blood red stripe spiraling around the inside of the plastic cup. "I borrowed Tutu's flippies. The strap broke on mine, and she prefers to go barefoot."

There are few men who could pull off wearing their grandmother's footwear. Juan Luna is such a man.

"She's pissed you haven't been by Palm Bliss to sample this year's theme cocktail."

I hold the cup to the light. "The spiral action is bitchin'."

"Tutu's latest art is syringe infusion in her drinks," he says, tossing back his own frozen treat with a long, "Ahhhh. You should see the crisscross in her Island Mind Bend."

I taste the drink. It's frosty, refreshing, and has her signature alcoholic kick. "Delicious. She must be making a killing at the booth. What's it called?"

"Red Sky at Morning."

I choke on my next sip at the well-worn adage—*Red sky at morning, sailors take warning.* "Is she being ironically or literally prophetic?"

Juan Luna slurps the rest of his cocktail. "At sunset, she's going to change it to Red Sky at Night."

"Sailor's delight." I hand my drink to him, and he tucks it inside his empty cup before downing it. For me, no buzz is a good buzz with the hour of the bonfire and live debut of my island rock drawing closer. "How very Yin Yang of her."

My friend levels a squinty gaze at me. "My man's Chi rocks some thorns. Are you freakin' about tonight?"

I fool with the whistle on my braid. "Once I name the new

owner of Cloudpath Music, the gate on my former life slams and locks behind me. Not exactly a high."

Juan Luna drops an arm around my shoulder. "Breathe into it, Bro. Grasp a new path. You're making life happen instead of it happening to you. That's powerful shit."

I turn into him for a full hug. "You're powerful shit." A trickle of icy liquid from the drink drips onto the small of my back where my palm print, short-sleeved button-down rides up. "Ach."

He laughs and grabs my arm when I try to wipe it. "Have your lady lick you clean after the bonfire."

A rush of heat bursts through my middle, imagining the sensation of Azure following the drop with her tongue.

Juan Luna nods toward the marina. "When do I get to meet your heart's fate?"

The rush kicks up a notch, hearing my friend speak the words *heart's fate*. The phrase anchors my truth down through the sands to the center of my beloved island. Azure is the love I've wandered through life waiting to believe in since the day Juan Estrella and *mana* began my tale in ink with the blue silhouette of a nameless woman. I can't wait to share Azure with Juan Luna, Juan Estrella, Granny Blossom, Tutu, and all my island family.

I've just got to get through tonight first and any fallout from Sulaa losing to Prospero. I check the marina again. Neither a shuttle from Miaqua or Prospero's yacht are in the slips reserved for them. The sky begins its shift from bright day to softening dusk.

"She'll be here soon." My eyes drift to the marina and then across the sand, the very colorful sand.

"Cool."

"J.L., what's with the rainbow sand?"

He fans an arm over the beach. "You like?" I saw the look in one of Tutu's design mags. Confetti raked into sand says bitchin' party."

"Paper confetti? As in flammable paper? Are you nuts?"

"Chill, my man. These teeny bits are harmless. You know sand kills sparks. To be hella safe, I told my peeps to rock a wide safe zone around the bonfire and scoot it closer to the water. We're covered."

I eye the specks of paper as if they're about to jump up and bite me on the ass.

He stretches. "I'm on duty with Tutu. Find me at Palm Bliss." Juan Luna flashes me the "hang loose" sign and shuffles into vendor village.

I turn my back on Juan Luna's party sand and close my eyes to search for personal bliss. It washes over me quickly as I imagine Azure strolling with me during our all-day festival, hitting every booth as I introduce her to the people in my life. We chitchat and then picnic at the lagoon. When the sun goes down, we take our party to the bonfire. My lovely mermaid will settle against me as we listen to the talent bust out their songs.

Reality stabs me in the gut. I'll never be given that day with Azure. Parts of it, yeah, but not the whole thing. Her scales don't last above the surface for a whole day. Our future will be moments of pick and choose. Fists pommel my insides. Azure's folks manipulated her life, set her limitations. I'll never let our bond prevent her from living her life the way she chooses.

Zeli jump scares me, popping out of nowhere. "Rai, I want to live in one of your tiny houses."

"My wife finally found someplace to match her proportions," says Justin Time, picking Zeli up from behind and swinging her in a circle.

As soon as her feet hit the ground, Zeli throws her arms around my neck. "I love your island. I love all the beautiful art and the cool peeps." She smacks a kiss on my cheek.

"It is a killer sweet vibe out here," says Justin. He punches my arm. "You hold out. This island is the jewel you kept hidden when we did the tour of your studios up in the big pink house." He stink-eyes the palm behind me. "The overabundance of these vandal palm trees does dull the appeal."

"Justin doesn't do palm trees." Zeli tips his face and kisses each of her husband's closed eyelids. I shudder, thinking about the eye gouging from a palm frond he survived during a B.A.S.E. jump gone wrong before this pair brought Gothel down. The act is so tender and loving it sets my own heart aching for Azure's touch.

Regret floods my chest. Maybe selling to Justin and Zeli at Rampion Records was the better move. They love my space, my world. If only I'd offered them the chance to fold island rock into their stable and avoided magical interference altogether.

I shake it off. There was one decision for me. Choosing Prospero is the only way to guarantee Azure's safety against Sulaa. His support of island rock is a fortunate sidebar.

Something near the marina catches Zeli's eye, and she shouts, "Chordaaaa." The pop diva's jubilant lope across the sand reminds me of Kitae. I'll invite Justin and Zeli out to Lalale Island again when they can enjoy its true stillness and meet my little fox dude.

Justin gazes at his wife as if there's nothing he'd rather do in the world. I totally get his look because I rock the same one for Azure.

"My lady and Chorda want to perform their new duet before the Lears bust out their father/daughter set," says Justin. "Cool?"

I nod. "Any and everything goes tonight, Dude. Give 'em the green light."

We watch the Rockin' and Rollin' Pantheon rock legend, Midas Lear, drag his wobbly legged son-in-law, Adair Holliday, down the dock.

Justin laughs. "I don't do palm trees. Adair doesn't do boats."

I hook a thumb toward the fair. "Take him to the Palm Bliss booth. Tell Tutu I sent you. She'll fix him up with her ginger/ginger/ginger."

"Ging-what now?"

"Ginger ale, ginger snaps, ginger hard candy. It's a freakin' miracle cure for seasickness." I grab his shoulder. "Don't let Juan Luna pass him one of Tutu's cocktails before he finishes the g/g/g unless you're willing to carry him to the boat."

"Thanks, man," says Justin with a fist bump.

I call to him as he heads over to his wife, Chorda, Adair, and Midas. "You and Zeli are on after The Mermaids open the show tonight."

He raises his arms with two thumbs up. I flip a rogue braid over my shoulder. I'm expected to mingle, but my head needs serious clearing before I bust out island rock songs with Azure and announce the sale of Cloudpath Music.

A wet tongue slithers up my calf. I scoop Kitae into my arms and cradle his snout in one hand so we're eye to eye. "What's an antisocial fox like you doing in a place like this?"

He nips my wrist, and I set him down. Following a series of quick barks and circles to make sure I'm paying attention, he darts along the outskirts of the arts and craft booths to the lagoon path. I follow. As soon as I clear the tree line, my heart hits overdrive the way it always does when I see my love. She sits with her back to me on sand tinted orange from sunset's glow. Azure hair dances in the sea breeze. I settle in next to her.

She leans against my side. "Is my dad or my mother and sisters here yet?"

I gently take her daintily pointed chin in my fingers to guide her lips to mine. The kiss is deep and slow as if nothing in our lives matters more than this moment.

"No, we've still got time before the bonfire." Azure hides her head against my shoulder. When I draw her closer, she trembles. "What's wrong?"

She speaks to the sand. "I'm afraid my mother and father will mess with each other and ruin your night."

"Your father promised me he'll keep everything under control once I make the announcement."

Azure grunts as she lifts her head, shaking a wild strand of hair off her face. "My father and control in the same sentence. There's a rare pairing."

I scoot her to face me and touch my forehead to hers. Shadows chase the color from the sand. "I'm working on a new song. Wanna hear it?"

"Is there time?"

"To sing to you—always."

With my lips a breath away from her, I sing.

"Don't be afraid.
This island is full of sweet noises that give delight and do not
*   hurt.*
Is it the music of instruments or voices humming in my ears?
I'll hear them in my dreams.
When I wake after a long sleep on the beach,
They're here waiting for me
And for you.
Tonight, my island will give you its sweetness and everything
*   will be right.*
I promise."

Azure rubs my nose with hers. "When did you write this?"

I smile against her lips. "Very, very recently."

"As in now?"

"As in..."

We kiss through a dozen sets of waves meeting their end against the rock clusters in the lagoon and hold each other while dusk swaps out for night. Down the coastline, a rumble sounds as people gather for the bonfire concert.

Standing, I pull Azure to her feet. "Which instruments did we decide to go with tonight?" We stroll to my collection of island music makers. I retrieve the abalone guitar. "Definitely this."

"And these." Azure grabs a wooden flute, short oak branch, and a nautilus shell.

"Perfect." The woman knows my new sound better than I do. My eyes fall to her pearl pouch. "Are you still at full charge?" I've been careless, letting too many minutes pass here at the lagoon when Azure's time on land is finite.

She laughs and places my hand over the pouch. I swear the swish of currents and tides move beneath my touch.

"I'm good to go." Her gaze falls over the sea. "If I do need to slip away, you'll understand."

I picture Azure hemmed in by the crowd at the bonfire. She's a famous musician as one of The Mermaids in her own right, but the two of us making island rock together live for the first time could zing her even farther into the spotlight. People will surround her, ask questions, take photos, and steal precious time. "We need a code word in case I need to cause a distraction so you can hit the water."

Her eyes sparkle. "Lighthouse."

We stroll down the main row of booths. When we pass the last cluster of palms before the sand, I pull up short. The bonfire is in full bloom. Sparks leap from the top of flames to take their chance in the sky. All my life, I've loved the raw beauty and power of these flames. That was before. Now, its sounds are horrible. Inside every roar, crack, and sizzle is a memory. My mother screaming. My father reaching for her only to be consumed by the out-of-control blaze. Piyo and Tani stumbling in panic seconds before they were overtaken.

"Rai?" Azure squeezes my arm.

I back up a few steps into shadow before anyone catches sight of us. My joints loosen and I'm on the edge of collapse. The bonfire signifies tradition. Since I was a child, I've been taught to believe the power of the flames are a symbol of the creativity burning within every member of the commune. All I see now is destruction, a raging beast with teeth of ash.

How did I ever think I could face a real-time copy of the thief who stole my family?

Azure's grip tightens. "See the fire the way it is now. Not that night. You told me they moved it closer to the water this year.

Look." She points to a trio of huge water tanks with hoses coiled at their bases between the bonfire and the marina.

I locate the poles ringing the fire to mark a safety zone and several commune members stationed as guards to make sure no one gets too close.

"Last year was a singular tragedy. How many years has your commune celebrated with the bonfire?"

I'd rather cry than speak. "Nearly fifty."

"Have there ever been any tragedies before the one last year?"

I shake my head.

"It will not happen again, love." She pulls me close. "Your heart is back there, at the accident, isn't it?"

It takes all my effort to nod through my pain.

"I'm here, Rai. You're not alone."

I sob and shake in her arms. My heart cries out to my family and Tani. In this moment, I know the pain, the loss is mine forever. Those I love should not be gone. I am helpless to bring them home.

My recent visions of Tani were the final notes of my family's song. Part of me wanted to believe so badly she could return for good. Now, I believe her return, however brief, was a test to help me move on. Fate's gentle way of easing me through a present with too many empty rooms. I draw breath deep from my soul and cling to Azure. With her, I can truly take a first step to swap bad memories for new ones to cherish.

I swipe the shirttail over my damp face. "I knew tonight would be a challenge. I didn't expect a punch to the throat."

Azure slides her hand under my shirt to my tattoo. The energy between her touch and my flesh breaks sorrow's hold on me. "Will you be able to sing?"

I nod and repeat the words I spoke to her on the sand. "To sing for you—always."

A flurry of high-pitched voices draws us out of the shadows. "Sisters," cries Azure and drags me to where Sulaa and The

Mermaids reach the end of the dock. She carefully helps each woman onto the sand as if she's worried they'll break once they set foot on the island. I study each sister for any sign of the gills or fins Tani told me about. There's nothing odd about any of the blue-haired beauties.

I'm included in each sisterly embrace with an intro. "Rai, this is Lapis, she makes the abalone guitars. Watch out for Bluebell, she'll tell everyone your secrets. Teal keeps the peace. We bribed Peacock with the tie-dye booth to get her to come. Cyan is dying to meet Kitae." They all giggle and fuss over me with hugs and cheek pecks. The sisters are everything sweet and charming.

Here in the whirlwind of family affection, I tear up again until Sulaa steps off the dock. Her dark purple stare is the antithesis of her daughters' open-hearted welcome. The weird color-wheel discs across her shoulders are twice as bright in the darkness as they were in Miaqua. They seem—agitated like fish swimming in too small a bowl.

"Mr. Cloud," says Sulaa, extending a hand with her signature glowing fingernails. "Thank you for including us in this monumental event." Sarcasm drips off every word.

"Thank you for coming, Ms. Kylock. It's an invitation long overdue."

My parents' avoidance of Miaqua stings. If The Mermaids had been invited to perform at the annual bonfire, how many years ago would Azure and I have found one another? Warnings and speculations from the spiritualists in the commune kept our two worlds separate. Now that I know how right the rumors were about sea witchery, I pray my gamble of inviting Sulaa doesn't turn into an ear-splitting record scratch.

Sulaa purses her lips at my apparently too-little-too-late olive branch. Her nails dig into the skin of my wrist. "I suppose it's time to leave slights of the past in the past?"

I rescue my hand before her nails drive deeper. "Absolutely." Acid creeps up my throat, picturing her reaction to the latest slight

I'm about to deliver when I name Prospero Tempesta the new owner of Cloudpath Music.

Sulaa shifts her attention to where Juan Luna charms his way into a reunion with The Mermaids. "Ladies, may I escort you to our humble entertainment venue?" says my friend with a wink.

I flash Azure a look to check in, and she reassures me with a smile.

"This way." She and Juan Luna lead her sisters to the raised platform where sand meets a small grassy hill. The stage is ringed with feathery Areca palms, giving the appearance of a green skirt. Azure helps her sisters onstage, settling each on a chair or stool and generally fussing over them. Tonight's performance will be small potatoes compared to the extravaganzas they pull off in Miaqua. They're clearly not used to a casual setting.

Once The Mermaids are ready, Emerson steps to the mic and faces the crowd of people in low-backed beach chairs and on towels that stretch along the sand. In the background, near the water's edge, the bonfire roils and hisses.

"On behalf of Cloudpath Music and the Lalale Island Artist Commune, I welcome you to our annual Festival of Island Art and Bonfire of Song." He answers the applause with a salute. "It's my honor to hand you off to Rai Cloud."

I give Em a thump-on-the-back hug. He whispers in my ear. "You got this."

Leaning into the mic, I start my roll. "Hey."

The audience answers with their own *heys, bros, Rais,* hoots, and whistles.

"Gratitude to everyone sharing the sand. Tonight is as much heart punch as it is party." It takes a sec for me to loosen my throat to continue. "Let's make it a celebration of music, the island, this incredible creative community, and the spirit of staying in the light Lucas, Corinne, Piyo, and Tani expect of us." I kiss my fist, press it to my heart and reach for the moon.

My people repeat the gesture, and I swear the moon brightens. Maybe Tani is up there increasing the volume.

"Make some noise for Teal, Peacock, Lapis, Cyan, Bluebell, and Azure—The Mermaids."

The group brings their ethereal music topside as they wrap us in the enchanting sounds of life from their underwater home. I wouldn't be surprised to see whale spirits and waving kelp forests overlay the stage. The way Juan Luna stares at the sky, he tuned in to his own visions. A pleasant fragrance of brine and island flowers drifts on the air. Reflections of firelight off palm leaves strobe in gentle flickers.

As the group sings, Azure watches me, her lips moving occasionally to add a note to a harmony. It doesn't seem fair her sisters can sing freely on the island when she can't. I'm eager to learn all her mermaid limitations so I can be a worthy partner. Under her gaze, I start to believe. I believe I can heal from the scalding gash of loss for my family. I believe Sulaa won't pull any rank moves when I make my announcement. I believe Prospero will handle the sea witch as promised. Most of all, I believe Azure, my heart's fate, is my forever.

I believe in believing.

It's glorious.

21

BONFIRE

THE SENSE OF BEING WATCHED CRAWLS ACROSS MY VACANT SKIN. IN my paranoia, I imagine Gothel with his black, fathomless gaze, Rubata's bright green cat eyes, and Sulaa's bruised plum stare tracking my every move. The trio thinks they own me. The three Dark Vinyl Artists all swim in the same sea of narcissistic cruelty.

I'm mentally and emotionally exhausted. Have I reached the last oomph of my spirit juice? I hate this feeling of depletion. Tonight, of all nights, strength is essential, strength of spirit, of willpower, of keeping my goals in sight. It is my last shot to claim my heart's fate. I must follow Sulaa's orders perfectly to find my way into Rai's arms. Once there, we'll fix all the sorrow, loss, and hurt each other carries in our souls.

Only a few people still hang at the artists' stalls and vendor booths. Tutu leans back in her wicker chair with bare feet on the counter of Palm Bliss, sipping something tall and peachy from a plastic daiquiri glass. I miss her strong arms around me and the filthy jokes she'd tell us years before she should. I miss Granny Blossom with her prophecies and promises. I even miss Juan Luna Azul and his endless cool dude flirt fest.

The Mermaids are on stage. I can't watch. The way their

misshapen forms adjust to chairs breaks my heart. It's clear Sulaa's enchantments that hide the truth of her daughters, her experiments, hold up here on the island or people would be freaking. Some naive part of me hoped the sea witch's strength diminished above the surface, compromising her power. No such luck.

I float to the top of the highest palm near the festival and search the crowd beyond the stage until I find the one person besides Rai I desperately seek.

I miss my father.

He looks older than I remember. Does he feel as alone as me? Is he drifting between realities that don't play nice with one another? I'll find a way to bring him happiness once I return. Rai will help me.

There is a face on the sand I won't find.

I miss Piyo.

A twinge of remorse trickles through me. Here I go, charging full speed back into a life with Rai as if I've forgotten Piyo. I loved Piyo. It never was the mind-bending passion I felt for Rai, but it was love of a sort. Choosing Piyo made my father happy. It made me happy to make them both happy.

Rai was like the scrub jay chick we saved one summer that was destined to fly off into the clouds to follow birdie dreams. I lost faith Rai would let me fly away with him.

I have faith in him now. Once I return, he will step onto the path leading us together. No matter what I'm forced to do to step onto that path. I will do it.

Will any of these people I miss besides Rai recognize me on some deep level even if I'm in a different vessel, or is such a secret to stay between my love and me?

Sulaa's last words weigh heavy on my soul. *"Tani is dead, but the you inside the shell will live again. Rai will know you in time if we succeed tonight."*

In time? As with any Sulaa exchange, you can ask for

clarification but only receive what she chooses to parcel out. If I dwell on her obtuse "you," I'll lose it, and I must stay focused on my task. What the hell will I be? Who the hell will I be when I slip back into life? I sigh and watch my moonbeam-colored hair fall over my shoulders. As long as Rai knows me and I am alive, I'll make it work.

The gathering at the bonfire bursts into cheers. It's time to join the party.

Midas and Chorda Lear finish their encore while I make my way to the steps leading to the stage. There's one act left. Rai and Azure will perform their last song together.

They move downstage to share the mic. Rai speaks first. "It's been too long since I shared music with you. I even began to buy into the totally flattering *One Hit Rai* title." The laughter at himself gives the audience permission to chuckle. "It took patience to let the music I knew I was supposed to make find me." He turns to Azure. "Love and the inspiration of this amazing woman and artist, Azure Tempesta, gave that music life." Right there, with the bonfire's mocking crackles and cackles, Rai kisses Azure with passion and depth that should belong to me.

Oh moon, I see it in his eyes. I see it in the way he holds her face in his hands. I see it in the way their bodies move through every note of the song. Rai loves Azure more deeply than he could ever love me.

I force down the weakness threatening to rise inside. Their display of affection doesn't matter. I will claim him. Rai Cloud is my bridge to life. He was promised to me first by the moon and then by a sea witch. He is mine. It will take tonight to finally make him accept the truth. This is my one chance to live again. Nothing will get in my way.

As I stare at the two on stage, my spirit is as dark as the obsidian blood Sulaa stole from my heart. I hate the love he sings to her in his songs.

Sulaa will make things right. Sulaa is my only hope. I will do what Sulaa has commanded.

Rai stands alone at the mic. Azure stands alone on the sand next to the stage.

Rai raises his hands for quiet.

"My parents started Cloudpath Music as an act of love. They wanted to share their vision of musical experiences with the world, and they did. It's time for a new chapter in the Cloudpath story." Rai scans the crowd but doesn't see who he's looking for. He glances at Azure, and she shrugs.

Prospero isn't here, the smug bastard. His triumphant moment over Sulaa was that cryptic dig about saving the date for tonight's bonfire. The witch knew then the sorcerer believed he'd won the prize of Cloudpath Music. The ass is probably preparing to toast his victory all over social. Well, won't Mr. Selkie Bad Ass be surprised after Sulaa makes her move tonight.

"At this time, I'd like to announce the new owner of Cloudpath Music will be—"

Before Rai seals the fate of us all, I float up behind Azure. My fingers reach for her pearl pouch and hesitate. Sulaa swore Azure will ultimately be fine. The way she fusses over her other daughters makes me believe even a sea witch wouldn't jeopardize her youngest's life.

Life. My life. That's what's truly at stake. Not Azure's.

I snatch Azure's pearl pouch and yank. The chain breaks, and I slink into the shadows with my prize. I can touch it since the pouch and I are both threads in Sulaa's magic tapestry. The pouch pulls against my grip as if desperately searching for Azure. I hug it tight against my chest where it burns my spirit with shame.

I've thrust Azure into blinding agony for my own self-serving end. Am I doomed to be this person when life welcomes me back? Was I always her?

Azure stumbles a few steps then drops to her knees. One long, sustained note flies from her lips before she clutches her throat, choking. She finds her feet and staggers toward the water. It's horrible to watch a woman drowning on land. When Azure falls again, she rolls past the safe zone, way too close to the edge of the bonfire. The moon looks on as the night explodes into mayhem.

Rai leaps off the stage, screaming Azure's name. The Mermaids cry out for Azure and for Sulaa. People in the audience call for a doctor. Granny Blossom pushes through the crowd. Her furious gaze rips through the air straight to Sulaa. Even the vermin, Kitae, flies to Azure and starts barking as if protecting her.

Rai falls onto the sand by her side. "Azure, tell me how to help you." The Mermaid's lips move. Only a weak, strangled cry escapes.

The sea witch takes her cue. With a sweep of her hand, she changes the landscape into the caliche forest with the bonfire blazing at its center. As if to mock the beauty of the island inside the monochromatic hell she creates, Sulaa spells the bits of confetti strewn across the ashy sand to blossom into paper flowers the size of a fist. The people of Lalale wail and cry as they find themselves trapped in the forbidden place on the island where ghosts and memories of murder dwell. Their terror is quickly silenced as every soul on the beach except for Rai, Azure, and Sulaa calcifies into a twisted tree trunk.

The gleam in the sea witch's freaky eyes proves how pleased she is with herself. The plan was for me to hand over Azure's pouch. As the sorceress wallows in her glory, defiance grows inside me.

I can't be her good little Calliwag and leave her victory unchallenged. The woman is risking her own daughter's life and torturing Rai with his own emotions. She is a horror. There's nothing about her I can trust, nothing I choose to trust any more. Not her motives, not her promises or deals. The possibility to create balance is before me. I wronged Rai in life. I've been given the chance to fight the wrong done to him now. My loyalty lies with Rai. If I can lessen his pain, his suffering, I will.

While any free will is still open to me, I'm sure as hell going to take it. I move to one of the petrified trees I judge to be in the same place a fern bed exists in real time. There, I stash the pouch under surface debris. I pray Sulaa is so preoccupied with her own treachery she'll assume I'm still holding Azure's scales, awaiting the witch's command. It may be self-sabotage, but if possession of the pouch helps Rai, I will be ready.

Realization strikes me like a blow. I love Rai enough to put his happiness ahead of my own. Not just his happiness, his life before mine, whatever the cost. My partnership with Sulaa is at an end.

The interlocking strands of blue on the sorceress's head writhe like Medusa's serpents. Her eye sockets are bruised pits, reflecting flame. The oval discs on her shoulders spark with black fire as she points a daggerlike fingernail at Rai's heart.

"See what your folly brought, stupid fool? This is what happens when you lure my child into a world she does not belong."

Tears stream down Rai's face. "Help me get her to the water." He lifts Azure into his arms, but there is no shore, no sea, only white dust, fire, and death surround him.

"You're killing her," he bellows.

Sulaa tugs at the invisible cord between us, and I'm drawn to her side. Rai's eyes widen.

"Tani, help us."

"Help you." Sulaa's laugh makes the trees tremble and the fire surge. "My tricksy spirit is only a diversion to muddle your mind."

Tricksy spirit. Diversion. I'm damn glad I hid the pouch.

Rai drops to the ground. Azure lies motionless across his lap. A death rattle wheezes from her lips. He doesn't spare me another glance. "If she dies, then kill me too."

"So dramatic." Sulaa flips her wrist at Rai.

Says the queen of dramatic.

The sea witch fans the air in front of her nose, shooing away stink. "No one has to die." Sulaa pokes a nail under Rai's chin. "All we need is a tiny rewind. You're going back up on that stage to announce Cloudpath Music is mine." The sea witch drags her nail across Rai's cheek, leaving a thread of blood. "I take my daughter home to recover. You never see her again."

Rai's look darts between Sulaa and Azure. I can't bear the expression on his face. Pain tightens the skin across his bones. I expect cracks to appear. He does not deserve the mountain of sorrow dumped on him with the loss of his family, his company, and now Azure.

Rai's gasping as if he's the one with lost scales. "You swear she'll be fine?"

"To prove my good faith, and give you a reason to keep living, I'll toss in your ghost to sweeten the deal. Excuse me, I mean..." Sulaa rips Rai's shirt open and presses a nail into his tattoo. "Your heart's fate." He hisses in pain as the ink of the moon pulses and the silhouette bleeds across his skin and reforms into—me. Sulaa shoves me onto my knees in the powdery white ground next to Rai.

Heat roars from scalp to face then neck, and I scream. When Rai grabs my shoulder, I feel his glorious touch. Fingers clamp tight as he says my name over and over. Wind from the bonfire sets my hair dancing around my face, the real maple-syrup-colored hair of a living Tani, not the white mass my spirit wore. I convulse as my human body slowly leaks down my frame, overtaking my spirit form. It's happening. Sulaa is giving me life. The witch still believes I'm on her side.

A ravaged voice so thin it could be a trick of the fire's high-pitched howl interrupts my transformation.

"It's all a lie, Rai, a performance," says Azure. "Mother can't bring Tani to life. I..." Her eyes roll back in her head.

Rai gathers Azure to his chest. "Azure, hang on. I'll give her whatever she wants."

The Mermaid's eyes blink and then open. "I've been keeping something else from you, my sweet Rai. Forgive me."

Confusion and a flash of hurt fly across Rai's face before he settles into gentleness. "Nothing matters but love." He presses his lips to Azure's as if he can kiss life into her.

She reaches a hand to touch the side of Rai's face. The thin golden string of Sulaa's spell that bound her singing voice leaks off her throat into the sand, and she begins to sing.

I'm watching the moment unspool the way it did the night of the storm. Azure on the beach with Rai's nearly drowned form in her arms. His voice asking her if she was a dream. The note he sang to join her song. This time, it's Azure slipping away in Rai's embrace.

As he did the night of the rescue, Rai answers her with his own note as he recognizes the voice. Tears stained red and orange from firelight run down his cheeks. "It was you. You fought the fury of the sea to save me. Your song gave me the sweet air of life. Oh, my love."

This mermaid's voice should never be hidden. Azure's smile of pure joy answers Rai's revelation for a heartbeat before the song diminishes into silence. Her head falls limp against Rai's chest.

Rai and Azure are destiny's message. They have been since the night he fell into the sea, but I'd refused to accept it. Azure, the mermaid, is Rai's heart's fate. She stole him from death, sang to him, and sealed their bond.

Their song lives again in these moments under star and firelight.

I was never meant for Rai. Sulaa fed the lie to tempt my spirit so I'd be hers to command.

A growl starts deep in Sulaa's throat. As her lips part, the caliche forest trembles. A moment later, a great gust blows through. The tops of dead trees disappear first, followed by trunks then all the way to the white ground as if the illusion was conjured of fragile sand. The whole damn caliche forest is gone. We're back on the beach. People fall to the sand in a daze of confusion moments before the screaming starts.

The sea rears up higher than the roof of the Cloudpath main building and thunders down to engulf the end of the marina. Above, the sky is a spiraling mass of clouds blacker than the night, punctuated with cascades of lightning. The stripping away of Sulaa's illusion drives sand into the eyes of people gathered in front of the stage. They cover their faces and stumble to the safety of the booths, retreating from the beastly attack of sand and sea.

Prospero's massive selkie form rides in atop a wave like a dark Helios bringing night with his chariot instead of sun.

"Sulaa." Prospero's bellow shakes the earth. "What have you done to my daughter?" He's about to make landfall when the sea witch thrusts her hands toward the swell, erecting a barrier of sea foam as fine as sheer lace between surf and shore that knocks the sorcerer backward into the water. The splatter from his fall erupts to block the moon.

"I've added her to the pile of my discards." Sulaa sweeps her gaze to The Mermaids. "You're not the only selkie in the sea, Prospero. I can birth a better mermaid than your disobedient whelp."

I'm horror stricken at the thought Sulaa will allow Azure to die to strike at Prospero. If it wasn't true, she'd call for the mermaid's scales to be restored. The sea witch is the darkest of fiends.

Instead of going under, Prospero rises, now playing the role of Poseidon in full-on naked human form surfing a monster, double-up wave.

Next to me, Rai jumps to his feet and flying-tackles Sulaa to the ground from behind.

"Rai, no," I scream. He won't last a minute getting in the middle of a magic smackdown between two sorcerers.

There's pain in my newly beating heart. Rai would never leave Azure unless she was dead.

Dead because I cut her lifeline to the sea. Dead because I didn't fight Sulaa hard enough.

The Mermaids sob and wail for their fallen sister.

"Go to her," I holler. They stare at me. Of course, they do. They have no clue who the crazy lady hovering over their sister is. The magic battle with Prospero short-circuited the enchantment that hides their poor, malformed bodies. The ones who can move at all make their way toward Azure while immobile sisters weep on the sidelines.

In the next instant, my body convulses, and I flop on the sand like a landed sea bass. My restored body momentarily granted by magic leaks away. I clutch my hips, my legs. as if I can stop the transition back to spirit form.

"Moon, please let me stay. Rai will need me."

The shift is over before my plea has a shot to reach any watching energies. I am once again the insubstantial essence formerly known as Tani. My return to life is the lie Azure claimed it to be.

The Mermaid's lifeless body lies next to me. The light of the bonfire lends a false healthy glow to her skin. I rest a palm at the base of her throat. Will I feel her spirit lift into the night? "I'm sorry. Oh, moon, Azure, I'm sorry. I wanted Rai so badly. I wanted life so badly. It all went wrong. You weren't supposed to be the sacrifice."

I wish I had tears to give. An almost imperceptible flutter whispers beneath my ghostly fingers. I stare at Azure. I can't touch or be touched in this form by anyone but Sulaa. Somehow, I do sense faint drops of a waning life deep within the mermaid.

"Get her to the water," I shriek. My connection with the living is severed once again. I am not heard. I am not seen.

It doesn't matter. The violence of a sorcerer-driven sea will not heal its daughter. Destruction is the only language it speaks.

It's all on me. Only I can save Azure. I fly to the fern where I left the pearl pouch and fling the leaves and dirt out of the way. When I turn to rush to Azure's side, a gale sends me tumbling into the bed of ferns. Pushing free from the mess, I lurch toward the bonfire.

I am too late.

22

TEMPEST

Roaring, shrieking, howling...every horrible noise surrounds me. Azure, my love, my heart's fate, the spirit who saved me from a storm at sea is dead. Killed by a hate-filled witch bent on stealing a record company.

This is the end of destiny's road. It's fitting to die and follow my love over the Cloud Path into the realm of the moon. Oh, if only I had power to transform this nightmare, but I am no sorcerer.

What I can do is fight. I hurl myself at Sulaa's back and take her by surprise. She sprawls on the ground for a single beat before twirling into a whirlwind of sand that knocks me toward the furious sea. I roll like a log downhill to the water's edge and stare up at the frickin' pocket of a killer wave high enough to snuff out the moon as it plummets in my direction.

I cross arms over my face. The sea is my fate. I've lived half-submerged since before I could walk. It showed me its wonders above and below the surface. The ocean challenged me on the night I buried my parents and broke Tani's urn. Waves brought me the love of my life. Now, the sea has come for me again. It's only bided its time until it regains its frothy grip on me to end our dance.

Above me, the voice of a naked Prospero, looking more godly

statue than man, slices through the cacophony. "I pull the wild waves and pour stinking pitch from the sky down upon you, Horror."

The chill in Sulaa's laugh threatens to turn the waves to ice. "Don't presume to lord control over the moon or the ebb and flow of tides over me, you selkie bastard."

Something slippery and wet slides beneath me. It scoops me out of the path of the wave about to throttle me then tosses my body as if I'm a sliver of driftwood, up and over the breakers into the dark ocean near the lagoon.

Strange quiet seeps over the currents. I watch the distant melee as spectator not participant. Sulaa strikes with spears of distorted air Prospero slices away by calling down his sorcerer's lightning. Each combatant bends and tears at the foamy curtain between them.

I'm irrelevant in a confrontation between Sulaa and Prospero. He made that clear when he pitched me away from their fury. If Azure was on shore still breathing... If there was any way for us to be together in this life alive, above or below the surface, I would swim to Prospero's side and fight. As if a minnow could aid a pod of orca on the hunt.

Treading water is beyond my sorrow-drained strength. I spread my limbs to float on my back and speak to the moon. "Thank you for bringing my heart's fate to me, if only for the breath of a moment." The swells rock more and more violently as Prospero churns the sea.

I sing farewell to my love under a defiant moon that refuses to be vanquished by the sorcerer battle.

"A man was claimed by greedy, stormy seas
Yet fate can change if love does life appease
In moonlight's claim, a heart's fate can be saved
By you, my love, beneath wild Azure waves."

The side of a tomol bumps my head.

"Rai, dude." Juan Luna shouts and grabs my hair to keep my head above the agitated surf.

I try to bat his hands away. He leans over the side of the tomol and clamps both hands in my armpits. "I got you." Juan Luna grunts in my ear as he attempts to haul me in. "A little help, man."

Twisting to grab the side of the canoe, I find Juan Estrella at the oars. The old man's gaze bores into mine. He smacks his own chest with his fist and then splays his fingers across it before pointing to my half-submerged chest. "Granny Blossom insists on your return."

Fate makes its move. If Juan Estrella and Granny Blossom are behind this rescue, there's *mana* involved, and only an idiot ignores *mana*. Juan Luna and I heave my ass into the tomol, causing it to dip dangerously to the side. Grandson and grandfather power row us to the sandspit past the lagoon in mere minutes while I lie crumpled like wet paper in the center of the canoe.

"How did you know where I was?"

Juan Luna hitches a thumb to the waves. "We were out here chilling. Didn't want to hang near the fire. Saw the nude dude send you into a bitchin' air flip. We totally almost got under you."

Juan Estrella jumps out to pull the tomol onto the sand. "Granny Blossom saw your path, Rainn. There." He points to the bonfire.

I'm ashamed as his message sinks in. Azure is my heart's fate. I need to love her into the next place, not abandon her in my despair. I tear down the path to the bonfire.

The scene is a hellish rewind of last year. That bonfire was too far from the water. Sudden ungodly winds carried volatile sparks to trees and dry brush around the beach, giving it deadly fuel.

Despite being placed at a safer distance, this bonfire has now become a living thing. It crawls across the sand fueled by Prospero's unnatural gale and thousands of confetti pieces turned to paper flowers by Sulaa to feed the greedy flames. Azure's sisters scream her name. Two try to get close to her, but the searing fire wind drives them away. I gasp when I see her other sisters in a heap near the edge of the sand. They are not The Mermaids I know. Some have gills or other strange affectations like macabre costumes.

Every one of them are way too fucking close to the blaze. The crowd scattered. No one mans the fire hoses. It's a landscape of panic.

The sea witch/selkie cage match is a painting created to scare the piss out of sailors. Screw krakens or other watery legends, the sorcerers are the essence of terrifying. Sulaa walks directly at a wave, holding her trident necklace in front of her. A molten stream of fire shoots out of the damn thing, beelining straight for Prospero's chest. While the sea begins to circle into a maelstrom of deep grays and white spume, he raises a hand to ward her off. The liquid energy from her attack pierces the battered foam wall and collides with water igniting a dozen towers of steam.

Prospero's next gale knocks me on my ass, and past becomes present. His sorcerer wind escalates the bonfire into a firestorm.

I leap to my feet and run to Azure. A solar flare of flame forces me to dive aside or get toasted. As I watch in horror, an offshoot of the fire runs across the ground and forms a circle around Azure's body.

I scream and wave my arms to get Prospero's or Sulaa's or anyone's attention to help. My face is covered in ash. I fight my way through the wall of heat one step at a time to get to Azure.

"Stop, Rai. Let me."

Tani soars past me, turns, and holds out a hand to keep me in place. She flies through the flames into the small pocket of sand left unburnt where Azure lies. Kneeling over the mermaid, Tani ties something around Azure's waist.

I crawl as close as I can without my eyes watering to blindness to see what Tani's done. Azure's pearl pouch is back at her hip. My love turns onto her side and begins to cough. She sits up, her sweet face distorted with terror inside the cage of flames. Rising on wobbly legs, she searches for an escape. I stand, screaming her name. Tani's name.

Azure sees me and shakes her head. There is no way through the wall of fire. To hell with any destiny that forces me to watch my heart's fate die twice. I coil, ready to spring through flames and grab Azure.

Tani appears at my side, voice urgent. "She can't hear me, Rai. When I go to her, guide Azure as close to me as possible." In an instant, Tani stands inside the burning circle with Azure and then steps within the arc of flames.

I scramble to position Tani between Azure and me. Waving my arms, I yell above the laughing conflagration, "Azure, face me. Walk close to the flames."

Azure nods, interpreting my hand signals.

"On the count of three, tell her to run through me," calls Tani.

"No, Tani." My vision blurs from the sweat pouring down my face. I pivot toward the water tank. Can I create an opening for Azure to run through?

Tani's voice is calm, soothing. It's as if her lips touch my ear as she whispers. "Trust me, Rai. This will work. On three."

In a raw-throated cry, I tell Azure what to do and wave my arms.

"One," says Tani. "Two. I love you, Rai. Three."

I count with her, and on three, Tani's spirit fragments as Azure plunges through her and collapses outside the ring of fire. Swinging her up into my arms, I run onto the grass.

"Azure, oh moon, Azure." I kiss her with fire-parched lips. "You're alive." I lay a hand over her pouch.

Her hands are in my hair, touching my skin, gripping my arms, convincing herself I'm real. Then her eyes widen in panic. "My sisters."

My gaze darts to the marina where I see Juan Luna, Juan Estrella, Tutu, Granny Blossom, and several others, carrying or helping The Mermaids to safety. Moon bless, my people. Despite the unnatural strangeness of Azure's sisters, the commune family leads with their hearts. A time for questions and explanations will come, but it isn't now.

Suddenly, a strange sensation like fingers jabbing through my skin to wrap around my ribcage yanks me toward the fire. Azure shrieks and grabs the back of my shirt. My body rips through the cloth. Sulaa stands beyond the bonfire, staring at me with ferocious glee, one hand outstretched in my direction while the other circles and thrusts at Prospero. Light blazes from her fingernails in a thousand colors along the glowing, ropelike energy dragging me forward.

My feet furrow paths through the sand as the sea witch summons me. The more I struggle, the more rigid my body becomes.

"Time to feed you to the sea where you belonged before Azure interfered."

Sulaa's attack on me is the distraction Prospero needs. Whatever sovereignty the Witch maintains to hold the tide at bay weakens when her attention splits between fighting him and drowning me. Behind Sulaa, Prospero leaps through the foam curtain to the edge of the water, his eyes blaze with blinding azure light. He raises both arms and thrusts them toward the sand. One, then two and three more colossal waves decked with a whitewash fringe of jagged teeth crash over Sulaa and continue to race along the shore, drowning the bonfire. One last feather of lightning flashes across the sky to reveal the unnaturally massive shape of a seal leaping into the air and diving beneath the surface.

When the waves recede, nothing remains but an empty beach and a rising plume of steam where the bonfire stood, hissing into the sky like the aftermath of a rocket launch. There is no Sulaa. No Prospero.

My knees give out, and I crab crawl back into Azure's arms. We hold one another and rock to silent music, afraid to let go.

"Rai."

Tani stands near us in a bed of ferns at the edge of the sand. Her figure blinks in and out. I kiss Azure on the forehead and whisper, "Tani." We stand, and I lead her to where my friend hovers in the night.

"I wish I could see you, Tani. I owe you my life," says Azure.

"I nearly cost you your life," says Tani.

I will have to stand as interpreter. "Tani says she nearly cost—"

Azure puts a finger to my lips. "No. This is all my mother's doing. You saved me, Tani."

The moment Azure speaks, Tani begins to change. The flickering of her shape speeds up, brightening her spirit form. Her body elongates and twists like a knot in her center fighting to untangle. She moans and her pain twists my heart.

"Tani," I cry and reach for her.

Above us, starlight intensifies. A dozen moonbeams cascade to the island and wrap Tani in a cloth of silvery light. Her body unfurls as a knot unbinding.

She grabs her waist, and a look of absolute peace graces her features. "I'm free."

Tani is whole and lovely, wearing the smile that made me fall in love for the first time.

We stand face-to-face, the woman who I once believed was my heart's fate.

"You're," I hold my arms out to her. "Moonglow."

She gazes into my eyes, then something high above my shoulder catches her attention and Tani gasps. "I see it, Rai. Look." She points. "The Cloud Path." Hands cover her mouth as she shakes. I can't tell if she's laughing or crying. "I never thought I'd find it."

I turn and see nothing but stars above an exhausted sea.

Tani looks back to me. "I'm sorry, Rai. I wanted to stay with you. I wanted my life, but..." She looks to the sky. "It's so beautiful. I'm meant to follow it."

Would she have found the Cloud Path sooner if I hadn't broken her urn and placed her in the path of a sea witch? Maybe it was my selfishness, clinging to what I'd lost, that kept my once love from her destiny. "I love you, Tani."

Her smile is wistful, neither joyful nor sad. "I will always love you, Rai Cloud." Tani moves in to lay her palm over the moon on my chest. Beneath her fingers, the ink begins to swirl the way it did when Sulaa altered my tattoo. There is no pain or scalding heat. Liquid coolness flows across my skin, and when she lifts her hand, there is a new chapter to the story Juan Estrella began on my flesh all those years ago.

My moon is a brighter white. A silhouette now floats in front of the orb instead of standing next to it. It is still a woman, but now luminous azure hair streams to her waist in waves. Her body curves into a perfect mermaid's tail.

The journey to my heart's fate is complete.

Azure takes my hand as I watch Tani rise gracefully into the air. She pauses above the highest palm to give me a final glance before she steps upon her Cloud Path and disappears into the moon.

23

SUCH STUFF AS DREAMS ARE MADE ON

"Is she gone?" asks Azure, staring at the sky.

"Gone home."

"I don't just owe her my life. I owe her us." Azure pets the waves in my hair. Not a braid in sight after being selkie launched into an offshore wind. "When Tani warned you at the lighthouse, she risked her eternity by defying Sulaa. Tonight, she brought me my scales when Sulaa would have let me die. If Tani hadn't been on our side..." She trembles.

Sulaa, not mother. Damn, did Azure hear the heartless barb the sea witch threw at Prospero about making more mermaids? This is a tragedy. Rotten or not, Sulaa is her mom. All six of The Mermaids shoulder a boatload of emo to deal with after their mother's performance tonight.

"Rai, I'm incredibly sorry. I didn't want to accept Sulaa was capable of going so dark." She clutches my arm. "Poor, Tani." Azure hisses in a breath. "Poor, Calliwag. Poor Miaqua. We should go to the station and make sure everyone is all right."

"Whoa. No one is going anywhere near Miaqua until we confab with your dad." A zing of fear travels along my spine thinking of the folks trapped underwater in Sulaa's playground. "Who's Calliwag?"

Azure runs her fingers over my altered tattoo. I lift her hand from my chest to kiss her palm. "Juan Luna Estrella inked the beginning of a story that was always supposed to end this way." I pull her into my arms, and we breathe together. "Why didn't you tell me it was you who saved me the night of the storm?"

She lays a hand on her throat. "I couldn't sing for you." She shivers against me. "Sulaa made sure of that. I wanted to tell you it was me the day I took you underwater. Then at the lighthouse, I heard in your song how desperately you wanted to find the woman who saved you, but without proof, without my voice, how could you believe a sea witch's daughter, one who might also be full of tricks and deception?"

"Azure, I let my dream of that woman go the day I fell in love with you."

She kisses my chin. "You've put it together they're both me?"

I hold her at arm's length. "If I'd found out the truth from the start, I'd love you out of gratitude. I believe it was destiny's test that I only realized you, Azure, were my heart's fate once I got to know and appreciate everything you are, your kindness, your creativity, the way your spirit shines above and below the surface."

Kitae leaps from the shadows and bumps against Azure's leg.

"And my fox loves you."

Kitae barks and nips the top of my bare foot.

"Excuse me, my associate loves you."

Azure scratches Kitae's head. Her movements are slow and wobbly.

"We need to get you in the water."

I want to lift her in my arms and carry her into the surf. She takes my hand, determined to walk on her own. My mermaid of steel.

"So, tell me, Rai, what does being your heart's fate entail?"

I cup the back of her neck. "I can explain it in two words—love and forever."

Azure slides her hands around my body to pull me closer. "My two favorite words." We fall into the sweetest kiss we can manage given we're both exhausted and a bit charred. The woman just returned from the almost dead for moon's sake.

A commotion in the direction of the marina catches our attention.

"Azure," booms Prospero's voice across the sand. "Where is my daughter?

The formidable human figure of Prospero Tempesta in clothes, thank goodness, strides down the dock.

Azure's strength gives out at the sound of her father. She slumps against me. "Rai, I don't think I can walk. Will you take me to him?"

I sweep her into my arms. "He can meet us in the water. Rumor has it, he's an excellent swimmer."

Azure lays her head on my shoulder as I carry her into the sea. "Over here, Mr. Tempesta." I wade in chest deep and bend, allowing Azure to dip her body below the surface. She exhales a long, relieved sigh.

Prospero splashes in next to us and plucks Azure out of my arms. He sinks low to keep her submerged as he crushes her to his chest. "Oh, my sweet darling. Your smile is indeed infused with the glory of the heavens. I feared I'd never see it again. When I raised this tempest against your mother, I never dreamed it would bring you harm. I vow to never use my powers in a rage or allow Sulaa to touch you again."

In her father's arms, Azure begins her tearless weeping. I see the faint glow of mermaid skin begin to cover her body.

Prospero strokes her hair and hums a low bass note. Slowly, he lifts his head to look at me. "It takes either Herculean balls or Herculean stupidity to make a rugby style tackle on a sea witch."

"It's the latter. Sir, I'm ashamed I gave Sulaa an opening for tonight's disaster. If I hadn't insisted on making a big announcement, she wouldn't have had the chance to hurt Azure. I thought it made the whole decision look above board and celebratory if we kept the sale under wraps until the bonfire. It was the type of gesture my parents always made, grand and joyful."

He waves me off. "I'm the one who had knowledge to foresee how far Sulaa dared to press any advantage." His eyes flick to Azure, bobbing with only her face above the water, peaceful, contented features covered with the delicate sheen of her bioluminescence.

"You saved the day, Stormbringer."

Azure coughs and raises her head when she hears me use her father's special name. Her tail flicks against my legs.

Prospero's face darkens even in the bright moonlight. I glance at the sky expecting gray clouds to roll in with a duet of thunder and lightning. "I sent the gale that nearly killed my child. There are amends to be made to you both." Prospero stares at my ink. His eyes glisten. Sentimental is not a speed I though he operated at. He switches a questioning gaze to Azure as he points at my chest. She smiles at the sorcerer.

Prospero's shoulders slump. "It's never been done before."

Azure swims next to me and slides her arm through mine. "Then we'll be the first. You said you believe there's safer magic than the pouch to allow me on land."

The selkie clicks his teeth. "I may have found provision in my art to create such magic for you." He kisses her head, then shifts those black seal eyes that always hold a touch of sadness over to me. "And for you, my daughter's heart's fate."

"Azure. Azure." The Mermaids are at the edge of the surf with the commune members who take on the role of protectors. We're far enough in the water to hide Azure's mermaid sheen from anyone not in the know.

Prospero turns to the chorus of voices. "And for your sisters. I will take up residence in Miaqua and care for these creatures born of Sulaa's deceitful liaisons with sailors, fishermen, and other men of the sea lured to her bed in a masquerade of love. A farce I, too, believed in for a time. I vow to find ways to ease the blights caused

by their mother's callousness in her zeal to breed a mermaid."
Those seal eyes turn even more soulful. "If I'd known all she
wanted me for..." His voice trails off and his gaze bores into Azure.
"No. I will never regret even the false love that created you, my
darling mermaid." He takes a slow breath, fogging in the cooling
night. "I give you my word, your sisters will continue to create their
unparalleled music despite what the witch has done to them."

"Won't Sulaa be back?" I ask. "Aren't you worried she'll
retaliate?"

Stormbringer stares me down. "It's bad luck to harm a seal."
There's a little twinkle in his eyes. "You'd best not forget." He
gestures to the group on shore coming our way. He lowers his voice.
"I chased her sorceress trace to Miaqua, but she'd already fled. Her
trail of rancid magic disappeared hundreds of miles away in
northern waters."

The sea witch blew her cover and skipped town. Still, I worry
the old research station is an underwater mine field of unfriendly
powers.

"Sir, how can you be sure Miaqua is safe?"

Prospero shows overly pointy teeth. His smile is going to take a
while to get used to.

"When a sorceress abandons her spelled dominion, she forfeits
her rights." He rolls up a soaked sleeve to show a totally ripped
forearm.

I'll share my island workout routine with him. I'm sure the dude
could do some serious tree chin-ups.

"I staked my own claim on Miaqua."

I can't help but notice he omits the terms *magical* or *sorcerer*
when describing his new claim. "Big night for you. Miaqua and
Cloudpath Music in one swoop." I don't mean to sound bitter, but it
sneaks out.

Prospero lays a sometimes flipper on my shoulder. I don't know
if he intends to push me deeper into the water or if he's oblivious to
his strength. I dig my feet into the sand to hold my ground.

"Mr. Cloud, your timing for this sale may be off."

I see Emerson out of the corner of my eye on the beach. I wish he'd had even the smallest moment with his daughter to say good-bye. When the clusterfuck of tonight is past us, I'll find a way to tell him she's finally taken her Cloud Path to meet the moon. Granny Blossom will help me with the words. Maybe I'll even bring Juan Estrella for backup. "Even if I agree with you, the numbers don't."

"Since I've been privy to your financials in preparation for the sale, I am unsettled."

Great. Prospero is going to pull out, and I'll be stuck starting the whole circus to sell Cloudpath Music over from square one.

"It's true Cloudpath is barely solvent. I'll be blunt. Your company has been sloppily handled, but you, Rai, have capacity and vision for a new direction with your island rock."

I feel as if my chest caves in. My mind can't handle any more input tonight. All I want is to be with Azure, a safe and restored Azure. "Mr. Tempesta, I'm wrung dry. Whatever the message is here, I'm not receiving."

"I don't think you should sell your company."

If I were Juan Luna, I'd tell Prospero he's totally *out there*. "I'm not going to disagree, but I'd be kidding everyone, including myself, to say I'm capable of pulling Cloudpath Music out of the dumper. If I possessed the brains to save it, I would have." I meet his gaze. "It's killing me to lose my parents' legacy."

"Then don't."

Pressure builds behind my eyes even imagining the effort taking his advice will suck out of me. I've known from the start business and creativity don't coexist in my brain. The time it will take for me to learn how to run Cloudpath and then actually do it kills my songwriting energy. On top of that, he's basically accusing Emerson of mismanagement. Totally unpleasant thing to face. I squeeze the bridge of my nose. "I can't see how to make it happen."

Prospero's gaze drifts to Azure and then to me. "Son, you look dismayed. Be cheerful. If you will allow me, I'll step in as a mentor to help you sort out business from artistry." He clears his throat. "I can facilitate putting the right people in play at Cloudpath Music. Your parents built a strong foundation. There is a successful balance between old and new to be found."

I'm a songwriter with no words.

"Thank you," says Azure and flings herself into his arms.

Prospero stares at me over Azure's head. "I surmise you're going to be around for a while. Consider my offer a first contribution to your future with Azure."

Azure floats out of his arms and snuggles against me. "A while? I don't think so."

Her statement causes my already cloudy mind to go full fog. What in the name of the moon does she mean?

Selkie Dad furrows his brow. I search his face for any sign of seal whiskers about to sprout.

"Does this look like a while?" Azure throws her arms around my neck, capturing my mouth in a kiss to prove she's well on the way to full charge. She pulls back and flips lovely bright blue hair over her shoulder. I'd love to see what she looks like with triple braids to match mine.

"I see it may be timely for me to share the second contribution to my daughter's happiness," says Prospero, stabbing a look my way that leaves no room to doubt he'll be monitoring my part in Azure's future joy. The sorcerer assesses the group at the marina and jerks his head toward an even more shadowy, private spot in the water.

Azure grasps my hand, and we follow Prospero into the darkness where no lights from the shore reach. It's still shallow enough for us to stand, but just barely.

"I believe I've found the path, an ancient spell, to grant you a balanced existence between sea and shore, daughter."

I step between them. "Believe or absolutely figured out?"

Prospero glares at me. "Belief is the gateway to change. If one never ventures through the threshold, there is no reward."

Azure's hand slides up my arm to my shoulder, easing my body around to face her and cups my face. "I believe in my father, Rai, and I'm asking you to do the same. This may be our chance to make a life together without always counting the moments until I return to the sea."

I lay a hand over hers. "You're asking me to trust, to risk you when I've only experienced the dark side of magic."

Her thumb slides across my bottom lip. "That's not true. We've flown together beneath the waves, and you witnessed Tani begin her journey across the Cloud Path."

Above the sea, the moon watches. Closing my eyes, I imagine its soothing energy filling me, guiding me. Like the beauty of a moonlit path across the calm ocean, Prospero's hope calls to me. I turn Azure's hand palm up and kiss it.

"Okay," I say, nodding to Prospero.

"Take my hands, daughter."

Azure reaches up to twine her fingers with Prospero's. As soon as they connect, a faint shimmer distorts the air and rains down the sorcerer's body as he gently shifts into selkie form. To my horror, that same ripple consumes Azure, turning her into a sleek, more graceful echo of her father's seal body. Instead of shining black selkie skin, she wears her bioluminescent mermaid glow. Pressed flipper to flipper, Prospero chants in a language of growls and quiet barks. Before I find breath to cry out for Azure, an opaque wall of pale green seafoam swirls around them, encasing the pair like a cocoon.

In a panic, I reach for Azure, but my hands meet only the cool softness of the thick mist. Has whatever magic Prospero attempted failed? Heartbeats are pain as I fear my mermaid, my heart's fate, is claimed by the sea.

Slowly, seafoam drifts downward and bleeds into the water to reveal a very human father/daughter pair. In its wake, fingertip-sized emerald gems flare on the surface for an instant before winking out. Azure's hair reflects moonlight, turning each blue strand into a string of sapphires.

"Give me your scales," says Prospero, holding out his hand.

Everything in me screams to protect her pearl pouch so she can't give away her scales, but I force myself not to interfere. If this goes south, Prospero will hand the scales straight back to Azure, and she'll be fine.

Prospero closes his fingers around the beautiful ovals Azure lays on his palm. "Now, breathe."

Azure stares into her father's eyes and takes one deep breath and then another. She nods as a smile blossoms across her face.

Prospero jabs a finger to the water swaying between them. "Beneath," he says.

She hesitates for a moment then shifts into mermaid form, head disappearing under the surface. Prospero and I lock gazes as I begin to count in my head. If she's not back up by the count of thirty, I'm going down after her.

Suddenly, Azure, the mermaid, leaps free atop a huge spout of water. She throws her head back as the sea explodes around her. By the time she lands in my arms, I'm holding Azure, the woman. She peppers my face with kisses. "Yes. Yes." With a twirl, she launches herself into her father's embrace. "You're brilliant. Thank you. Thank you."

Then there is silence from all three of us, reverence for the power of magic in all its ancient glory.

"For you, my daughter, I would drown the moon to forever light the sea," says Prospero. With a kiss to the top of her head, the sorcerer disappears into the tide.

Azure drifts away from me, staring down at her body. "I feel... different. No." Her gaze lifts to mine. "I feel complete, as if the whole of who I am was locked inside and now it's free." She shakes her head. "I don't know how else to explain it."

I float over to her and pull her body against mine. "You explained it perfectly." Placing a finger beneath her chin to angle her lips to mine, I kiss her slowly and sweetly. "I love you, above or below the waves and every place in between, my Azure."

She rests her palm over my tattoo. "'Til the tides turn to glass and the moon ends its shine. The heart's fate before me will be for all time."

"Hey," I whisper against her mouth. "You're writing our next song."

EPILOGUE

GRANT GOTHEL CAUGHT THE REFLECTION OF SULAA KYLOCK GLARING out the passenger side window at the streets of Hollywood.

"Flash and trash," she sneered.

"I prefer to call it home," said Gothel from behind the wheel of the Rolls Royce Wraith they'd stolen from a ritzy beach house far north on the Olympic Peninsula in Washington. The place had been buttoned up with no one in residence. He was confident they had time to forcefully borrow the car and dump it before being discovered.

"If you'd stuck to the script on Lalale Island, our transition wouldn't be so fraught, my dear sea witch."

Sulaa *harrumphed* and glared at him.

"Soon, we'll bring the briny deep to you and brighten the city's appeal," said Gothel before he refocused on traffic. *Thank God for tinted windows.* It was imperative not to be identified before they bled into Hollywood's shadows.

He silently cursed Sulaa for the necessity to flee so far north until Prospero abandoned the hunt. The twenty-hour drive to Hollywood was unbearable with Maisie and Rubata whining while Sulaa whispered spells that filled the car with the stink of burned popcorn. Turns out a sea witch is not a supreme asset when taken too far from the waves. During the insufferable drive, they'd sketched a plan to recharge Sulaa's power once they were again under the glow of the Hollywood Sign. Home field advantage would soon be in Gothel's fiery grip.

"Right there, Maisie. The best sushi," said Rubata, closing her eyes. "Ummm, I can taste the dynamite roll."

"Sushi is nasty," said the kid.

Sulaa grunted while Rubata smacked her lips.

Gothel felt the skin on the back of his neck super heat. He mourned the demise of his Rampion Ranch where other people dealt with the children, especially precocious pains in the ass like Maisie. Zeli had never been the irritant this child was. Gothel winced. Until the end, when his pop diva destroyed everything he'd worked for: Rampion Records, his ranch, his Opus program for procuring, raising, and harvesting platinum-hit-making children.

Visions of impending vengeance calmed him. "Look, Maisie. The theater with all the bright lights is where I met your mother." He smiled at the memory of luring Maisie's pregnant mother, Maisie Sr., and her violin into his Opus program. More teeth showed as he remembered wiping the child's father, Jaycee, out of existence while peppering the pregnant violinist with Rampion Tea until she gave birth to a daughter who cried the golden tears to fuel his own powers. Once he lost his hold on Zeli and her tears, Maisie became essential instead of the reserve he'd intended her to be.

"Grant, slow down," screeched Rubata.

Gothel hit the brakes and scanned the street around them for the cause of Rubata's cry.

"I can feel my goddess's power," said Rubata, lowering the window to let wind blow through her cherry red hair.

"Are you certain?"

Rubata was totally cut off from her goddess and her magic in Miaqua. This was progress.

"The Mórrigán," whispered Rubata. "She waits for me."

Gothel allowed himself the briefest smile as the lights of his Hollywood set off the nearly imperceptible sheen of gold on Rubata's skin. He pursed his lips and took inventory. At present, Dark Vinyl Artists consisted of one temporarily out-of-service sea witch, one spoiled, Irish green witch with a goddess connection, a brat with enchanted tears, and him, Grant Gothel, a fire-maker who'd walked free from the prison he'd set ablaze.

One side of his lip curled. Once the rest of his invitations to join his new label were accepted, he'd shape this motley crew into a force to punish every vandal responsible for the shredding of his power. Soon Zeli, Justin Time and his ragamuffin Hollywood Boulevard rabble, Midas Lear and family, Prospero Tempesta, Rai Cloud, and his mermaid would be reduced to dust beneath Gothel's black crocodile loafers.

He slowed in front of the Hotel Caliwood then turned left down the side street next to the pool before coming to a stop near a double doorway lit only by a piss yellow light. In the distance, the stacked blue neon discs of the Rampion Records Tower, his Rampion Records Tower, rose as a beacon calling him to arms.

As soon as he stepped out of the car, the hotel doors slammed open to reveal a blinding beam of pure white light. From its center emerged a throwback to a 1950's Hollywood blonde bombshell, dripping in pearls and a dress that gave off its own twinkling luminosity.

"Tressa Divine," said Gothel in his silkiest voice. "You do know how to make an entrance."

The woman held out a hand for Gothel to kiss as the beacon harkening her arrival faded. The dress continued to glow. "Nice car."

"It's yours. I do suggest you"—he cleared his throat—"redecorate the plates and the vin number."

Tressa swept a hand over the car, which changed from black to platinum. The plates now read *NCHNTRZ*. "And it's not even my birthday."

Gothel glanced behind her into the shadows. "Your contributions to our team are here?"

Tressa locked gazes with him as she crooked a finger to summon something from the dark.

A man in his sixties wearing a stylish suit and an air of authority swept past her and extended a hand to Gothel. "Welcome to the Caliwood. I'm Leonato Andante. Anything you need during your stay is my pleasure to give."

After they shook hands, Gothel pulled Tressa aside. "He has no memory of me?"

Her grin was a mirror of his own predatory smile. "None at all, and when you're ready to consume his sweet, little Caliwood, Inc. record company, he will sign whatever you put in front of him."

"Well played, Enchantress."

"Well met, Tea Master."

"And the other?"

Tressa's face shifted as if a foul odor had wafted in. She snapped her fingers and pointed to the ground in front of Gothel.

A hulking shape lumbered through the shadows and ducked under the doorway. Gothel felt bile rise in his throat as details of the thing were brought into sharp relief under the triangle of dirty yellow light.

"Grant Gothel, meet Beast."

Thank you for reading! Did you enjoy? Please add your review because nothing helps an author more and encourages readers to take a chance on a book than a review.

And don't miss CRIMSON MELODIES, book four of the *Rockin' Fairy Tales* series, available now. Turn the page for a sneak peek!

You can also sign up for the City Owl Press newsletter to receive notice of all book releases!

SNEAK PEEK OF CRIMSON MELODIES

Once I step inside the Hotel Caliwood, I'll have to admit she's gone. My irrepressible, garage sale couture, brilliant, sharp-tongued lyricist and singing partner will not be waiting. She won't be waiting anywhere for me. Beatrice is no longer mine.

Was she ever?

God knows I was completely hers.

Fumes from the departing tour bus that's been our home for the better part of a year, gag me solidly in the present. The bus wrap with *Ben and the Boulevard Bunch's* logo will be peeled off tomorrow as our mobile digs are repurposed for the next band eager to hit the road. I'm blindsided with an urge to chase the bus and proclaim, "*The tour must go on.*"

It's all glamour and roadies until you find your ass home and off the Caliwood, Inc. record company's per diem dime. A bankroll we cranked into overtime partying too hard and long in Vegas after our final stop of the tour yesterday. We were scheduled to pull an all-nighter drive home, hitting our neon clad stretch of Hollywood Boulevard in the early morning, but our tour manager couldn't gather everyone's drunken asses onto the bus until this afternoon. Everyone being my band bros, Claude, D.G., and the two horn players and keyboardist we'd added to jazz up the tour. In the band's defense, the performance high from a sold-out crowd for a tour finale impairs one's power of good decision making.

Alfie, our bass guitarist, the keeper of the link between the melody and rhythm of the band's sound, thwarted my temptation to disappear into the oily shadows of Vegas and embrace a state of oblivion. He lovingly strong-armed me into the bus somewhere between round three and full shit-face status of our post-show champagne and whiskey fest. My personal saint knew a semblance of mental clarity would be required for me to hit the ground running today and finish the already overdue songs for our upcoming album.

I squeeze my eyes shut, a catalyst for calm. If I wasn't facing a blazing deadline to hit the studio in less than a month to record *Ben and the Boulevard Bunch's* next album, I'd have fought Alfie off and let Vegas swallow me whole. Anything to prevent the syrup of dread seeping through my veins at the thought of returning to the apartment I shared with the woman who was the damned love of my life until I royally detonated our relationship.

The combo of hangover brain and closed eyes hit me with a wave of vertigo. I flail for anything to support me. The stack of D.G.'s drum cases accommodates my sway. Luckily, I don't knock his precious babies to the asphalt.

My album deadline is a finger snap away. I've got a full roster of songs and not a single lyric. B.B., before Beatrice, I was shit at lyrics, but with the help of a mountain of poetry books, I cobbled together passable phrases. A.B., after Beatrice, every line I attempt to write is utter crap. The rhymes—empty and flat, cadences—pathetic, basically a reflection of who I've become.

The peeling sticker for *B 'n B + 3*, on D.G.'s drum case insta-grows a lump the size of a chinchilla in my throat.

B 'n B + 3.

It's a glaring reminder of my band's rebrand during that magical stretch when Beatrice wrote and performed with us. *Beatrice and Benedict Plus Three* chokes off the last of my wind.

Beatrice and Benedict

Even our damn names sound perfect together. The friction, the fire we conjured making music, and making love burned the world into beautiful glowing embers, until they reduced us to ash.

Benedict without Beatrice

A clingy pocket of L.A. heat permeates the late September evening. I lean my damp forehead against the stucco wall of Hotel Caliwood, feeling its texture press into my skin. The mixed bag of melancholy and relief that usually captures me at the end of a tour is totally out of whack. I'm all melancholy and no relief.

The last remnants of bus-following groupies who slipped in from Hollywood Boulevard while we unloaded, collect autographs and kisses from my OG bandbros, Claude, D.G., and Alfie before the lovely ladies scoot their booties toward the clubs. Our temporary brass and keyboard bandmates grab their gear. After a round of dude hugs, they Uber away.

Claude, our rhythm guitarist as well as the voice filling the holes left from our failed attempts at keeping a female vocalist, slaps me on the shoulder. "Holding up the Caliwood, my man?" He offers me his beer bottle. "Top off your tank and help us load in."

D.G., our drummer, wheels out a flatbed trolley. "Leonato says to set up in the Ghost Lounge for the start of the Haunted Hollywood Bar Crawl before we crash."

Alfie groans. "It doesn't start until tomorrow night. We can do it in the A.M.."

Claude downs his beer. "Dude's making us do it now as penance for the bus overtime." He sniffs his underarms. "I need fifteen so I can get fresh before my baby sees me."

Alfie carefully lifts one of D.G.'s drum cases onto the trolley. "Which baby?"

"The only baby that matters, my men—the beauteous Hero."

I explode with the hybrid of a snort and guffaw. "Beauteous, is she? I'm shocked you remember her name." After Claude's social media-documented tomcatting across the U.S., I can't believe the dude is deluded enough to think the daughter of our boss, Leonato Andante, the Caliwood's owner and C.E.O. of our label, will greet him with anything less than a kick to the balls.

"Yes, beauteous, Captain Moody," says Claude, tossing his empty bottle into the trash can by the Caliwood's service entrance.

Residual whiskey from last night mixes with disdain for Claude's callousness toward Hero to gift me with acid stomach. "You broke up with her before we left on tour. Hero's a worthwhile woman, Claude. Don't go sniffing around for a replay of something you discarded."

"Says the reigning king of the relationship fuck up," says Claude.

Heat explodes along the back of my neck. My face must telegraph imminent combustion because Alfie and D.G. step in.

"Claude, dude, cut Ben in on your intention," says Alfie, nudging Claude out of the reach of my right hook.

"Ben, I'm not talking about a quick trip to *Pound Town* with Hero."

I aim a finger between his eyes. "Says the reigning governor of *Pound Town*."

Alfie taps a finger to his chin. "I think you mean mayor of *Pound Town*. Towns don't have governors."

"He could be the count of *Pound Town*," says D.G. "Count Claude of *Pound Town*."

My three bandbros laugh. Usually, I'd dive right into their bawdy banter, but the thought of Claude going after Hero again because she's the closest thing available disgusts me. Hero became Beatrice's closest friend when we all lived in the Caliwood before this tour. I feel responsible to defend her since Bea isn't here to do it.

I must look tame enough because Claude clutches my shoulders to stare me in the eye. "Truth, bro. Before we left on tour, I liked Hero. I ended things because it would be a shit move to keep her tied down while I was gone."

I shrug him off. "You broke up because you wanted to screw your way across America."

"And you didn't?"

Claude's right to call me out. I slapped multiple coats of one night hook-up paint on my miserable carcass to assuage a splintered soul after Beatrice disappeared without even bothering to flip me off. The series of women I used during the first half of the tour didn't deserve my disrespect, my indifference to satisfy anything besides the package behind my zipper and the freakin' Beatrice shadow in my heart. I was a selfish bastard. Claude makes empty sex look easy, but the aftermath of guilt for me only confirms I'm a self-serving piece of crap.

My dick-flinging behavior came to a grinding halt, pun intended, after an insane night at an upscale bar in Louisville where I indulged quite publicly with a post-show hookup against what I thought was a dark and secluded wall. Discretion had left the building, but cell phones had not. My social media shaming was one hundred percent deserved. I was not only mortified by my lack of decency but gutted at the thought of Beatrice seeing the pictures. I went cold turkey on hook-ups after that.

The sound of Claude's voice pulls focus from my musings back to the dingy alley.

"Ben, swear I'm going to do things right with Hero this time."

"I'll believe it when I see it." I walk away from him to our pile of equipment and suitcases.

Claude grabs my arm and spins me to face him. "Seriously, Ben. The shit I pulled on the road was meaningless. Flings without the feels. I'm ready for heart. Hero has always been the one for me, I just denied it. I'm going to go for it, bro, the whole deal. Hero Andante is the person I want to become a lifer for."

I stare at Claude. His sincerity is out of sync with the player he's been on tour. The shift is jarring.

"Truth, Ben. My man, Claude, is totally all in," said D.G. "Hero's more than a knuckle bulge for him." Our drummer grabs his crotch to illustrate.

Before Alfie can school D.G. to tone down his crassness where Hero's concerned, Claude flies at him and shoves the drummer so hard, he ass plants on cement.

Claude looms over D.G. shaking a fist. "Respect only when it comes to my baby."

I dart between the pair to drag Claude away as Alfie helps D.G. to his feet. "Dude, chill. We've got whiplash from your romantic lane change."

Claude gets right in my face. "I get I screwed up, Ben. You of all people should know how much Hero means to me."

I give him a gentle push away. "Claude, there's not a drop of blood in your body able to be seriously touched with love. Hero is a whim, a convenience. Not a forever."

"Shut it. You know she's a keeper. She's smart and sweet, and tolerant."

D.G. and Alfie snort in a duet at Claude's last adjective. Clearly, we share the opinion that anyone involved with Claude must be the essence of tolerant.

I shake my head. "If you're trying to talk me into the idea of the two of you, Claude, forget it. You had Hero, and you blew her off."

He meets my gaze with no hint of backing down. "I don't need to talk anyone into believing Hero is a rare jewel. She is as beautiful in looks and spirit as the first day of spring after a harsh winter."

Those aren't bad lyrics. Maybe I should tap Claude for words to my music. I level a look at him. "What do you know of harsh winter, dude? We live in L.A."

"It's a metaphor, Ben. Try a few and you might pull decent lyrics out of your ass before Leo kills our next album."

My mouth bobs open and shut at the low blow.

"New flash, Benedict. We're sick to death of your lectures on the evils of falling in love. You can preach all you want, but I've seen you sick in love. I bet a hundred bucks I'll see you that way again if you can ever cut your Beatrice cord."

"Claude," says Alfie, giving him the *lower your volume* signal we use on stage.

I purposefully raise my volume. "You'll see me sick with anger, with fever, or with hunger, but never again with love. If freaking

Cupid comes sniffing near me, I'll stab the bastard with his own arrow."

The pity on their faces makes me wish I had an anti-love arrow to drive through every heart, sparing humanity from the pain surging through my body. I spin toward my suitcase, preparing for a spectacular mic drop of an exit. My step falters. These dudes are my band, my creative partners, my family. Our dynamic will repair itself over the next few weeks and when we get in studio after we've decompressed from a year of relentless togetherness. It's wrong of me to project my pain of being home without Beatrice on them. Time to rip off my emo bandage and assume my proper place as the decent and productive leader of *Ben and the Boulevard Bunch*.

A human whirlwind spins through the service entrance doors, and Santino Fedele lands in our midst. "The warriors have returned from battle. Welcome home, gents."

His positive energy dilutes the tension I splattered over the band. After what Santino endured, it's a freakin' miracle the dude retained his gift of erasing shadows. Fading scars crisscross his face from the multiple skin graphs and other surgeries that put him back together. Santino barely survived a massive explosion on the night he led the charge along with the singer, Justin Time, to free pop diva, Zeli, from Grant Gothel's stronghold, Rampion Ranch.

In the aftermath, Gothel landed in a prison that burned down in a killer fire. Justin and Zeli got hitched and now run Rampion Records. It was during Santino's convalescence the musical duo hooked Santino and me up. His cyber makeover for *Ben and the Boulevard Bunch* resulted in sweet ticket sales for our tour. I snagged him pronto as our permanent Internet marketing magician.

Santino scratches at the riot of tight brown curls on his head. Our tour stylist once attacked me with a perm in an attempt to create a fresh look after Beatrice bailed, and we returned to four fellows making music. Epic fail. What works au natural on Santino makes me look like a tool in search of a hip vibe.

"Lookin' good, Tino," says Alfie, embracing our friend.

Santino bounces on the balls of his feet. "I'm a dude filled with gra*titude*. Glad it shows."

Damn. Everyone comes up with better lyrics than me.

Claude nods to the superhero print high-top tennis shoes on Santino's feet. "Those fellows have nothing on your superpowers, man."

The two bust out a ridiculously complicated handshake routine before dissolving into laughter when it falls apart.

Claude raises his palms to beg off. "Out of practice." He grabs a beer from our dwindling supply and twists the top off with a flourish before presenting it to Santino.

I remember Claude encouraging the choreography of their goofy handshake in the days when Santino was rehabbing movement in his hands. It reminds me to appreciate the good guy Claude is at his core. I'm being too snippy about his renewed focus on Hero. Sometimes a dude must run the gauntlet of being ridiculous before he realizes what's important in life. If Claude is ready to appreciate Hero and thoroughly return her feelings for him, who am I to cut that down?

I wish I'd drunk from a romantic well of truth before I chased Beatrice from my life.

Santino takes a long swig and then smacks his lips. "You guys always stock the good stuff. What's with this swill?"

D.G. roots around in our Styrofoam cooler and lifts a handful of ice that he lets cascade through his fingers before shaking the water off. "We did when Caliwood, Inc. was footing our beer bill. Here's hoping Leonato stocked the Ghost Bar with primo brew for the bar crawl."

Santino windmills his hands. The guy's energy is a renewable resource that could power all the neon on Hollywood Boulevard. He's having a good day. Occasionally on video chats during the tour, he'd go dark and angry over what I thought was insignificant crap, rip me a new one, and then disappear for a while. Later, he'd hail me full of embarrassment and regret. It broke my heart when he confided in me that his hair-trigger rage was lingering nastiness from his accident and painful recovery.

"Speaking of..." Santino jerks a thumb over his shoulder. "The boss wants to meet as soon as you're finished unloading."

I whip out my cell to check for a Leonato summons. Nothing. Hopefully, he just wants to brief us on any last minute deets of the crawl tomorrow night before we crash in our own cozy beds.

My lonely bed.

It'll be the first time back in it without Beatrice.

As I help Alfie lift the last piece of equipment onto the trolley, my gut drops to my shoes.

Shit. I'm sure Leo's going to troll me for an update on lyrics and a title for the album.

All I have to offer is a flatline.

Don't stop now. Keep reading with your copy of CRIMSON MELODIES, available now.

Don't miss CRIMSON MELODIES, book four of the *Rockin' Fairy Tales* series, available now, and find more from Leslie O'Sullivan at www.leslieosullivanwrites.com

A year ago, lovers Benedict Boyd and Beatrice Sharpe, lead singers of the rock band, B & B + 3, made Hollywood history with a spectacular break up at Hotel Caliwood that ended with Beatrice in the pool, ruining a wildly expensive designer dress. Beatrice dropped off the grid, leaving the band without a lyricist.

After a year on the road, Benedict and the band are back in Hollywood, preparing to go into the studio to record a much-anticipated album to resurrect the singer's tainted fame. Although Benedict is a genius with music, he's a disaster with lyrics. If he can't deliver completed songs for the album, his band's future is in jeopardy.

Back at Hotel Caliwood, Benedict encounters Beast, a mysterious, harpy poetess who's taken up residence in the abandoned library. Following a prickly beginning, the two forge a musical partnership that promises to save the band.

To his surprise, Benedict forms an attachment to Beast which blossoms into unexpected affection. Unbeknownst to Benedict, any possibility of a future for the unconventional pair is tainted by the curse slapped on Beast by a jealous enchantress.

Will help from the ghosts of Hotel Caliwood and Beast's beautiful lyrics allow Benedict to let go of his past and embrace this new love, or will he turn away, dooming Beast to remain a harpy forever?

The snap and spice of *Much Ado About Nothing* meets a gender swap *Beauty and the Beast* in this enemies to lovers, rockstar romantasy set at Hollywood's haunted Hotel Caliwood.

Please sign up for the City Owl Press newsletter for chances to win special subscriber-only contests and giveaways as well as receiving information on upcoming releases and special excerpts.

All reviews are **welcome** and **appreciated**. Please consider leaving one on your favorite social media and book buying sites.

Escape Your World. Get Lost in Ours! City Owl Press at www.cityowlpress.com.

ACKNOWLEDGMENTS

A tsunami of thanks to all the readers out there who love fairy tales, Shakespeare, and romance. Hugs to all the booktokers, bookstagrammers, and the Plum Canyon Book Club, who make love of reading the coolest thing in the universe.

Tides of humble awe and admiration for every actor who has trod the boards in a Shakespeare play, launching stories off the page into tangible, relatable reality.

A tempest of thanks to my amazing editor, Lisa Green, who fills this writer's journey with endless laughter and support.

Waves of love to my fellow City Owl Press and Mystic Owl authors and editors who are a constant source of inspiration, and to Tina, Yelena, Heather, and MiblArt who make the magic happen.

Currents of appreciation to the folks at the Channel Islands Visitor Center in Ventura, CA who helped so much with my research for this book.

Whitecaps of thanks to Jillian Tempesta whose last name was too perfect to pass up for this story.

As always, love as deep as the sea to my family: Melissa, Cameron, Rich, John, Sidney, Chuck, Heidi, Caity, Ben, Joe, Karen, Bobby, Jon, Jane, Kristie, and friends who are family: Diane, Flo, Laurie, Rob, Tiffany, Gwynneth, Trillian, Shannon, Gail, Anthony, Lizzy, Sarah, Julie, Katharyn, Shona, and Jeff. Your love and support keep me going when those big scary waves try to pull me under.

ABOUT THE AUTHOR

LESLIE O'SULLIVAN is the author of *Rockin' Fairy Tales*, an adult romance series of Shakespeare/fairy tale mash ups set against the backdrop of a fictional Hollywood music scene. Coming in fall of 2022 is her *Behind the Scenes* contemporary romance series that peeks into the off-camera secrets of a wildly popular television drama. She's a UCLA Bruin with a BA and MFA from their Department of Theater where she also taught for  years on the design faculty. Her tenure in the world of television was as the assistant art director on "It's Garry Shandling's Show." Leslie loves to indulge her fangirl side each year at cons.

www.leslieosullivanwrites.com

facebook.com/leslie.osullivanauthor
instagram.com/leslieosullivanwrites
twitter.com/LeslieSulliRose
tiktok.com/@leslieosullivanwrites

ABOUT THE PUBLISHER

City Owl Press is a cutting edge indie publishing company, bringing the world of romance and speculative fiction to discerning readers.

Escape Your World. Get Lost in Ours!

www.cityowlpress.com

facebook.com/YourCityOwlPress

twitter.com/cityowlpress

instagram.com/cityowlbooks

pinterest.com/cityowlpress

Made in the USA
Middletown, DE
01 October 2023

39810654R00172